No Cure for
the Dead

ALSO AVAILABLE BY CHRISTINE TRENT

No Cure for the Dead

A FLORENCE NIGHTINGALE MYSTERY

Christine Trent

CROOKED
LANE

NEW YORK

Published in the United States by Crooked Lane Books, an imprint of The Quick Brown Fox & Company LLC.

Crooked Lane Books and its logo are trademarks of The Quick Brown Fox & Company LLC.

Library of Congress Catalog-in-Publication data available upon request.

ISBN (hardcover): 978-1-68331-544-5
ISBN (ePub): 978-1-68331-545-2
ISBN (ePDF): 978-1-68331-546-9

Cover design by Melanie Sun
Book design by Jennifer Canzone

Printed in the United States.

www.crookedlanebooks.com

Crooked Lane Books
34 West 27th St., 10th Floor
New York, NY 10001

First Edition: May 2018

10 9 8 7 6 5 4 3 2 1

*For the millions of nurses in the world
who endure exposure to disease, pestilence,
and all manner of miasmas, simply for the love
of their patients.*

*Especially the nurses who work in the MedStar
Health System, who exhibited this love during
my mother's final years.*

It may seem a strange principle to enunciate as the very first requirement in a hospital that it should do the sick no harm.

—Florence Nightingale,
Notes on Hospitals, 1863

CHAPTER 1

September 1853

Some said I must have been possessed by a demon to take on the position as superintendent at the Establishment for Gentlewomen During Temporary Illness. On exhausting days like this, I was in total agreement.

Shaking out my hat and gloves on the stoop outside the Establishment, I determined that the smuts swirling through the London air in a never-ending cloud of ebony flakes were the most repellent thing I'd ever encountered. They say it's even worse once winter sets in. I had been out for a mere hour to visit my family's banker, and in my short walk to and fro had accumulated enough coal dust in my hat and on my gloves and shoulders to form a diamond.

Satisfied that my accoutrements were as clean as possible for the moment, I twisted one of the massive brass knobs to open one side of the equally massive mahogany entry doors. The building offered a grudging, creaking acceptance of my entry, and I tossed the hat and gloves onto the mirrored stand along one wall of the spacious vestibule. I had been employed as the superintendent of the Establishment for only a week and breathed a sigh of relief to be back. I was eager to return to my growing list of plans and tasks for the hospital.

The week prior to my arrival had been taken up by a move from the old Cavendish Square location to this one in Upper Harley Street. The front part of the new facility had a gleaming white front and was full of multipaned windows. It had once been the glorious home of some Georgian-era lord, but it had fallen into disrepair, been sold at auction to the Establishment committee, and then hastily reconstituted into a small hospital. It had been joined in the rear to another abandoned home, and the intent was to eventually turn that rear section into a proper surgery and add more wards.

I had been permitted no opportunity to advise on the alterations to the old home, and now I was faced with making adjustments after the fact. However, it was my first chance at the life I had craved for years, and I was not about to complain.

Upper Harley Street might be a newer location with more beds, but it was still in terrible need of proper sanitation and organization. Worse yet, the nurses hardly knew how to take care of themselves, much less the women who came here to convalesce from a variety of ailments. Some of the ailments were real and some were most certainly imagined, but all of the patients—or inmates, as they are known—had been given the same level of inadequate care prior to my arrival. I planned to change all of that, quickly.

The walls of the corridor I now proceeded down on my way to the hospital library were a glaring example. Covered in what probably had once been a cheerful yellow wallpaper, the walls were now dingy, and the framed landscapes on them were covered in dust. Disgraceful.

The odor of the building was the same no matter which of the four floors I walked, and I paced through them all daily. I fully intended to replace the stench of stale urine and unwashed linens that had befouled Cavendish Square with the orderly smells of carbolic soap and vinegar. Heaven only knew how long that would take, especially since it was blended with the odor a building takes on when it has been abandoned for a long time. It is a peculiar smell—the essence of loss and despair.

However, what was unique to the place, and it was oddly comforting to me, was that instead of unvarying wards full of beds in long orderly rows, the large rooms of the home had been carved into smaller rooms. Thus, each inmate had privacy, almost as if she were being treated at home. It meant fewer inmates could be accommodated, and was certainly more work for the nurses, who must constantly enter and exit rooms rather than shifting from bed to bed, as was typical. But in the experience of my youth, caring for family members and local villagers, I had done exactly that—gone from home to home and room to room.

I had many ambitious plans for refurbishing the Establishment, but right now I only wanted to confirm a theory about the spread of malaria. The supposition had popped into my mind while I waited in the bank's lobby to conduct my business.

The sound of my heels echoed on the oak floors as I made my way to the library. The floors were scraped and worn, as though large trunks had been carelessly dragged along them by servants. It made for a very poor presentation to inmates and visitors to the facility. I made a mental note to ask the hospital's committees for money to have the floors refinished. I sighed at the thought of the verbal battle this would entail, not only with Lady Canning, who had originally conceived the idea for the hospital and who chaired the Establishment's ladies' committee, but also with the men's committee. Those gentlemen in a short time had already proved to be very miserly fellows.

I was halted in my mission by the distinctive thud of the door knocker, a silly thing in the shape of a leopard's jaw. It was obviously an absurdity of the original owner, and I intended to have it replaced with something far more dignified.

I hurried back to the door and opened it. Before me stood a scowling, middle-aged woman wearing a bonnet that seemed far more fashionable than her dress. I wondered if she had borrowed the hat.

"Miss Nightingale?" the woman asked, still looking all the world as if she were angry with me.

"Yes, how may I help you?" I did hope she wasn't about to ruin my day.

"I'm here to apply," she said stoutly, her threadbare reticule slapping against her midsection as she crossed her arms in front of her.

I raised an eyebrow. "To apply for what, Mrs. . . . ?"

"Gilbert. Maisie Gilbert. I understand you're the new superintendent here. My husband has left me and I need work, so I've come to join as one of your nurses."

This was curious. I had not advertised for any new staff members. So much had been happening that I hardly knew who was on staff as it was.

"I see," I said.

As I considered the woman before me, she began scowling again. "Will you not let me in?"

I opened the door and stepped back. "Of course."

Maisie Gilbert swept in and surveyed the entry hall with apparent disdain. "This does not look like a hospital. I have visited St. Barts, you see."

I was actually amused by the woman as I shut the door and turned back to address her. "Indeed?" I asked. "The more important question is, for whom have you served as a nurse?"

I could tell she was resisting the urge to roll her eyes. "I cannot say that I have taken on a position in the formal sense. But I did my father's bedside vigil in the weeks before he died, putting cold compresses on his head and reading to him."

"Is that all?" I said.

Gilbert looked at me uncomprehendingly. "Is that all? What do you mean? What more is there to nursing?"

I sighed. "Mrs. Gilbert, today I intend to instruct my nurses on the proper cleaning of a hospital. Are you experienced with stewing rhubarb to make a rust treatment?"

"What? Rhubarb is for pie and jam." I had thrown her a little off balance.

"I see. Today my nurses will also learn how to remove stains from our inmates' clothing by rubbing raw potatoes on them before sending the clothing off with the laundress. Are you willing to learn to do this?"

Now Gilbert was distinctly uncomfortable. "Miss Nightingale, I don't mean to tell you your business, but this is all work for the maid and the laundress."

"Is that so? When I have trained them on both of these cleaning techniques, I intend to show them how to make medicinal plasters. Have you made one before? A blend of wax and healing ingredients laid atop a thin slice of leather and applied to the affected area."

"I—er, Miss, a nurse just sits and watches the patient and brings him some food and maybe serves up some physic prescribed by the doctor, which is always delivered by the chemist."

I clasped my hands together in front of me. "Not in my hospital, Mrs. Gilbert. I have plans to train up women to become not just caretakers of the ill but healers of them."

Mrs. Gilbert's expression returned to incredulity. "That is simply ridiculous. Decent women won't do such work. You're fortunate enough that a respectable woman like me has graced your doorstep. Don't think I don't know what most nurses are like. Mucking about with wax and leather—it's preposterous and I'll not be part of it. I'm certainly not that destitute that I need to reduce myself to such circumstances. I'll go and live with my cousins first."

I went back to the door and swung it open wide. "Then that," I said firmly, "is exactly what you should do. Good day, Mrs. Gilbert."

She swept back out in a huff, and I was none too happy with the encounter, either.

With the door firmly closed on Mrs. Gilbert, I retraced my steps back toward the library. A nurse scurried down the corridor from the opposite direction, dropping into a quick curtsy as she approached me. She had likely been a maid in some London household that had gone bankrupt, or perhaps she had been terminated for some sort of improper behavior. I hoped it was the former.

"No need for that. Nurse Hughes, isn't it? You need only nod and acknowledge me with a 'Good afternoon, Miss Nightingale.'"

The nurse, who was clearly wearing an old maid's uniform that had recently been embellished with some ribbon trim and a lace collar, bobbed her head up and down and seemingly parroted me. "Yes, Miss Nightingale. Good afternoon, Miss Nightingale."

The nurse's plain face was worn thin with the endless days and sleepless nights of household service, making it impossible to know if she was twenty-five or fifty. She wore her hair back in a simple fashion, which I liked, although her expressionless face was unnerving. Her eyes were such a pale blue as to be nearly without color at all.

I really needed to sit down with each woman for a lengthy interview, not only to know each one personally but to determine whether they were fit for the sort of nursing role I intended to cultivate here.

As washed out as she was, the nurse did obey me without question, and thus seemed to have some promise. "Good afternoon to you, Nurse Hughes," I replied, inclining my head.

Hughes caught herself in midbob and blushed, the pink tingeing her cheeks so that she appeared much more alive. She then hurried down the corridor away from me. At least she wasn't slovenly, nor a slug. Yes, Nurse Hughes had promise.

I once again reached the library, which was tucked away at the back of the building. It was unusually dark and unoccupied in the middle of the day. The librarian, Miss Persimmon Jarrett, was probably pestering Cook, hoping to stuff herself with pigeon pie and custard tarts. The librarian was one staff member I had already come to know quite well, since the library was my favorite location in the building. Miss Jarrett had held some other sort of position at the previous location but had apparently pleaded for the role of librarian here, and it had been granted by the hospital committee.

She had an enormous capacity for food, yet nothing she ingested had any impact on her, for she remained as thin as an iron bedpost. I imagined Miss Jarrett would be killed in a jealous rage by another woman one day for her ability to consume so much without consequence. In the meantime, though, I preferred the library empty, and so was grateful for Miss Jarrett's absence.

The library had been carved out of a previous ballroom and was a peaceful place for inmates to spend time outside their rooms in inclement weather. Its new walnut bookcases were pleasingly stocked, not only with the expected romance and mystery novels along with a smattering of religious texts, but also with medical texts and journals. I even noted a copy of *Uncle Tom's Cabin*, by that American authoress, Harriet Beecher Stowe. What a shame that the Americans were still arguing about a societal curse we Britons had eliminated two decades ago. The library was an unexpected benefit of my new position. What I especially loved were the two side alcoves—one on either end of the library. They were cozy square spaces lined with shelves and topped with horizontal windows whose panes filtered the sun. Those familiar and comforting rays, teeming with floating dust particles, provided a shadowy sort of light.

In each alcove were a small study table and chair crowded into an opening between two bookcases. The gasoliers that hung from the ceilings did not work anywhere other than in the main area, but that was to be expected of such newfangled machinery. Candles are so much safer and less costly, but they say gas is the future. I remain doubtful.

I was glad of every opportunity to settle myself among the tomes and read all I could about medicine, away from the suspicious looks of the Establishment's committee members. Some of them had already appeared at random moments to inspect me, as if they still weren't certain that a woman with a background as privileged as mine had any business embroiling herself in so lofty a field as medicine and so disreputable a pursuit as nursing.

Because Miss Jarrett wasn't there, there were no lamps lit in the main room, so I searched around on the librarian's messy desk, heaped with volumes needing repair, dripping glue pots, long needles, twisted thread cones, and stacks of paper that presumably detailed what books were in the collection. Eventually my hand stumbled upon the handle of a lamp. Lighting and holding it aloft, I made my way to my favorite alcove in the north end of the library.

It was here at the entrance of the alcove that I stopped so suddenly in shock that I nearly fell backward in my skirts. Recovering my balance and holding the lamp aloft, I tried to understand what I was actually seeing while willing myself to keep from screaming like a wounded soldier having a limb amputated.

Dangling from the chandelier, which had been nearly yanked out of the ceiling from the weight, was the body of a young woman. Her face was purple and bloated so as to be unrecognizable, her eyes half open. She spun on the rope at an inexorably slow pace as though she were looking deliberately about the room, taking inventory of the books on the upper shelves. Just behind her, the study table had been pulled away from the wall and now lay on its side in the center of the alcove, a mute but guilty participant in the dead woman's jump. The alcove's chair had been pushed neatly against a bookcase as if someone had been seated in it, watching the morbid proceedings as though they were nothing more than a stage play.

I took several deep breaths in an effort to calm my nerves.

Take charge, I told myself sternly. *You are a nurse and the superintendent of the Establishment, not some young ninny to go running to her mother's skirts.*

But I was only a year out of my training at Kaiserswerth, and no one had ever offered a suggestion as to what to do when confronted with a suicide. At least not a suicide as astonishing as this one. I couldn't possibly manage this by myself. I needed help, immediately. Heart still pounding and legs shaking, I walked as confidently as possible back out of the library. I summoned John Wesley, the Establishment's errand boy, and sent him to fetch a constable, swearing him to secrecy about his mission.

Which undoubtedly meant that everyone in the building would know about it before the little jabbernowl returned with the officer.

I returned through the library, shutting and locking the door behind me. I gripped the lamp's iron ring harder, determined to ignore my hammering heart and go and bravely inspect the body. I was a nurse, after all, and therefore accustomed to taking care of people. Most of those people were alive and relegated to beds, of course, not dangling lifelessly from the end of a coarse length of hemp.

I edged around the body and set my lantern down on the table, the place where, by now, I should have had my nose happily buried in lists and graphs about malaria. *Well, a superintendent should expect her days to go awry once in a while*, I thought.

One of my greatest interests lay in gathering figures and statistics and then using that information to establish patterns. What could I ascertain from what lay before me?

I returned to the body. The woman's feet were suspended at the height of my waist. She wore shabby, side-laced boots, the kind normally worn outdoors. Actually, she wore only one boot. That was curious. Had she been so distraught that she forgot to lace on both boots before climbing onto the table and—

And why did she choose to do this in my *favorite alcove?*

I shook my head in disgust at my own selfish, irrelevant thought and resumed my inspection. I bent down and looked at the bottom of the woman's boot, which was worn. The insole of her stockinged foot was soiled.

So she had walked in here with one boot missing? That didn't seem right.

I dragged the chair so that it was in front of the body and climbed onto the seat. I reached out both arms and put my hands on the woman's waist to stop her drifting. Now my face was much closer to the dead woman's. I considered who she might be. A nurse? A patient? A visitor?

How was it going to look when I had to tell a constable that the superintendent had no idea who was hanging inside the library?

However, the woman's clothing offered clues. Her skirts were coarse—although not so lowly as homespun—and I noticed patched seams and worn places in the fabric. The stitching, though, was expertly done in an interesting zigzag pattern one would not normally see in utilitarian sewing. It was as though it had been performed not by the wearer but by a trade seamstress. I wouldn't have said, though, that the needlework had the uniformity of one of Mr. Howe's new machines.

Her blouse had not been fashionable for a few years, but it had been well maintained. My gaze traveled down the length of one sleeve, startled by what I saw there.

Seeping beneath the cuff was blood. I unbuttoned the cuff and rolled it up. The woman's wrist was cut. By instinct I held up her other arm, no doubt looking as though I were attempting to dance with the corpse.

Blood had seeped through the bottom of that sleeve, too, and a quick unfastening proved that the other wrist had also been slit.

I frowned as I realized that the cutting had been performed after death. Although sloppily done across the artery instead of along the artery line to ensure a more forceful blood flow, the cuts had resulted in a dripping, oozing discharge that was dried and crusted on the woman's hands but hadn't pooled in any significant way on the wood floor below. If her wrists had been cut while she was alive, wouldn't there be blood everywhere?

This, of course, brought up the most obvious question. Had someone murdered this poor girl and tried to make it look like a suicide? But why employ two different methods of death? It only served to suggest that someone wanted to emphasize the suicidal nature of it. And I was supposed to believe that a young woman would cut her wrists and *then* jump off a table? Or put a rope around her neck and *then* attack her wrists with a knife while she dangled?

It made me think that whoever had done this had very little medical training. Of course, that could be anyone in the building, other than Dr. Killigrew.

I shuddered to think that such base perversity might be walking the halls of the Establishment right now in the guise of a friendly face or an obedient pair of hands.

I was still consumed with cheerless contemplation, the woman's lifeless hands in my own, when I heard the banging of truncheons at the outer library door. The loud thuds were accompanied by imperious, masculine shouts of, "Metropolitan Police! Open this door immediately!"

The chattering behind the police indicated that, indeed, every nurse and ambulatory patient was crowded behind the officers, having listened to John Wesley's passing gossip and wanting to know what required both the police *and* a locked door.

I stepped down from the chair and returned it to its place, then calmly smoothed my skirts and schooled my features into neutrality before unlocking the library door. As the police burst in, I turned the switch on the wall that connected to the gas pipes, and in a few moments, hissing chandelier light filled the room.

The officers were young and very handsome. The taller one—who introduced himself as Sergeant Warren Goodrick—had an expression that suggested he was far more aware of his magnetism than the shorter man, Constable Douglas Lyon, whose dark, curled hair and cleft chin reminded me of—it was of no matter anymore.

"I am Miss Nightingale, the superintendent here," I said firmly. "I called for you."

Without explaining why, I shut the door on the gawkers in the hallway and led the officers to where the poor woman hung. Their reaction was quite the opposite of my own, showing no shock or revulsion as they peered up speculatively at the body.

"Suicide, eh?" Sergeant Goodrick said blandly. "Always a shame when a woman does it. Probably rejected by a suitor or some such thing."

"Don't be daft," I snapped without thinking as two pairs of startled eyes riveted their gazes upon me. "This girl no more committed suicide than I turned into an ostrich this morning."

They both shifted uncomfortably, and I immediately regretted my outburst. It made no sense to make an enemy of the police. I cleared my throat and spoke in a more conciliatory way. "If you'll check her wrists, you'll see that they were opened after death."

Goodrick examined the woman's arm. "I suppose. If she'd been bleeding herself regularly, she might not have good circulation."

That made absolutely no sense. "You're saying she drained herself of blood and then managed to hang herself?" I asked, feeling as incredulous as Mrs. Gilbert had been earlier that morning.

"No, Miss Nightingale," Goodrick replied patiently, as if I were a child. "A suicidal girl like this was probably getting bleeding treatments to cure her melancholy. She probably had very little blood circulating in her system when she died. Anyway, it's best to get her down. Lyon?"

Before I could argue against his foolish theory, he nodded at the other man, who looked so much like Richard that my heart began its familiar ache. The feeling was much like an old wound that has long healed, yet will sometimes throb with a faded, dull pain that doesn't really hurt but simply serves as a reminder of the ancient injury.

Lyon dragged the chair back while Goodrick righted the table, and together the two men worked to get the hanged girl down, laying her out gracelessly on the floor.

"Mr. Swan, the coroner, should be summoned. See that she stays undisturbed until he arrives, do you hear?" Goodrick ordered.

I nodded in deference to the constable's demand. My specialty was caring for living bodies, not dead ones. However, to leave the girl here in the library, in this reading alcove, was a bit too, too—"I think it would be more dignified if she was removed to an empty inmate room."

Truth be told, I also didn't particularly care to have a dead body confined in my reading alcove.

Goodrick shrugged. "Very well." He and Lyon lifted her, Lyon holding her half-shod feet at the ankles and Goodrick hoisting her under her arms. The noose was still around her neck, the length of rope trailing along the ground, and it was all vaguely disturbing to witness.

Not nearly as disturbing as the scene that awaited us outside the library, though.

CHAPTER 2

Patients—recognizable by their middle-class garb, their walking sticks, and rolling chairs—as well as the more roughly clad members of the staff, were congregating anxiously outside the door as I pulled it open for the constables. The officers brought the body out and the group separated like broken carriage axles, murmuring like witnesses to an overturned coach in the middle of Piccadilly Circus.

I had to maintain control of the situation. The first recognizable face was Miss Jarrett's. I had to assume she had most reluctantly put down her fork when word spread that there was a dead body in the library she oversaw.

"Miss Nightingale!" she gasped in horror. "What has happened?"

I quickly pulled the librarian aside as the crowd made to follow the constables.

"Who is that young woman?" I asked, nodding to the dead girl, who was being jostled around a corner by Goodrick and Lyon.

Miss Jarrett frowned. "Why, that's Nurse Caroline Bellamy. Don't you know her?"

Bellamy. Yes, I recalled something about Bellamy coming to the Establishment from . . . was it Mrs. Fry's training school? Or a private posting? I would have to check my notes. However, I wasn't about to admit to Miss Jarrett that I had had no idea who the poor girl was.

"Right you are. I had forgotten her name." I hurried away from the librarian to resume leading Nurse Bellamy to her temporary resting place, for the moment ignoring all the pressing questions in my mind. I also had to ignore all the chattering women behind us who were plaguing me with questions about the unfortunate victim.

We passed the room vacated by Mrs. Moore, who had recently departed with an unresolved bout of melancholia, which I understood to be a regular occurrence for the lady. I felt a tug on my skirt. I paused at the doorway next to Mrs. Moore's room, gestured toward the bed for the constables, then turned to see who was at my side. It was John Wesley again. The boy was an enigma to me. He had apparently appeared at the Cavendish Square location one day, seeking work, and had followed on to Harley Street. He did not speak of home or family, and he came and went as he pleased. No one knew where he slept or what he did when he wasn't at the Establishment. Actually, no one even knew what his surname was. He was just John Wesley.

"I fetched the constables, just like you said, Miss Nightingale," he said, his brown eyes large as he studiously avoided looking into the room. Most children John Wesley's age had experienced the death of at least one sibling or parent. I had noticed that young ones coped best with tragic events by stoically pretending they hadn't occurred.

"It seems you fetched most of the hospital while you were at it," I replied sternly, but I reached into my pocket for a coin, placing it in his outstretched hand. "However, I need you to do something else."

John Wesley kissed the coin and bent down to tuck it into his shoe. The crown of his flaxen-haired head was littered with coal smuts. "Yes, maum," he said, his expression registering his anticipation of another threepence.

John Wesley's actions instantly reminded me of Nurse Bellamy's missing boot, but there would be time enough to dwell on it when I was through with what I was sure would be a very long afternoon and evening.

"I want you to go to the coroner. His name is Mr. Swan. Do you know where he is?"

John Wesley shook his head no. Quite frankly, I didn't know where he was, either. I'd never had need of him, since I had never encountered a death that wasn't due to illness, disease, or an obvious accident. I sighed. "Do you think you can manage to figure it out for yourself?"

"Yes, maum," he replied, and I watched as he cocked his ten-year-old head to one side, as if already calculating which street waif to ask.

"After you see Mr. Swan, I want you to go to the undertaker. Ask Mr. Morgan to come in the morning."

John Wesley immediately scampered off as I informed the constables that the coroner would be coming presently.

Satisfied that their work was done, Goodrick and Lyon took their leave, and I shut the door to Mrs. Moore's room so that there would be no further gawping at poor Nurse Bellamy's corpse.

I may have literally shut the door on the horror of Nurse Bellamy's death, but I still had at least a dozen faces staring at me in expectation, waiting for their superior to explain what had happened and to reassure them that it was all just some strange dream they were having.

I smiled at the assembled group, knowing that my smile was tremulous but hoping they wouldn't notice. I clapped my hands twice, speaking as loudly and firmly as my nerves would allow.

"As you have already seen, there has been an unfortunate accident with Nurse Bellamy. We are all grieved, to be sure. But we won't dishonor her by dwelling on it, or by grieving too harshly. We especially won't be gossiping about her death, will we?"

At that moment, I realized that the worst was yet to come. After I was finished dealing with the coroner and the undertaker, I would have to face the Establishment's committee, who would be none too happy to learn that their new superintendent had permitted a woman to be murdered right under her nose. Yet another unpleasant thought to be shoved into the recesses of my mind until I was forced to deal with it.

I stopped.

Of course, if I chose to agree with Sergeant Goodrick's assessment that it was merely a suicide, it might go more favorably for me with the committee.

I actually considered this for several moments. I suppose it is a basic human instinct to shield and protect oneself.

However, a desire for justice is another human instinct, one that I hoped would always devour the selfish desire to preserve the self.

I sighed inwardly. No, I could not walk the easy path. I would have to do what I could for this poor woman.

I returned my attention to the scene before me. I could see that there wasn't a single woman standing before me who wouldn't be dishonoring the victim with gossip the moment she left my presence.

"Nurses, I'm sure you have bedridden patients who need attending. Those of you who are convalescing should continue to do so and not be worried about one poor girl's unfortunate demise."

One of the more slovenly nurses, Miss Wilson—or was it Miss Williams?—spoke up, and the fumes from her noxious breath enveloped me from several feet away. "I didn't do nuffin', Miss Nightingale. I just been mindin' me own business."

Where had the previous superintendent found this girl? Her speech was as appalling as her presentation. This was another aspect of the nurses that required attention.

"Of course not," I replied, holding a finger under my nose in a vain attempt to ward off the woman's stink. I hoped I sounded sympathetic and not as if I would prefer to smack a sense of hygiene into her.

The nurse wiped a sleeve across her snuffling nose.

"You should never—" But I stopped and inwardly sighed. There would be time enough for comportment lessons later. "Nevertheless, some of you may have known Nurse Bellamy and her . . . state of mind, and I—the coroner—will wish to learn more about her."

Miss Wilson or Williams and the others shuffled away

reluctantly. I made it down to my study just in time to receive the coroner, which turned out to be yet another unhelpful experience.

★   ★   ★

He introduced himself as Mr. Jasper Swan, and I invited him to sit down. He said he was a local towpath warden who worked on the Regent's Canal. He smelled of the Thames, too, a combination of offal and damp that was peculiar to that body of water. It was a scent far more pleasant than Miss Wilson's exhalations, though. I imagined he had the side business of coroner as a favor his family was owed by some local official. Coroners were appointed and might be judges, shopkeepers, bankers, or any manner of men. On occasion an undertaker or doctor might be appointed, but only rarely.

It could have been worse, as he seemed a congenial enough fellow, with his balding head, wire-rimmed glasses, and ready smile. However, his nose was bulbous and pitted, and I was distracted by it despite his pleasant demeanor.

"Your boy told me you had a suicide here?" Mr. Swan asked. "Not the first one I've seen, I'll say. Poor souls without jobs or hope just give up sometimes."

"Yes," I said. "Except that Caroline Bellamy was employed as my nurse here, so there was precious little reason for her to be 'without hope.'"

"I see. Perhaps she had been jilted by a lover?" He pinched his nostrils together as he echoed Sergeant Goodrick's opinion. The gesture was probably a lifelong habit of his, but it flustered me.

"I couldn't possibly say," I said, looking off at a framed picture on the wall. It was an old Cornwall seascape with a chipped and bedraggled frame surrounding it, no doubt left behind by the previous owner who had taken only his finest artwork with him. It was another reminder that there was much to clean up inside the Establishment.

Willing myself back to the present subject, I realized that I should have spoken with my staff before summoning the coroner, but it was difficult to know what to do in such a situation. After all, I had never before encountered a body that hadn't succumbed naturally to age, disease, or accident.

"I should take you up to see Nurse Bellamy," I said, standing. "It is my opinion that she did not commit suicide but that someone intentionally did away with her."

Mr. Swan began his nose-pinching again. I turned away and led him up to the next floor to see the body.

I thought Mr. Swan's assessment of Nurse Bellamy's body was exactly what was to be expected of a towpath warden, which is to say that it was a poor one, borne of his ignorance of medical knowledge. I pointed out the woman's cut wrists and the fact that surely they had been cut after death, but the man was insistent that she must have done herself in as the result of a broken heart. He advised me to simply see her sent off to her family as quickly as possible for burial, and stated that he saw no reason to suspect foul play. "Besides," he added dismissively, "there aren't really enough constables out there to look into such a thing. And if there's no actual reason for her to have been murdered, then there's no sense in looking for a particular quill in a goose pillow, now is there?"

So there would be no satisfaction from that quarter.

★ ★ ★

After going through the Establishment's records on Nurse Bellamy and learning that the woman had never admitted to having any family, I retired for the evening. My parents had insisted on my having separate lodgings nearby where I could retire more respectably than among the sick, but already I found that most nights I was too tired to trudge the several blocks there. It was just simpler for me to have rooms in the hospital. I had selected a connected bedchamber and study at the opposite end of the upstairs corridor from where the nurses slept.

I tossed about all night on my pillow—stuffed with common duck feathers and certainly not goose down—but in the morning made myself presentable enough to appear confident before my staff.

I started by summoning Miss Jarrett, the librarian, to my study. Although small, it contained a glass-paned door that let in light from the corridor wall sconces and led to a small balcony overlooking Upper Harley Street.

I was particularly curious as to why Miss Jarrett had not been at her post the previous day. The librarian trudged her way into the study, her eyes downcast as if on her way to her own execution. I immediately wondered if she was hiding something and decided to try to startle it out of her.

"Sit down, Miss Jarrett. I shall be forthright with you. I found Nurse Bellamy yesterday afternoon in the library, the space that *you* manage. I should like to know where you were for so long that she could have been brought in there and hanged without you knowing of it."

"I-I-I was in the basement, ah, I was a bit thirsty and decided to seek out a bit of tea, you understand . . ." The librarian shifted nervously in the oak armchair she occupied.

I frowned at the librarian. "That's all? You left your post to fetch tea?"

Miss Jarrett dared to look up at me. "I was also hungry, Miss Nightingale. I hadn't had anything since breakfast . . ." Her voice faltered.

I would have to add strict staff mealtimes to my list of hospital improvements. But for now, I needed to know about more than the librarian's eating habits.

"How well were you acquainted with Nurse Bellamy?" I asked.

Miss Jarrett shrugged. "Not very, Miss Nightingale. She wasn't too friendly."

"Do you know if she had any family?"

The librarian wrinkled her nose as if in careful thought. "Not that I can remember. She sometimes wore a locket around her neck. Maybe it had an image in it of her mum and dad . . . or maybe a beau?" she added hopefully.

I couldn't recall that Bellamy had been wearing any jewelry when I had found her body, but perhaps I wouldn't have noticed. However, a photograph would have been a frightfully expensive item for her to have been carrying around. I would have to see whether she still wore this locket.

"What did the other nurses think of her?"

Miss Jarrett considered this for a few moments, finally meeting my gaze as she spoke. "She was a peculiar sort, you know?"

"How so?" I asked.

"A bit of a loner. Didn't want to associate with us much. Some of us planned to go see *The Barber and the Beadle* at the Pavilion Theatre about a week ago, and she wouldn't go. Said she was too busy for the likes of us."

I was skeptical. "She said it just like that?"

"Well, maybe not exactly so. It was right snippy, I will say that."

"Were the others offended?" I wondered if Miss Jarrett was either being overly sensitive or if she was trying to provide me with a story she thought I'd like.

"I can't say, Miss. I do remember that Nurse Wilmot told Nurse Bellamy that it was her last invitation."

Wilmot! That was it, not Wilson or Williams. I made a surreptitious note on a piece of paper at my elbow.

I asked a few more questions, but the librarian seemed to have nothing else to offer. It would probably be the other nurses who would be able to give me real insight into Nurse Bellamy's life.

I considered admonishing Miss Jarrett again for not being at her post the previous day but saw no point in it. Instead, I instructed the librarian to ask one of the nurses to come to my study.

"Which one should I fetch?" she asked.

"Anyone; it doesn't matter," I said.

"Anyone?" She looked doubtful. "Just . . . tap someone on the shoulder?"

"Yes, yes, just bring up one of the nurses."

She rose to leave. "And Miss Jarrett," I added, more kindly this time. "Please go straight there."

The librarian blushed furiously and nodded. I doubted

she'd be able to refrain from disobeying the order by stopping off to see what our cook was doing. Actually, my own stomach grumbled at that moment, and I began to wonder myself what Mrs. Roper might be working on.

CHAPTER 3

Nurse Wilmot sat before me about fifteen minutes later. Unlike Miss Jarrett, who had studiously contemplated the floor for most of my interview with her, Nurse Wilmot was pert and bold. I disliked her more with each passing moment, especially since being in an enclosed space with the woman was bringing tears to my eyes. Did the nurse not realize her own stench?

I stood and went to the balcony door, throwing it open to let in air. I figured I stood a better chance of surviving the smuts that were sure to come swirling in than I did the poisonous miasma Nurse Wilmot was emitting. How was it that a young woman who couldn't possibly be more than twenty-five years of age was already so repugnant?

I knew that Wilmot had come to the Establishment through typical circumstances: both parents dead and distant relations tired of supporting her. The Establishment provided a room and a wage, and it was of no relevance to the family whether Nurse Wilmot was suitable for the work.

It was difficult to tell yet the extent to which Nurse Wilmot was one who resented her circumstances and expressed it in a brash personality, or if that brashness had played a part in her relatives' decision to scuttle her off somewhere.

The gaze from her sharp brown eyes was one of challenge. "You sent for me, Florence?" she said with impudence.

"Miss Nightingale," I corrected her. Already Wilmot was testing the bounds of my patience. "You will not be so familiar with me, Nurse."

Wilmot lowered her gaze briefly, but I knew there was no sincere remorse in it. I would have to watch this one very carefully.

"I suppose you know why you are here?" I prompted her to start the interview.

Wilmot nodded. "Because of Nurse Bellamy."

"Yes. You knew her?"

"We all work together here, don't we?" A very caustic response, one I would ignore for the moment.

"How long have you been here?"

"Mebbe a year. It's not real important, is it?" She lifted a shoulder to let me know how inconsequential the question was. That shoulder was covered in a chartreuse yellow poplin that had seen better days but was still serviceable. I imagined it had been a parting gift from her exhausted and guilt-ridden relatives, although the putrid shade of it—making the nurse's already sallow complexion even more waxy—practically implied that her relations had been playing a joke on her with such a hideous gift. Perhaps I was judging Nurse Wilmot a bit harshly, given the woman's circumstances, but it was difficult for me not to meet the woman's sarcasm with invective of my own.

"Do you happen to know when Nurse Bellamy came to

work here?" I asked, maintaining my temper, which was attempting to claw its way out and swallow me whole.

"She's newer than me. She's been here about six months. Oh, she *was* here about six months. I guess she no longer is." She offered a toothy smile, which demonstrated that one of her front teeth was much shorter than the other, as though its development had been stunted. Much like her manners.

"Indeed," I replied. "And what did you know of her personal habits? Did she have many friends? Were there any gentlemen interested in her?"

"She weren't much for friendliness. As for a beau, I remember once seein' Caroline—I mean, Nurse Bellamy—slippin' out through the kitchens one evenin'. Her room is next ta mine, and I heard her return in the wee hours of the mornin'. I always wondered if she sneaked out ta meet someone."

This revelation deserved further questioning.

"How did you happen to see her leaving through the kitchens? What were you doing down there at night?"

Wilmot was nonplussed for only the briefest of moments before responding carelessly, "I remember I was a bit green around me gills that day. I skipped me dinner but was hungry later. That's how I ended up there."

Was she telling the truth? I couldn't be sure.

"You said your room was next to hers, so you must have seen her frequently. Did you notice anything else that Nurse Bellamy did?"

"I had me own business; she had hers. I'm not one for pryin' inta others' affairs." Wilmot sat back in her seat, supremely satisfied with her performance.

It was then that I noticed the nurse's fingernails, which were encrusted with dirt. Quite unacceptable. I was quickly growing weary of this chit, no matter what sort of discontented background she might have. Nurse Wilmot was in desperate need of training, and her lessons would begin immediately.

I folded my hands on the desk and said quietly, "Nurse, are you of the impression that I am an idiot?"

The question startled her. "What?" was all she managed to say.

"Do you believe that I am so foolish that I would permit you to behave like a churl in my presence without any repercussions for you?"

"I never said that, Miss Nightingale."

"Is it your opinion that because I have not been here long I am not fully aware of when I am being flimflammed by someone? Do you also think that I am not capable of discipline?"

I leaned forward to make my next point. "If you wish to be sent back to your family in disgrace, I am more than happy to oblige."

Wilmot shifted once more in her seat, this time uneasily, but kept her gaze steady. "It wouldn't matter to me, Miss Nightingale, whether I remain here or go back ta my aunt and uncle. Either place means me drying up an old spinster."

Wilmot rose without permission, thus concluding the conversation. After she was gone, I stayed at my desk a considerable time, thinking, with no regard to the layer of coal dust settling down over my desk.

That girl was going to be trouble.

★ ★ ★

After Nurse Wilmot, I chose to remain alone for a time to gather my thoughts. As was my nature, I pulled some sheets of paper from my desk and uncapped my fountain pen. I am a firm believer that by collecting data and compiling it into tables, one can analyze and come up with the answer to nearly anything. I am, in fact, quite certain that disease outbreaks can be halted by studying the characteristics of who becomes afflicted, where they live, and what is in the air they breathe.

I had explained my methods on many occasions, but few in the medical community were doing more than patting me on the head as though I were a puppy who had just fetched and dropped a toy at its master's feet. Among other goals that I kept to myself, it was my great hope that in my new position as superintendent of a recuperation facility, I could finally prove the value of my tables and charts.

For now, though, perhaps I could make sense of Nurse Bellamy's death using my methods. I plotted out one chart with a list of the Establishment's employees down the left side, and their responsibilities—nurse, cook, manservant, etc.—across the top. In the intersections I would indicate whether the employee was friendly with Nurse Bellamy. As I interviewed more of the staff, perhaps I could establish that the nurse tended to associate with certain types of people or in certain areas of the hospital.

It was a weak start, but most of my charts began that way.

I was suddenly reminded of having seen Nurse Hughes coming down the hall away from the general direction of the library just before I discovered Bellamy's body. Was it possible the nurse knew something or had seen anything? Nurse Hughes would be next on the list of interviewees.

As I put down my pen, a face appeared in the doorway. I checked the watch pinned to my dress. The undertaking company had been punctual to a fault ever since my family had known them, which is to say since Graham Morgan's grandfather, then his father, and now the young man before me, had been serving us.

I greeted him cordially. "Ah, Mr. Morgan, thank you for coming. We have a sad situation here, I'm afraid."

After accepting his congratulations for my new position, I led him into the hallway. I was surprised to find an attractive, dark-haired woman waiting there, dressed in the layers of black that signified either mourning or the undertaker's trade.

Graham Morgan stood behind the woman, placing his hands on her shoulders. "Miss Nightingale, this is my wife, Violet. We were married last week, and she is working with me."

Violet Morgan had a surprisingly firm grip as she shook hands with me. I held her clasp for a moment too long, though, as I took in the image before me: the handsome young merchant gazing adoringly on his beautiful new wife. Such an enviable marriage would theirs be, between a husband and wife who would work alongside each other the rest of their days. There would certainly be children and bickering arguments and holiday trips and long nights wrapped up in each other's arms.

I imagined myself in Violet's position, with Richard standing behind me, grinning deliriously in happiness at having made me his bride, as I leaned back against his broad shoulders, letting his spicy cologne envelop me. My eyes misted to think of what had not transpired, what would never transpire. If only that constable hadn't been here the day before to dredge up—

"Miss Nightingale?" Morgan asked in concern, breaking into my reverie. "Are you quite all right?"

I blinked away my useless thoughts and tearful regrets. "Of course. Let me take you to the body."

Chapter 4

Nurse Bellamy's body had certainly not improved overnight, but at least it wasn't starting to rot. I waited as Morgan and his new wife inspected the bloated corpse, impressed at how fearless the young woman was at the sordid example of death that lay before her. She would have made an excellent nurse.

"What is your opinion?" I asked, knowing they would understand exactly what I meant.

Morgan shook his head in deep concern. "This was no suicide, Miss Nightingale."

"No," I sighed. "It wasn't."

I remembered that I needed to check for the locket. Morgan had removed the noose, and it was plain that there was no necklace there. I didn't bother asking him if he'd found it upon her, since there was no imprint of it on her skin, which would have been readily evident had the locket been trapped under the noose.

Either the murderer had stolen it or she simply hadn't been wearing it at the time of her death. I needed to go through

Nurse Bellamy's belongings to search for it. Maybe it would provide me with a clue as to her background.

"How do we reach her kin?" Morgan inquired, as his wife gently wrapped Nurse Bellamy inside the bed's blanket.

"I don't know of any relations."

He gave me a sorrowful look. "So not only unconsecrated ground if she is officially a suicide, but a pauper's burial."

Violet Morgan looked up from where she was gently patting Nurse Bellamy's face before shrouding it with the blanket, seemingly affected by the ignominious end for the nurse.

"Yes, it looks as if Nurse Bellamy has been served a double helping of injustice," was all I could manage.

Once the Morgans had taken Nurse Bellamy away, I went to her room on the third floor and surveyed it, deciding where to begin my search. However, I had hardly put my hand on the key protruding from Nurse Bellamy's thickly painted wardrobe when I heard a throat clearing noisily from the doorway.

I turned, dismayed by whom I saw there. It was Roderick Alban, an influential member of the Establishment's men's committee. By the glowering expression on his face, I knew that he had learned of the nurse's death, and that my life henceforth would become adverse enough to make me envy the now-deceased Nurse Caroline Bellamy.

"Mr. Alban, how may I help you?" I asked, folding my hands demurely in front of my waist. I hoped my calm voice and demeanor would placate him.

The fussily dressed Roderick Alban didn't enter the room

but chose to chastise me from the doorway. His dark hair, tinged with gray, was perfectly coiffed. His face was lined from all forty-eight years of his life, but it only served to make him more handsome. And somehow more acidic. Mr. Alban was like a bottle of vinegar on a shelf, never decaying or changing composition but always maintaining his bitter bite. While I was glad he didn't approach me, it was also impossible to escape him.

"It has come to my attention that a tragedy has befallen the Establishment," he said. "A tragedy never known in the three years it was located in Cavendish Square. What have you done?"

I had hardly opened my mouth to respond when he forged ahead, seemingly determined to bring me to heel. "You've hardly darkened the door to this place and already there are women committing suicide here. How can we endure the bad reputation that will ensue from this? Do you know how much I have personally invested in this project, not to mention how much I have raised from investors? I ask you again, what have you done to drive them to such despair in only a week?" The man's voice became deeper as he vented his anger. And yet Alban had a remarkable capacity for appearing civilized and polished. It was disconcerting.

"It would seem the misgivings I expressed to Lady Canning about employing an unmarried, inexperienced young woman for such a responsible position were well-founded." His lips curled into a feral smile.

I had turned thirty-three years old in May, so I was hardly a naive little miss. But even my parents had harbored serious doubts and misgivings about my ability to lead a hospital—no matter how small—not to mention the appropriateness of it all. They had finally given their grudging permission, but only after I had argued with them nearly my entire adult life about my desire to enter nursing. My sister, Parthenope, still sent me letters full of hysterics over my insensitive and cold-hearted decision to abandon the family for "the profession of prostitutes." Nursing had long been considered work that was just a step above harlotry, given that it had no standards whatsoever and was frequently pursued by low women.

If I was not careful in this very moment, I might find a swell of support for sending me back to Embley Park to be replaced by someone more "suitable" for the position. After all, I had just replaced another lady superintendent myself.

"Mr. Alban, I assure you that everything is well in hand." I prayed God would not strike me dead where I stood for that colossal falsehood. I still barely knew who the dead woman *was*, much less had anything under control.

"Ah," he said, stroking his clean-shaven chin as though contemplating my assurances. "Then perhaps you can explain to me how it occurred," he invited crisply, offering me no quarter whatsoever and appearing to desire nothing more than to watch me squirm. I couldn't give him that satisfaction, not when I was trying so hard to build my authority at the Establishment.

"At the moment, I obviously cannot, although I have started interviewing the staff here to figure out what anyone may have seen or heard prior to Nurse Bellamy's death." I squared my shoulders and stood at full height to bolster my next statement. "I am sure I can discover what happened, given a little time."

Alban shook his head in disbelief. "I am expected to believe that a wisp of a woman will ferret out who may have murdered a nurse?"

I stilled. "I did not say that she was murdered, sir. And you yourself just said that she committed suicide. Who or what has led you to believe otherwise?"

Alban's self-assurance evaporated in that moment. "I, er, well, I'm sure that someone here told me. So many people are prattling about the situation that I cannot remember who specifically suggested she was murdered. It is quite beyond the point, of course. What is of utmost concern is your ability to manage this facility properly."

"Again, I assure you, Mr. Alban, that—" I began, but to no avail.

"I'm going to see Lady Canning straightaway, and *I* can assure *you*, Miss Nightingale, that we shall see then what your future is to be." Having regained his cold, elegant composure, Alban stalked out of the room haughtily without waiting for a response from me.

I felt a moment of relief, not only for his departure, but also because I was sure Lady Canning would defend me for the time being. However, if I did not ascertain quickly who had killed Nurse Bellamy, I knew I would find my employment abruptly terminated. I heard the front door of the Establishment slam in the distance as Roderick Alban made his final statement on the matter known to everyone in the building.

Everyone, that is, whom I needed to face with placid competence and confidence. I took a deep breath and determined that I would let no one—not even Roderick Alban—interfere with my resolution of Nurse Bellamy's murder. In doing so, I would retain my position and continue unimpeded to improve conditions at the Establishment.

What clue could her room provide me?

I surveyed it once more. Most of the staff rooms on this floor were shared, but this one was particularly small, so Nurse Bellamy had it to herself. Most of the staff stayed on the premises, with the exception of our cook and Miss Jarrett, the librarian.

Like all the rooms, this one was outfitted with an iron bedstead with white coverings, a small wood table with chair, and a locking wardrobe for clothing and other personal belongings. Her bed was made and the room was generally tidy, other than a sheaf of papers scattered on her table. I turned the key to her wardrobe and searched through it, but there was naught but clothing hanging on the hooks inside it. In the top drawer at the bottom of the wardrobe were old, worn underlinens, a few hair combs, a watch with a cracked face, and a broken fastening pin. I did not see a locket.

In the drawer below this one were a couple of hairpins, a touring guide from the Museum of Manufacturers in Somerset House—which had just opened three years before to exhibit art and science collections—a box of lavender-scented pearl powder, and a jar of Crème Céleste.

This was curious. How could Nurse Bellamy afford such an expensive cosmetic as Crème Céleste, or "Heavenly Cream," as it was known? It was made of white wax—a substance from the sperm whale—sweet almond oil, and rosewater; my sister had a great affection for it, claiming that it hid blemishes and made her complexion light and smooth. I opened the jar and sniffed at it. It was fresh and had hardly been used. I closed it and returned it to the drawer. Regardless of how Caroline Bellamy had come to be in possession of a container of emollient, it wasn't likely to have anything to do with her murder.

Shutting the wardrobe, I turned my attention to the table and its untidy stack of papers. I sat down on the pale-green, painted cane chair, imagining myself to be the young woman I had so recently seen dangling from the ceiling. What had she known or done to get herself killed?

Among the papers were several bills for dressmakers, which had recently been marked paid. That was odd. Nothing in her wardrobe matched the quality of the dresses described in the bills, what with their dropped shoulders, ruffled sleeves, and matching, ornamented bonnets. Where was this clothing and how had she gotten it? Perhaps she had obtained it for someone else, maybe another family member. But it was still inexplicable how she could have afforded such garments.

I continued my search through Nurse Bellamy's papers and came across a haphazardly folded letter, dated just a week before. I scanned the contents and knew with certainty that whoever had killed her had done so in a cold rage.

CHAPTER 5

I read the letter again, this time more slowly to absorb the contents, written in a ragged hand.

> I know What you have dun. Do not Think you are not GILTY, or that you will avoid PUN-NISHMNT. The Book says the Wages of sin is DETH. You have Sinned but justis is at hand.
> -From the One who Knows

Was I holding a letter written by a killer? The thought chilled me. I didn't mind vomit, blood, and sputum, but ultimately I came from a refined family of good breeding. Murder was as foreign to me as a Chinaman.

Perhaps it would be best if this piece of paper was not left out. I folded it and placed it in my dress pocket, to lock away in my own room. On second thought, I decided I would remove the letter from the premises and store it in my lodgings a few blocks away.

It occurred to me then that if the police and the coroner

wouldn't be helpful, I would seek advice elsewhere. And who best to confide in than my old friend, Elizabeth Herbert?

★ ★ ★

Before I could arrange a meeting with my friend, though, there was the matter of burying Nurse Bellamy, which the Morgans helped accomplish with a minimum of fuss the next morning. Most of the staff accompanied the simple funeral cortege on the three-mile walk to Kensal Green Cemetery, where the nurse was laid to rest in a discreet, out-of-the-way area of the Anglican section. Graham Morgan must have fixed things with the minister and the cemetery director for Bellamy not to be buried as an outcast.

With that done, we all trudged back to Upper Harley Street to resume our daily lives, such as they had been before being shattered by Nurse Bellamy's death. Of course, the nurses and other staff still chattered incessantly about it, and who could blame them? I almost wanted to know what their thoughts were, but couldn't allow myself to be seen as flailing about in the matter. Once back inside the building, I offered a brusque little speech about doing one's duty and avoiding the temptation of being a busybody. I'm sure no one paid any attention to my words as they returned to their assigned spaces.

It flitted briefly through my mind that I had not agreed to pay for Nurse Bellamy's funeral, but someone must have done so. I would have to ask Morgan about it next time I saw him.

I then visited all the patients currently convalescing at the Establishment. The facility currently had just a handful of patients but could accommodate up to ten. We would eventually be able to house twenty, when the rear building was finished. Most of the inmates who had been brought over from the old location were no trouble, but there were a couple who were overrun with problems. Such a one was Alice Drayton, whose room I now entered, who would have tried the patience of Job, Abraham, *and* all the Israelites who wandered in the desert for forty years. None of them had had to cope with poor old Miss Drayton, who was a medical muddle. She had been a governess for many years, never marrying because of her great devotion to the family she served. I believe she had reared almost three generations of children for them. But her declining health meant she could no longer chase after her wards, so the family had turned her out with the tiniest of pensions. She lived with her sister and her sister's family somewhere but had come to the Establishment with a beastly case of thrush.

The white ulcers all over her tongue and inside her mouth should have made it difficult for her to speak, but nothing stopped Miss Drayton. Her chattering wandered as much as her mind. She was seated in a chair next to her bed and perked up considerably upon seeing me. "Miss Nightingale!" she exclaimed. "Finally someone is here. I've been waiting for *hours*. Even a *dying* person would have been granted a glass of water or some sort of attention by now."

Miss Drayton's sense of time was none too keen, so there was no point in arguing with her that the nurses visited each patient regularly to tend to their needs and that a carafe of water was kept full at each patient's table.

"How may I assist you?" I asked, surveying her room to

ensure that the window was open and that her bed linens were fresh.

"I wish to return to my bed." She pointed at the bed, only three feet away, with the end of her walking stick.

"Of course, madam," I said, moving to assist her.

I struggled with lifting her into an upright position, even though we had her walking stick and the back of the chair as tools to help us. Although Miss Drayton must undoubtedly have had plenty of exercise when she had been an active governess, the years since her retirement had clearly been spent in solitary eating, for she was quite rotund and unsteady on her feet. By the time I had her situated in bed, I was exhausted and sweating, as the woman outweighed me by at least eight or night stone. She, too, was perspiring, her thinning gray-tinged hair damp at her neckline and her considerable bosom rising and falling heavily several times as she caught her breath from the exertion.

"Now then," she said brightly, her thick lips breaking into a wide smile as her personality changed mercurially, as it always did. "Let's have a chat, shall we?" She still held her walking stick, and she now used it to tap the seat of the chair she had just vacated.

I sat in resignation. It was not in dislike of the poor woman, who certainly was not in control of her current condition, but because my mind was elsewhere and Alice Drayton required considerable care. I attempted to focus as she launched into a speech that babbled like water flowing downhill. "I've noticed that the maids are using a new laundry soap on the bed linens. Don't like it. Too much lye. That little imp John Wesley taught me to play backgammon yesterday. I do think he cheats, but I don't know how he does it. I must say I am glad that that Nurse Bellamy is gone. Did you know she was trying to poison me? I received a letter from my sister this morning. She plans to visit me on—"

I interrupted her rambling monologue. "Pardon me, Miss Drayton, what did you just say?" She had just completely shaken me out of complacence.

She began to dutifully repeat, "I received a letter from my sister this—"

"No, Miss Drayton, what you said before that. About Nurse Bellamy." I found myself gripping the hard wood seat of the chair.

The elderly woman paused and frowned, trying to reach back that far in her memory. "Oh, yes. That nurse was trying to murder me. With arsenic."

How had this gone unremarked upon till now? Had Miss Drayton told another nurse, who dismissed it as one of the patient's frequent rambles? Or was Miss Drayton simply twisting around what she may have heard about Nurse Bellamy to thrust herself into the story? It was impossible to know.

"Miss Drayton," I said slowly. "Can you tell me how you knew Nurse Bellamy was trying to murder you?"

She was only too happy to comply with the request. "Naturally I can. Because I witnessed her doing it. She sprinkled it into my morning tea before serving me."

CHAPTER 6

I was speechless. My mind was racing furiously, though. How could I verify what this patient was telling me? Where had the arsenic come from? The better question was how Miss Drayton had even realized it was arsenic . . . and why she would agree to drink it. This was a potentially serious matter, but first there was the matter of Nurse Bellamy and—

Miss Drayton interrupted my train of thought. "I'm glad you finally arrived, Miss Nightingale," she declared, frowning. "I've been waiting for *hours*. Even a *dying* person would have been granted a glass of water or some sort of attention by now. I want to sit in my chair."

Poor Miss Drayton and her deteriorating mind. I was saved from moving her again by the arrival of Dr. Killigrew, the Establishment's doctor. He entered with a hearty, "How are we today, dear lady?" directed at the patient as he placed his brown leather medicine bag, beaten and scratched from years of use, on her table.

He was Lady Canning's personal physician, and she had somehow convinced him to serve here one day each week as charity work, setting aside his customary guinea-per-visit fee.

I think he was reluctant to do so, not because of the money, but because he worried that it wasn't good for his reputation as a gentleman practitioner. After all, he had trained at Oxford and had been made a Fellow of the Royal College of Physicians, a prestigious appointment.

However, he also did not want to say no to one of his patronesses, and so he had agreed to come to the Establishment every Tuesday afternoon. This was his second Tuesday since my own arrival here, and he had concluded his prior visit by meeting with me in my study to discuss the patients' cases without condescension or pretension. I had to admit that he seemed to be a reasonably competent man in most cases.

Alice Drayton proceeded to enumerate her difficulties. "Why, I was just telling Miss Nightingale that I've noticed the maids are using a new laundry soap on the bed linens. I don't like it. I like John Wesley, though. Except he taught me to play backgammon yesterday and I think he cheated, but I don't know how. I have also noticed that I'm not walking as well as I was just yesterday. Of course, they are practically starving me here. I cannot even obtain a glass of water. Even a *dying* person . . ." She continued into her litany of complaints while Dr. Killigrew listened patiently.

The doctor had demonstrated an easy manner with the patients to which they all responded well, sometimes even tittering like young girls. The patients' swooning reaction was surprising, given that Dr. Killigrew was shorter than I, was almost completely bald with mere tufts of dark hair above his ears, and suffered from a shortsightedness that he refused to recognize, leaving him with a perpetual squint. However, these shortcomings were overcome by a ready wit. Beneath

Killigrew's hairless pate was a mind that was a veritable arsenal of amusing jokes and stories.

As Miss Drayton's monologue ran its course and she began wandering into the past, Killigrew cut her off skillfully. "That reminds me. I have a puzzle I've been meaning to share with you. What is the difference between a watchmaker and a jailer?"

Alice was stumped by the question. "A watchmaker and a jailer? Hmm . . . one is a criminal and one is not? One has rich customers and the other deals with thieves? I don't know."

Killigrew held up a finger. "I shall tell you. The difference between a watchmaker and a jailer is that one sells watches, whereas the other watches cells." He burst into laughter, and she followed suit, her own laughter more like a confused cackle.

Admittedly, some of his jokes bordered on the ridiculous.

Now, though, he turned serious. "I should like to try another treatment for your thrush, since the honey cure was not effective."

Alice nodded in childlike trust. "Yes, doctor. I was just telling Miss Nightingale that I've been getting poisoned here by one of the nurses."

I held my breath, waiting for Killigrew's reaction, but he just laughed gently. "I wouldn't exactly refer to your honey elixir as poison, given how greedily you drank it, Miss Drayton. But I've been reading about a new cure that might work. I will need you to, er, evacuate your bladder. Can you do this?"

Alice bobbed her head up and down, and reached out an arm to me. I helped her get up from the bed and escorted her to the toilet located behind a curtained screen in the corner of the room. While she relieved herself into the chamber pot, I waited on the other side of the screen with the doctor.

"Miss Nightingale," Killigrew said over the multitude of grunts, wheezes, and splattering sounds Alice Drayton was making behind the screen. "I should like a bit of sugar water in a cup, to help with the taste."

"Sir?" I said, blinking at the implication of his request.

"One of my textbooks suggests the drinking of one's own urine to cure ulcers in the mouth and throat. I think some flavoring will help it be more palatable for her. I shall have her drink it each afternoon for the next three days to see what happens."

Now, I am of the belief that nurses should take their cues from doctors, and that it is not our privilege to speak against them, no matter how much we might disagree with them. And indeed this was an instance in which I thoroughly disagreed with Dr. Killigrew. Although it is impossible to know exactly how diseases are spread, there are several theories that exist. In my own studies, I have become a firm believer in the miasma theory, which seems to be the only logical explanation, as it postulates that internal diseases are caused by noxious odors. Since I have already seen that making patient rooms as spotlessly clean as possible, and opening windows to let in as much fresh air as can be had, has restorative effects on patients, what other answer could possibly make sense?

"Dr. Killigrew," I said, going to Miss Drayton's fireplace and stoking the smoldering coals as I considered my words. I didn't wish to cause trouble but was very disturbed by his planned treatment. Once the flames were flickering again, I put the poker back on its stand. "Do you not think that the miasma caused by her urine will further aggravate her condition? Not to mention that what you propose is rather . . . repulsive."

Fortunately, Killigrew took no offense. "Most medical advances are borne out of what is repugnant to our sensibilities, Miss Nightingale. We shall consider this an experiment. If it works, then thrush sufferers will happily drink their own waste. If it doesn't work, we shan't bother trying it ever again."

I could find no argument against what he had suggested, so I went into the hall where I had the misfortune of finding Nurse Wilmot. However, she did obey my instruction to fetch a glass half full of sugar water with a minimum of fuss. By this time, Alice was finished draining her bladder.

"Miss Nightingale," came the plaintive cry from behind the screen. "Is there no one to help me back to bed? I've been waiting for *hours*, and even a *dying*—"

"Yes, Miss Drayton," I replied, cutting her off to save Dr. Killigrew from this repetitive complaint. I went behind the screen with her, ensured she was tidily arranged, then escorted her to bed. Then I emptied a portion of her chamber pot into the glass of sugar water that Wilmot had delivered. She had done so without breathing heavily upon me, for which I was grateful.

For his part, Dr. Killigrew sat in Alice's chair and watched me perform my work. It is the way of gentlemen doctors that they mostly instruct without ever *doing*. It is why I believe nurses are far more important to a patient's recovery than doctors.

He did, however, stand next to me as I administered the drink to the patient. Miss Drayton blinked in concentration as she took her first gulp. To my great relief, she didn't spit it out at me, although she did grumble about every mouthful. "Even a dying person wouldn't drink this and instead would wait for hours for a glass of water." Dr. Killigrew offered comforting words while I continued to offer her the cup, and eventually she drank it all.

"Not so bad, was it?" he encouraged her. "Before I go, you must answer this riddle for me. What is that which a young lady looks for but does not wish to find?"

Alice did not even attempt an answer, and I was worried that she suddenly looked a bit unsteady and pale.

If Dr. Killigrew noticed this, he did not comment but instead finished his joke. "A young lady looks for a hole in her stocking, even though she does not wish to find one, is that not right, Miss Drayton?"

She smiled weakly at him, and within a few moments I could see that color was returning to her fleshy face.

I heaved a sigh of relief and was about to tell her that I would check on her within an hour when Miss Alice Drayton suddenly belched, loudly and open-mouthed. It was as if a sewer had just exploded in our faces. I attempted to maintain a steady gaze at her, but my eyes watered from the stench. Even the good doctor took several steps back as I retreated to the window and pushed up against the sash handles to open it even further. The old Georgian window squealed against my weight but went up another six inches, and I breathed deeply of the outside air. It was full of coal smuts but fresher than what existed in the room.

How could Dr. Killigrew doubt for even a moment that bad smells carried disease on them?

★ ★ ★

I accompanied Dr. Killigrew as he went to visit another patient, Mrs. Ivy Stoke. She had had periodic asthma attacks, and a recent one had been so severe that her husband had insisted she come to the Establishment in hopes of a cure. She was unlike Alice Drayton in almost every way imaginable, except that they both flitted from topic to topic. However, Ivy was at least ten years younger and was a tiny hummingbird of a woman. She was inclined to quick movements, as if she were darting from flower to flower and inserting her needlelike beak into each one to taste what was there.

Despite the fact that she could change subjects without warning, it was never in a completely insensible manner, as could be true with Alice Drayton. Sometimes I wondered if it wasn't simply that Mrs. Stoke was highly intelligent and didn't care whether other people in the room were capable of keeping up with her varied interests. One of her particular interests was death, although I suppose that is common for people who have engaged with death on their dance cards and are waiting for the band to strike up the tune that will waltz them to their graves.

No doubt some of Mrs. Stoke's more serious asthmatic episodes had made her think she was embarking on those complicated dance steps. However, she certainly kept the building lively.

"How is Jasmine feeling today, Mrs. Stoke?" Dr. Killigrew asked, once more setting his bag down, this time on Mrs. Stoke's chair.

Jasmine was the woman's Blue Persian cat, without which

she refused to go anywhere. It spent most of its time draped over its owner but had been known to pick off a rat or two down in the kitchens, so I had no objections to its presence. It currently lay curled up in its owner's lap and blinked in irritation at the interruption.

"She is having a little trouble sleeeeping, sir," Mrs. Stoke said, a faint wheezing emitting from her as she exhaled.

"I see. She is perhaps having the same symptoms as her mistress, yes?" Dr. Killigrew said. He withdrew an ear trumpet from his case and handed it to me. Not only did physicians not perform the sort of manual labor involved in touching patients, but they particularly did not have contact with female inmates. I or another nurse assisted the doctor regularly on his visits.

Mrs. Stoke brightened at the suggestion. "I've always thought Jasmine was very empathetic." Mrs. Stoke coughed repeatedly but eventually caught her breath. "I told John that she could probably be of service to a meeeeeedium, sensing spirits in the room and such, although I'd never give up my darling girl for it. Have you ever been in contact with the dead, Miss Nightingale?"

John and Ivy Stoke owned a reasonably successful pet shop. The business specialized in Blue Persians, which were well known as Queen Victoria's favorite breed, thus attracting many people and their purses to the shop. So consumed were the Stokes with caring for their animals that Mr. Stoke had not yet been to the Establishment to visit his wife, and Mrs. Stoke spoke of her husband only in connection to whatever feline enterprises were in progress.

Ignoring her question, I sat at the edge of her bed, thus

jarring the offended Jasmine, who mewled in feline disdain at me and jumped off the bed. Her fluffy gray tail switched back and forth as she stalked off through the open door.

"Mrs. Stoke, if I may?" I held up the foot-long ear trumpet and she nodded. I leaned over and placed the flared end of the wooden tube against her chest and set the narrow end at my ear. As I moved it to different locations, I heard the distinct whistling sound that was uniquely Mrs. Stoke's whenever she was in an asthmatic episode. I handed the ear trumpet back to Dr. Killigrew and stated, "I believe Mrs. Stoke is in some distress."

Killigrew tucked the equipment back into his bag and frowned. I had read of a newer trumpet that used a flexible tube to both ears, which was reportedly more effective. Dr. Killigrew, though, tended to be more experimental with treatments than with diagnostics.

The doctor frowned. "Dear lady, have you been smoking your Potter's cigarettes, as I instructed?"

Mrs. Stoke made a face and shook her head, her burnished blonde curls flapping about her face. "I don't like them, sir. They taste dreadful."

Dr. Killigrew made an exaggerated face right back at her. "I am not interested in your satisfaction with your treatment, madam, but in curing your symptoms. I know Miss Nightingale has a devil of a time getting you to obey my instructions. However, I have been given a new recipe for cigarettes by a fellow physician, which we shall try to see if you like it better. Some American has invented it." He dug around in his coat pocket and pulled out a sheaf of papers. He thumbed through them until he found the one he wanted and handed it to me. "You will see that the chemist prepares this?"

"Of course." I examined the new concoction as he continued to address his patient.

8 parts stramonium leaves
8 parts green tea leaves
6 parts lobelia leaves
2 parts plantain leaves

The leaves were to be minced, moistened in a combination of potassium nitrate and water, then packed in an airtight jar.

"You will smoke one cigarette of wrapped leaves each night before settling down to sleep, but no more than one, do you understand?" The doctor then directed his patient, "Smoke it slowly, inhaling the smoke as deeply as possible. It will excite the airways, you see, and help you to breathe. If I see that after a week you are breathing better during the day, I shall send you home with the recipe."

As with Alice Drayton, I was concerned that the smoke would create a miasma that would aggravate someone in Ivy Stoke's condition, but I rarely argued with a physician. I would simply keep her room aired out as much as possible.

Fortunately, each patient room inside the Establishment had a window in it, even if they did not all have fireplaces. Although the main floor of the mansion had been hastily carved into various patient rooms, there had at least been an eye to ensuring that each one incorporated one of the building's many windows. It made for some inconsistently sized rooms, but the windows were far more important than room design. I firmly believe that only through the constant circulation of fresh air can a patient improve, no matter what his disease or condition.

The paints, wallpapers, carpets, and many of the pictures belonging to the previous owner had also remained behind. At least, the prints and paintings that were of little value endured. Rectangular dark areas stained the walls where long-hanging portraits and landscapes had been removed to settle in with their owner at his country estate in some far-flung county.

Ivy affirmed that she had understood Dr. Killigrew's instructions, but was immediately distracted by other thoughts.

"Where is Jaaaaasmine?" the woman wheezed, laboring to breathe.

"Probably down in the kitchen for a bit of Cook's veal, I imagine," I told her. "Or maybe she's cleaning out the vegetable larder of rats."

"She's a good girl," Ivy said. "She saves on the expense of rat poison, doesn't she?"

Tins of poison were cheap compared to feeding and housing our inmates, but I did agree that the cat had her uses. "Jasmine is quite a help downstairs, saving Cook time from setting so many traps."

Ivy's breathing was easing, although it would be only a matter of time before she had another attack. I would have to have the doctor's recipe fulfilled right away, but first I went to the fireplace to quickly stoke the coals before Dr. Killigrew and I took our leave. The area above the narrow mantel was dominated by a chipped, but detailed, porcelain crucifix. The

Christ figure gazed down at me in sorrow, and I involuntarily shuddered.

But Mrs. Stoke wasn't finished with us yet.

"Tell me, Miss Nightingale, have you experienced any more deaths here since that nurse was found?" she asked.

My hand froze while stoking the coal. Out of the corner of my eye, I saw that the doctor had also stilled in the midst of picking up his case. Naturally, he would have been aware of Nurse Bellamy's demise.

"Why do you ask, Mrs. Stoke?" I replied carefully, replacing the poker in its stand and turning to face her.

"Father Bradshaw says there is no absolution from murder or suicide," she announced, blinking innocently at me. "Anyone who dies of anything other than old age, accident, or disease creates a moral burden for someone somewhere, is that not so?"

My mind was whirling. Did she know something about Nurse Bellamy? Or was she merely repeating a theological discussion she had had with Bradshaw, a man of the cloth who I had been told spent considerable time at the Establishment visiting the inmates? Mrs. Stoke and her husband were devout Catholics. Catholicism had made a resurgence in England over the past couple of decades, what with Parliament granting the Catholics full civil rights in 1829. Just three years ago, Pope Pius IX had reinstated Roman parishes and dioceses, and the religion was now flourishing.

Flourishing enough, in fact, that many people were disturbed by it. Lady Canning, a staunch Anglican, had declared that no Catholics could be permitted entry into the Establishment and that it would treat Protestants only. However, I had made it a strict condition of my employment that we would treat any sick middling-class woman without question as to her worship. A Unitarian myself, I dance along the edge of Protestant theology and am probably one flip of a Bible page away from being sent to Coventry, as they say. I find that the whole lot of Anglicans, Lutherans, Methodists, and Presbyterians are so focused on arguing their doctrines that they never act out what they purport to believe. In my opinion, God watches what we *do*, not what we *say*, as the former speaks to our character and the latter speaks to our weakness.

"Father Bradshaw has a mind for deep matters," I replied neutrally to Mrs. Stoke.

"Oh, yes," she agreed, waving her hand in the air. "Father and I speak on many topics. Where *is* Jasmine? Have you been reading the latest serialization by Mr. Dickens, *Bleak House*? So engrossing, isn't it? He certainly writes fiction with a social purpose. So many people die in his books, though, don't they?"

I had little time for reading novels, but I knew that Mr. Dickens was also a proponent of miasma theory, so I considered him to be a like-minded soul. I understood that many of his books focused on London's poor and beleaguered, living in unsanitary conditions, who did tend to bear the brunt of most diseases. Of course, cholera had been springing up in various places over the past year, and that disease had no respect for social station.

Mrs. Stoke shook her head and clucked her tongue. "Death is a mighty terrible thing. Miss Nightingale, you simply must let me know if there are any more funerals to be had. I do so enjoy the solemn services and the incense. I also do believe I am feeling peckish. Might I have a tray? Maybe with a little of that apricot cream Cook made yesterday? Did I mention that I had a bit of a walkabout in the gardens yesterday? Mr. Lewis was pruning back the honeysuckle. Such a delightful fragrance, bringing back memories of my childhood."

Mrs. Stoke had caromed off the walls of three topics in under thirty seconds. Perhaps her mention of death had nothing to do with Nurse Bellamy, per se, but with a fascination with funerals. In any case, the Establishment's cook, Polly Roper, really had quite outdone herself on the molded fruit dessert the previous night.

"I shall talk to Mrs. Roper straightaway," I assured her, ready to leave. But Dr. Killigrew had parting words.

"Mrs. Stoke," he said, a ready grin on his face. "What is that which a cat has but no other animal?"

"You mean my Jasmine? Whiskers? No, many animals have those. Claws? No. I know! A sweet disposition."

Killigrew shook his head. "A cat is unique among all other animals because it has kittens." He laughed uproariously, and Ivy Stoke joined him.

As Dr. Killigrew and I left, Mrs. Stoke sat up in bed, humming. I wished I could be so placid.

*　*　*

I deposited Dr. Killigrew in the library while I went down to the kitchens so that I could request trays not only for Mrs. Stoke but also for Dr. Killigrew and myself. As I had assumed, Jasmine was prowling around under Mrs. Roper's feet as the cook casually dropped down bits of meat to her that she had pulled out of her burbling stew pot. With her back to me and unaware that I had entered, she cooed and crooned at the cat while stirring and sniffing at whatever creation she was making.

Polly Roper was unlike any cook my parents had ever hired, for she was as slim as a young girl, despite the fact that she must have been in her midthirties. Her face, though, was incongruent with the rest of her, as it was so chubby that her eyes were nearly blinking slits when she smiled. I attributed this to what she claimed was Germanic descent. She had once even insinuated that she was a very distant relative of the Austrian emperor, a proposition I highly doubted. She had no hint of an accent, but she certainly did produce some exotic dishes reminiscent of her supposed homeland.

Mrs. Roper's face may have made her look like a cherub, but she was anything but an angelic figure. I found her to be overly sensitive to any criticism whatsoever about her food. Likewise, she wasn't hesitant to offer her considered opinion of anyone who inadvertently slighted her dishes by asking for more salt or daring to leave a morsel behind on the plate. She was yet another problem I would have to find time to address, but she was a fleabite compared to the plague that awaited me regarding Nurse Bellamy's death.

I cleared my throat and the cook whirled around, a shred of sauce-laden meat in her hand, which immediately plopped to the ground and disappeared inside Jasmine's mouth.

"Miss Nightingale," she said, while the cat licked the ground at her feet. "I was just in the middle of my goulash for tonight's supper and didn't hear you. How may I help you?" The cook smiled, and her eyes almost completely vanished.

"Mrs. Stoke would like a tray, with some of the apricot

cream if there is any left over," I said. "She was quite enamored of it."

The cook preened at this, waving her apron as if to shoo away my fancy compliment. "I'll have to check the cool pantry. I'll get her something."

I also instructed that trays be delivered for Dr. Killigrew and me in the library. Within fifteen minutes, he and I were seated in front of our plates, as far away from the place where Nurse Bellamy had been cut down as I could manage. As a physician, Dr. Killigrew occupied a high rung on the social ladder, much as I did because of my family's position and wealth. Hence it was appropriate that we dine together. Besides, I wished to seek his advice on Nurse Bellamy.

I waited patiently while the good doctor spun a joke about Macbeth being the greatest chicken-killer in Shakespeare's plays because he committed murder most fowl. I also listened quietly as he speculated on the causes of Ivy Stoke's asthma. He postulated dust, vegetable irritants, and the climate, then expressed dissatisfaction with all of them.

I poured him a second cup of tea while he finished his bread, thickly lathered with pork gravy left over from the day's earlier luncheon. I ventured onto the topic of the dead nurse, first verifying that he had heard about what had happened. When he nodded solemnly that he had—at this point, who in all of London didn't know?—I broached my concerns.

The typically jovial man turned very serious as I described for him the manner in which I had found the nurse. I elaborated further about the contents of the letter I had found, my interviews with Miss Jarrett and Nurse Wilmot, and Alice Drayton's claim that Nurse Bellamy had been trying to poison her. I held back the fact that Roderick Alban had verbally annihilated me, as there was no point in humiliating myself a second time in the retelling of the incident, nor did I wish to risk the appearance of disparaging Alban.

"Where, exactly, did you find your nurse?" Killigrew asked. We rose from our finished meals and I showed him the alcove, where everything had been set back in order again, as though the grisly death had never happened.

"How well did you know her?" he then asked.

I sighed. "Truthfully, sir, I didn't even recognize her when I first found her. The past week of my employment had whistled by like the East Coast Main Line train from London to Edinburgh. I've hardly gotten to know the inmates, much less the staff. An unhappy circumstance I regret at this moment."

"So you don't personally know whether she was in a quarrel with anyone else here?"

"Based upon the letter I found, I would say she was in a quarrel with someone, but I cannot say with certainty that it is someone located here on the premises." It chilled me to imagine that there might be such squabbles and spats going on inside the building's walls that would result in murder.

Dr. Killigrew continued to question me, as if by staying in his role as a physician and simply eliciting some critical piece of information he could eventually come to the right diagnosis. "Have you overhead anyone talking about Nurse Bellamy? Had she been employed here more or less time than the other nurses? Was she well liked among the inmates?"

I shook my head in frustration, as I had few answers for him. "As I said, I hardly knew her. The librarian claims that Nurse Bellamy was very standoffish with the others. Nurse Wilmot implied that Nurse Bellamy had inappropriate gentleman callers in the middle of the night. But that's all hearsay, isn't it?"

"Hmm. Perhaps. Did Nurse Wilmot tell you who the gentleman callers were?"

"No," I admitted. "I had the impression that Nurse Wilmot may have just been spiteful."

"Hmm," Dr. Killigrew mused again. "Or maybe not. Perhaps someone else saw the gentleman—or men—in question coming or going."

Dr. Killigrew seemed fixated on this point. Did he believe that a romantic interest of Nurse Bellamy's might have killed her in some sort of crime of passion?

"I don't know. When I resume my questioning tomorrow, I can make further inquiries."

He seemed satisfied at that. Killigrew squinted now as he looked around thoughtfully, stroking his chin. "If I were a murderer, why would I hang my victim in the location known to be the favorite of the Establishment's new superintendent? It seems as though someone was making a point, doesn't it?"

That hadn't occurred to me, and I shivered at the thought.

"You believe Nurse Bellamy was murdered to prove something to me? But then what of the letter I found among her belongings, which suggests that whoever it was had a complaint directly against her?"

"True." Killigrew stepped out of the alcove and I followed him, happy to leave it. This would certainly no longer be my favorite location in the Establishment.

"May I ask where the letter is? I should like to see it for myself," he said.

"I have it in safekeeping among my things." Leaving him alone in the library once more, I went to my room and retrieved it, mindful that I needed to remove it from the premises at the first opportunity. I brought the badly creased square down to the doctor, who read it in mere seconds.

"The writer would appear to be both uneducated and enraged, eh? That could implicate any number of people, both inside and outside your doors."

He folded it up again and started to hand it to me, then stopped.

"You know, I have a friend with the Metropolitan Police who might take this a bit more seriously than the constables who came and took down the body. Perhaps I could take this letter to him and convince him to open an investigation."

Although I had sought out—and valued—Killigrew's advice, I had no desire for that sort of intercession unless it could come from on high. I took the letter from him and tucked it safely into my skirt pocket. "Thank you, but no. I'm afraid this is my own problem to sort out."

He inclined his head toward me. "As you wish, Miss Nightingale. And now I have my regular patients to see, so I will bid you good day."

It was only once he had gone that I realized he had left without completing his visitation with the rest of the inmates inside the Establishment, and so they would all have to wait until next week for their evaluations.

★　★　★

I remained quietly secluded in my room for the remainder of the evening. I attempted to calm my nerves by adding to my chart of employees at the Establishment, now including not just staff but inmates and regular visitors like the doctor. I left spaces for any information I could glean in my interviews, filling in what little had been told me by Jarrett and Wilmot. Finally, as my eyelids drooped heavily with sleep, I put the chart away and retired to bed. I could not really call it resting, though, as my night's sleep was fitful.

In the morning, I quickly did my ablutions and donned one of the few stylish day dresses I had brought with me from home. It was my intent to have a regular, somber uniform at the Establishment, but I saw no need to attire myself like a nun, wearing the same bleak clothing no matter where I was. In fact, it quite lifted my spirits to be wearing my bold plaid skirts of cranberry and gold, topped with a cranberry velvet cloak over my starched white shirtwaist. The bonnet I settled atop my head was new, a cream-colored, ruffled confection edged with gold ribbon.

Once I checked on all the patients, most of whom were still sleeping, I could finally spend the rest of the morning in a visit to my friend, Elizabeth Herbert. She had followed a very different path in life, yet I admired the steely strength that lay behind her delicate, genteel features.

First, though, I returned to my room for my reticule, gloves, and the threatening letter, which I intended to drop off at my nearby lodgings.

My bag and gloves were in my wardrobe, where I always left them. The letter, however, was gone.

CHAPTER 7

I spent a half hour combing repeatedly through all my possessions looking for the letter, but I knew from the start that it had been lifted from my room in the hour I had been downstairs checking on the inmates. Other than the doctor, though, who knew I had found it?

I supposed it would be natural for the killer to think I had it if it was no longer among Nurse Bellamy's things. Dear God, that meant that anyone in the building might have taken it out of my room. I would have to start locking my door as a safeguard for my valuables and, quite possibly, my person. I made a mental note to have Charlie Lewis, the Establishment's manservant, install a secure lock. I then decided to keep my plans to visit Elizabeth so as not to make anyone think I was upset or agitated.

It was two miles to her home in Belgrave Square, which I chose to walk even though I could have easily afforded a cab. Being this far outside my parents' reach made me feel like a fledgling chaffinch, having taken wing out of the nest in an attempt to fly. My mother would have said Nurse Bellamy's death was a sign that I was still dependent on parental care in the nest, but to mingle among the crowds in this congested part of London made me feel both alive and free. It was as if I were soaring above the treetops, even though I was just a tiny flotsam of flesh in a sea of humanity.

I made my way out of Marylebone and down along the edge of Hyde Park, getting yelled at twice by arrogant young men dashing around in their smart, two-wheeled curricles with no regard for pedestrians. Even that didn't dampen my enthusiasm for being out on my own.

I paused before passing by Wellington Arch, that grand piece of architecture behind Buckingham Palace and on the edge of Hyde Park. A bronze of the duke himself on a noble steed sat atop the grand, columned structure, which faced the corner entry to Hyde Park and served as an outer entrance to the grounds of Buckingham Palace. Many holidays of my youth had I spent in other countries, admiring iconic palaces, statues, and other structures. My parents were great lovers of travel. In fact, the first two years of their marriage had been spent traveling in Italy. My sister and I had been born during this time, Parthenope having been born in Naples but named for its Greek title. I, of course, was named for my own city of birth.

But never had I had an opportunity—unfettered and free—to admire sights like this. My life had been a continuous circle of my parents, governesses, and family friends holding my hand wherever I went. I knew that everyone loved me, but no one had ever understood that the mind remains cramped until it has room away from others to take wing. My father had filled my head full of math, science, and Latin, but then I was never permitted to contemplate, to reflect, to

merely *think*. Finally though, with my position as superintendent, I had found a way to wing my way out of my nest.

I neared 49 Belgrave Square, Elizabeth's own nest. It
was a dazzling mansion, built for her and her husband, Sidney
Herbert, just two years before. It was constructed as though
the architect had thought to place an octagonal tower against
a round tower against a third, square tower. Overall, it was
four stories of pleasing effect in gleaming white stucco. Unfortunately, Elizabeth's spacious nest did not permit her much
room for thought, either.

I twisted the doorbell key, and in mere moments after I
heard the bell trilling inside, the front door opened. My gloves
and bonnet were taken by a servant, and I was ushered into an
opulent sitting room that I confess momentarily made me miss
the comforts of my parents' home, Embley Park.

Ironically, I had met Elizabeth while traveling in Rome
five years earlier, when she and her husband had been newly-
weds on the Grand Tour. Embley Park was within visiting distance of Wilton, the Herberts' country home, and our friendship
had continued upon our return to England.

It had seemed natural that our friendship would not long
survive Liz's marriage, given that Sidney Herbert had held
the prestigious position of secretary of war for over a year now,
while my father had become disgusted with politics early
on. However, our friendship had flourished through correspondence, and Liz had brought her influence to bear in rec-
ommending me to Lady Canning for the position I presently
held at the Establishment. Now that I had moved from Hamp-
shire to London, we could see each other on a more regular
basis, even if she and her husband would be fleeing the city

for the countryside and its leisurely pursuits come next June. In fact, the Herberts were in London ahead of Parliament's opening this year, because war was rumored to be brewing against the Russians in the Crimean Peninsula.

I highly doubted Herbert was even home at the moment, as he was surely locked away somewhere in Westminster with some stuffy generals and heavily marked-up maps in a room full of cigar smoke.

Liz joined me shortly and we sat together on a long, brocaded settee. After we exchanged pleasantries about my own family and her four children—two girls and two boys thus far, including her husband's namesake, Sidney, born just six months previously—I quickly pivoted to more serious matters.

"Is Sidney home?" I inquired politely. I hoped not, as I wanted Liz to myself at the moment.

Liz laughed. "Of course not. He is planning and plotting with Prime Minister Aberdeen and Home Secretary Palmerston. I expect his career will be boosted considerably by the recent turn of events. You know that the Russians have gathered along the northern banks of the Danube River, don't you?"

I had not known this. My interests did not extend too far out from issues surrounding the care of patients and the study of diseases. Although I was aware of world events enough to be cordially conversant about them in society, a conflict with the tsar was of no immediate concern to me. Liz, though, was the daughter of a senior British Army commander who currently held the colonelcy of some Welsh regiment, so such events held great fascination for her and, no doubt, made her a valuable ally in her husband's career. It was obvious that

Sidney Herbert esteemed his wife in return, if the flawless rubies dangling beneath her looped hair and adorning her right wrist were any indicators.

Such thoughts reminded me of Richard again, and if I dwelt upon him, I would soon forget my true purpose in being here and end up gloomy and morose. Planting him firmly in the furthest recesses of my mind, I once again took up the mantle of storyteller and described for Liz in detail what had happened at the Establishment. As she was a dear friend, I also told her about my unfortunate visit from Roderick Alban.

Liz listened without interrupting, her large brown eyes silently registering shock and sympathy. When I was done, she reached out a hand to cover mine. "Oh, my dear, how positively dreadful."

There was a tapping at the sitting room door, and a maid entered with a tea tray. It was heaped with ham sandwiches, thinly sliced bread, and molded butter in addition to the requisite silver urn, cream pot, sugar bowl, and teacups. She set up a table next to the sofa, and soon we had warm cups in our hands. I put the mint-green queensware cup to my lips, and the steam delivered the smoky aroma of souchong to my nose.

Liz finished stirring milk and sugar into her cup and carefully tapped her sterling spoon on the rim. "If Dr. Killigrew is correct in his assumptions about the murder intentionally being committed in your favorite room, who do you think might have a grievance against you so strong as to do this?"

I rubbed the raised, cream-colored decoration of trailing ivy on my saucer as I contemplated her question. I like to think myself a realist, unafraid to confront truth wherever it lies, but to decide who might be disturbed enough by me to take *another* woman's life was almost too much to bear.

"Since my arrival at the Establishment, I have been a bit strict with the nurses, but they need discipline. You should see how slovenly some are, Liz. One nurse in particular, Nan Wil—"

Liz cut me off gently with a pat to my cheek. "Florence, dear girl, you needn't explain to me. I know you wish to make improvements right away, but may I suggest that sometimes you can be a bit . . . abrasive? You are almost always correct in your observations, but patience is not your strongest quality." She dropped her hand back down to her cup.

I bit my tongue on a retort. Leading the Establishment was a difficult endeavor, beset as I was by the nurses, the committees, and my own family. It was a simple thing to accuse me of impatience, not understanding the duress under which I toiled. Liz didn't have to contend with anything similar; she just had to pour advice and guidance into a husband, who was a willing vessel. Even if I was a bit snappish, how could that possibly be a cause for *murder*? But Elizabeth was trying to be helpful, and I greatly needed help, so I merely nodded my head. "Perhaps," I conceded, hoping it sounded gracious.

Satisfied with my response, Liz also nodded and then completely changed theories. "It seems to me that Dr. Killigrew makes an excellent point about the killer's motive, but then, the good doctor could also be completely wrong. The police and the coroner believe she committed suicide from a broken heart. But what if it was her lover who had a broken heart and killed her in return? The location of your library may be mere coincidence. Or perhaps the library had meaning for Nurse Bellamy herself."

I was mentally adding all of this to my chart as Liz pondered the situation. Could that be true? That Nurse Bellamy was an unfortunate victim of a rejected suitor? It was still a tragic—and unnecessary—occurrence, but I admit it made me feel a bit less worried that there might be a madman—or woman—skulking about with an intent to destroy me or the Establishment.

"I don't know how the library would have meant anything to Caroline Bellamy, other than perhaps as an assignation place." I was revolted to think of my library being defiled in such a manner.

Liz shrugged, her slim shoulders lifting in the delicate, graceful way that marked all of her movements. "And the significance of the murder's location isn't as important as who the murderer himself could be. I think it may be important to ascertain whether she had a beau who lived on the premises."

I frowned. "But Nurse Wilmot claims that she witnessed a man leaving through the kitchens."

Liz smiled. "Flo, I have been around adulterous men in Parliament long enough to know that they will commit any number of elaborate acts to cover their tracks. The secret exits might be staged for anyone watching. Do you have men living at the Establishment?"

"Just the manservant, Charlie Lewis." Of course, Dr. Killigrew and members of the men's committee had occasion to be in and out of the building. Roderick Alban's bluster over Nurse Bellamy's death flitted through my mind. And there were any number of delivery boys, repairmen, and such in and out on a regular basis. But only Charlie lived there.

"Are you suggesting that someone would make it obvious that he was leaving the building to hide the fact that he really *wasn't* leaving?" I asked. I decided in that moment that Mr. Lewis would be sitting in my study as soon I arrived back at the Establishment.

"I don't know, but isn't it a possibility?" Liz poured herself another cup of tea and offered me more, which I declined. My stomach was knotted up in contemplation of all she was suggesting.

"If the trouble is a scorned lover, whether inside or outside the hospital," I said, "how in the world do I capture such a killer?"

Did I really think I could call Charlie Lewis into my study and he would immediately break down into a confession? Then what would happen? He would attack me?

"I do wonder if Sidney might be able to help you," Liz mused.

"How so?"

"Well, I'm sure that, with one word from him, the police would be forced to treat it more seriously than as just a suicide. That would deliver some help into your hands." She drained her cup, then placed it and her saucer on the tea tray.

"Wouldn't that simply alert Parliament, and thus every London paper, about the scandal that has occurred at the Establishment?" I said in dismay, my stomach souring even more at the idea.

"But Parliament is not in yet. It could be, shall we say, our *secret.*" Liz's eyes sparkled more brilliantly than her jewels as she warmed to the idea.

I turned her suggestion over in my mind. How helpful would the police be if they were forced back into the situation at the behest of the secretary of war? The image that came to my mind was of a resentful, irritated Sgt. Warren Goodrick. That hostility would probably not lead to a productive relationship.

I shook my head. "I think that until I have something more definitive to go on, it is best not to agitate the police. Perhaps I will take you up on your kind offer at a later point."

The light in her eyes faded, but she ungrudgingly accepted my rebuff. "The offer stands at the ready," she said.

I wondered whether Liz wasn't a little bored in her role as the wife of Secretary Herbert. Wise counselor she might be to her husband, but doubtless most of her days were spent molting in this spacious, opulent cage. I couldn't risk what might happen with Lord Herbert's involvement, though, just to satisfy my friend's sense of adventure. No, for the moment I must proceed cautiously on my own.

★　★　★

I summoned Charlie Lewis to my study the moment I returned to the Establishment. He appeared in the doorway, worrying his tan wool cap in his hands. "Miss Nightingale? You wished to s-s-s-see me?"

Charlie was tall and lanky, with a weathered face that, like that of Nurse Hughes, made it impossible to determine whether he was thirty or fifty. If I hadn't known he was in his midthirties, I might have guessed by his reserved demeanor that he was much older.

"I did. Please sit down, Mr. Lewis."

Charlie took a chair across from me, his long legs almost touching the burr of my desk. He took no notice of the rich and intricate knotty whorls in the wood grain but instead slouched in the chair, the posture of a man embarrassed by how overly tall he was and completely unaware of the precautionary coal poker I had at the ready on my side of the desk. I guessed that he must be six and a half feet upright, and even in the chair he towered over me. As I studied him while deliberating on my first question, I realized that he was yet another member of this hospital whom I didn't really know. I had talked to him only in passing, asking for his assistance with unsticking heavily painted window sashes, or moving furniture, or removing items from high shelves. Charlie tended to spend much of his time out of doors, puttering around in the rear garden where the inmates could stroll or be pushed about in wheelchairs on pleasant days. As consumed as I was with ensuring that the inmates were comfortable and beginning to address the problems with my nurses, I had had scant thought for someone who said little, obeyed me without question, and was unobtrusive. All I had noted was his stutter, which became worse the longer he talked. That was probably the root of his reticence.

He licked his lips nervously. A lock of sandy brown hair fell into his right eye, and he ran fingers through it to brush it back off his face. As I still said nothing, he began tapping his left foot rapidly on the floor, quite a sight in such a long-shanked man.

I folded my hands together on my desk. "Mr. Lewis, I do not recall: were you in attendance at Nurse Bellamy's funeral?"

My question startled him. "Ma'am? I-I-I-I had an errand to run at the ironmonger's. I-I-I-I needed some n-n-n-nails and a new h-h-h-hammer. I'm s-s-s-sorry, ma'am, if I should have been there. I d-d-d-didn't mean to—"

I held up a hand. "There is no need to apologize. Did you know Nurse Bellamy well?"

He ran a hand through his hair again. "No, ma'am. I k-k-k-keep to myself mostly. Most women don't like Charlie, although I-I-I-I am a great, a great admirer of them."

"I see," I said. "And you did not greatly admire Nurse Bellamy in particular?"

His mouth dropped open and there was panic in his eyes. "I-I-I-I swear, ma'am, that I am most 'spectful of the l-l-l-ladies here. My unwanted affections I-I-I-I keep to myself."

I wasn't sure what sort of answer that was, but I also realized that I had leapt into questioning the man without getting to know him. I took a deep breath before starting over. "Mr. Lewis, I confess that I don't know much about you. How did you come to the Establishment?"

The topic switch confused him once more, and I was beginning to realize that Charlie Lewis was not as sharp as most people. However, he valiantly carried on, presumably to please me. "I'm just an old tar, ma'am. Served Her Majesty from the time I was a lad of fourteen until last year."

I noticed that when he spoke of the Navy, he no longer stuttered, and in fact sat up straighter and gained some confidence.

"Why did you leave Her Majesty's service?" I asked.

" 'Twas my own fault, ma'am. I'm ashamed to say that I copped a ter'ble case of green gills in my last year. I dunno how it happened after so many years. But my mates couldn't take me constantly offering up my daily rations on deck, and no amount of lashing 'cross my back fixed it. So 'twas asked to leave. Did some odd jobs, I did, until Lady Canning found me when I was a painter's helper working on her ladyship's iron fence. Now I have my job and I'm very happy for my security here, ma'am, 'deed I am."

So Charlie Lewis had been drummed out of the Navy for seasickness. It was ironic and amusing actually, but it was obvious that the man had been devastated by losing his position in the Navy and considered himself to have found a safe place in the Establishment. Still, that didn't prove or disprove anything.

"Lady Canning assigned you your room in the basement near the kitchens, didn't she?" I asked. I was becoming increasingly more uncomfortable with how much I *didn't* know about this place.

"Yes, ma'am. Lady C–C–C–Canning wanted to make sure all was proper, and that the w–w–w–women were kept separate from me." The stuttering had returned.

But that meant his rooms were near the kitchen where Nurse Wilmot claimed to have seen Caroline Bellamy's inamorato depart.

It was time to be blunt with the man. "Mr. Lewis, I will tell you that someone here says she witnessed a man leaving late at night through the kitchens after, ahem, visiting Nurse Bellamy. I am wondering if that man was you."

More bewilderment. "Ma'am, I have no n–n–n–need to leave the building 'cept to pick up tools and supplies. I–I–I–I never do that at night."

This short interview was convincing me that Charlie Lewis was an uncomplicated man who had no wherewithal to conduct a thought-out murder. What had happened to Caroline Bellamy had certainly not been a fit of rage or a spontaneous occurrence, but rather had been devious and well planned. I didn't think it possible that Charlie had done it. That didn't mean though, that he wasn't lying to me and that he didn't have "affections" for the nurse that he kept to himself. Because of my vocal suspicions, I doubted he would confess them to me, either. I would simply have to keep my eye on him, much as I needed to do with everyone in the building, staff and inmates alike.

I glanced down at the new chart I had developed. I had already interviewed Nurse Nan Wilmot, our librarian Persimmon Jarrett, and our cook Polly Roper. I traced a couple of the other names on the list. "I wish to speak to either Nurse Hughes, Nurse Frye, or Nurse Harris. Will you fetch one of them for me?"

"Harris," he repeated dumbly. "Yes, ma'am."

In that instant, though, I had another idea. "Never mind, Mr. Lewis. I don't need to see any of the nurses at present. You may return to your duties."

It was after four o'clock, and the nurses were likely taking afternoon tea. It was a bit stealthy of me, but I thought it might be a good time to go over those three nurses' particular rooms to see what might present itself to me.

★ ★ ★

I went up to Nurse Marian Hughes's room first. It was located across the hall from Nurse Bellamy's and was also private. It was furnished in the same simple manner, but Hughes's surroundings were far more interesting, to say the least.

Fabric-covered boxes in a kaleidoscope of colors and textures adorned every available table and windowsill. On the wall above her writing table was a piece of embroidery in a scratched, bent walnut frame. I went to peer more closely at it.

The design was of a thatch-covered cottage with "Cleanse thou me from secret faults, Psa 19:12" written beneath it. The name "Marian Rose" had been stitched in varying hues of blue to form a border on the piece.

My sister had always been the needlewoman of the two of us, much to my mother's despair. It had always been Mother's plan that I should be accomplished in needlework, music, and scintillating conversation, so that I might attract a titled or monied husband into our family. Her hopes were thus concentrated because my father's property was entailed and would be going to my Aunt Mai and Uncle Sam when Papa died. She had even managed to have Parthenope and me presented to the queen at one point, the most terrifying experience of my life.

In a great irony, I had instead adopted my father's interests in math, science, and languages, which no desirable suitor would ever care about in a wife but made me a perfect candidate for striking out on my own to raise the standards and stature of nursing for the sake of inmates.

I had also already developed an interest in checking on ailing relatives and villagers and was developing skills in keeping the sick nourished, hydrated, and warm or cool, depending upon what was needed.

I ran my finger along the edge of the two-story cottage's jagged roofline, done expertly in silver, brown, and tan threads.

The cottage was a sweet representation of an idyllic home where children could be raised and tranquility would be de rigueur.

Poor Mother. She had had just such a vision for me, despite my boyish tendencies. Although Parthenope was the more perfectly cultivated one, I was the one who had been graced with beauty. Mother had assumed that my perfectly white and straight teeth, my creamy complexion, and my dewy eyes would overcome my lack of feminine skills.

It had seemed to be true when Richard Monckton Milnes came to court me. I had met Richard when I was twenty-two. He was older than me by eleven years but was still ludicrously handsome. I was as besotted by him as he seemed to be by me. He was already a member of Parliament as a conservative member for Pontefract, and was known for his literary and poetic wit. He had also been noticed by men like Lord Palmerston.

My mother had nearly swooned over Richard's attentions to me, particularly since I had already rejected a proposal from Henry Nicholson, one of Mother's brilliant, hand-picked suitors, who also happened to be a cousin of mine. Had she really thought I would entertain an offer from so close a family member? As Richard and I had drawn closer through a love of reading the philosophers and debating theology, my mother had essentially declared the family future secured.

Parthenope had also been relieved, as her suitors had been sparse and she, too, was relying on me for her salvation.

But being a savior is very distressing work, and I wasn't formed for such lofty efforts.

Besides, my encounter with God in my seventeenth year

had shown me clearly that my purpose was far from being anyone's pathway to heaven. To the contrary, He had shown me clearly in a vision that I was to be set aside for a specific purpose, although it would be several years of waiting and seeking before I understood that purpose to be caring for the sick and infirm.

I can still remember the day of my vision as a great flash of light coming upon me while I strolled through the February gardens of Embley Park. I had clutched my cloak as I enjoyed the solitude and silence of walking among the frost-covered boxwoods, their bright green leaves juxtaposed against the bare branches of all the other flora around me. I have always tried to walk every day, not just to stay robust, but because it is precious time to think in private. My mother and sister would never have dreamed of parading around anywhere that their breath would crystallize in front of their faces, so I never worried that they would try to join me. As I strolled that day—my nose and ears numb and my throat burning from the cold air—my line of vision was consumed with a fullness of light, as if the sun had descended to earth directly over me. As I stood there, stunned, I truly heard a voice say, "You will hold yourself apart for the task I will assign you."

I froze in abject fear, of course, as I wondered whether I had lost my senses before ever approaching my dotage. After all, any normal person who starts to claim to hear voices might find herself tossed into Bedlam forthwith.

As I quailed, though, the blinding light lifted like a curtain, and once again I stood in normal daylight, grateful that I had at least not embarrassed myself by evacuating my bowels.

Naturally, my parents and sister believed me to be inventing tales so as to avoid my presumed role in life. No amount of pleading, cajoling, and isolating myself in my room could convince them that I had had a genuine vision from God and was determined to follow and obey it.

Richard, though, was the first and only reason I ever wavered in my determination to wait patiently on my divine destiny. He was utterly devoted to me and respected my intellect. His hand folded around mine like a perfect, comfortable glove. His laughter was rich and infectious. He sought my opinion in every decision he made.

Oh, yes, I would have done well with Richard Monckton Milnes.

His first proposal to me wasn't unexpected, but I was still tortured by having to make my response. I finally told him no, describing the vision I'd had. In true Richard fashion, he didn't mock me but asked serious questions about what I'd experienced.

A week later, Richard returned to me and declared that my vision was not incompatible with marriage to him. He assured me that he would be perfectly pleased to let me do as I would as his wife, as he, too, wished to obey whatever God's leading was.

God help me, I believed him wholeheartedly. He *would* have permitted me just about anything, and I desperately wanted to say yes. Only I knew I could not, for I had a destiny that did not involve the natural feminine triad of wife, home, and motherhood. The day of my formal refusal was the worst of my life, as I saw the tender light leave Richard's eyes, to be replaced with confusion, incredulity, and anger. I would never forget watching the back of his finely tailored jacket as he walked away from me, grabbed his velvet-trimmed hat from the hat stand, and stormed out of the house.

I took a deep breath and dropped my hand from the stitching on Nurse Hughes's wall. Remembering what had happened next served no purpose, and I had a murdered nurse to worry about. And one of that murdered nurse's peers had an odd collection of boxes. I suppressed only a moment's twinge of guilt before picking up one of the boxes from the desk. The container and lid were covered in a coral-and-white-striped taffeta with a small brown stain along one side. I pried off the lid and was puzzled by the contents.

Inside were numerous squares of heavy paper, and in the center of each was a different button, tacked to the paper with a small pin that was bent at the back of the paper to keep the button attached. As I poked through the contents of the box, I saw that most of the buttons were common ones of plain brass or fabric-covered wood. But there were some ornamental buttons with stamped designs on them, a few studded with paste diamonds, and a lone enameled button. Several were jet-glass mourning buttons.

How very odd.

I picked up another box and found another assortment of card-backed buttons. Surely they were not all filled in the same manner?

I walked over to her window, which had a panoramic view of the rear gardens below. A brick-patterned walkway spoked the gardens where Charlie was on his hands and knees, fixing some loose bricks in the section of walkway that approached a figural vase standing proudly in the center of the space. The gardens were still green but had little left blooming in them.

I lifted another box that rested on the sill, this one covered with an old, mottled gray piece of wool. Again more buttons. I tried two more boxes before realizing that that was all I would find in any of them. I was baffled by why Nurse Hughes had them. Did they belong to every piece of clothing she had ever owned in her life? I doubted that, for she would have had to be quite wealthy to own this number of articles. Had she stolen them? Perhaps, but for what purpose I couldn't fathom.

I abandoned examining them and went to her armoire. It contained what I would expect from someone of her station: plain underclothes and a nightgown of thin unbleached muslin, as well as a couple of serviceable dresses in cheap fabrics. However, they were well maintained, much like the dress Nurse Bellamy had been wearing when I found her. Maybe the two nurses had hired the same seamstress, although I couldn't for the life of me understand why they would spend precious money on such an extravagance instead of making repairs themselves.

A search of her desk drawers revealed nothing of interest either, just a matted hairbrush and tortoiseshell comb with two missing teeth, plus a jar of tooth powder and a worn boar-bristle toothbrush.

Nurse Hughes's worldly value seemed to be in the enormous button collection she owned. It was odd, to be sure, but not criminally suspicious in any way. Maybe I would discover something more incriminating in the room that Nurses Frye and Harris shared next door.

I gave the embroidered sampler a final look, unsure why I

was so drawn to it, given how much it caused me to dwell upon the past. The past was a far more dangerous place for my mind to reside than the investigation of my dead nurse. Yet I traveled back one more time as I ensured all of the button boxes were arranged as they had been before.

I had attempted to rearrange my life after Richard stormed out the door that day. As if I hadn't been heartbroken enough on my own, my mother compounded my misery by wailing like a banshee over my "stupid, insipid selfishness." My sister took to coming to my bedchamber at all hours of the night to plead with me. With tears coursing down her face, she would beg me to reconsider Richard's offer and thus save the Nightingales from penury.

On two of Parthenope's nightly visits, I tried to explain my reasoning and to make her see that I wanted to marry Richard even more than she and Mother wanted it. Unfortunately, as much as Richard himself might grant me absolute freedom, society itself would not be so open and easy about it. I also reiterated my firm belief that I had been called for a divine—if yet unidentified—purpose, in an attempt to appeal to her own deep religious sensibilities.

Parthenope had looked at me blankly, then started weeping again.

I stopped trying to make her understand and instead locked my door at night so that I could be alone with my own tears.

At least there had been some relief in Papa's indulgent shrug. "You know our girl, Fanny," he reminded my mother. "She will have her own way in all matters. I won't force her to marry where she does not wish." Which only sent Mother into more grief-laced tirades.

I believe he was secretly glad of my decision, because by remaining unmarried, I would be at his side longer. It was disloyal to my family to consider it, but I often thought that my life was frequently Mother and Parthenope pitted against Papa and me. My father and I had few victories in Mother's march to secure the family's salvation.

Naturally, my mother had no sympathy for my own personal misery and seemed oblivious when I stopped eating and lost interest in my books and friends. I suspect she viewed my listlessness as just punishment. After a couple of months, when my already-spare frame had shed enough flesh that even Parthenope was becoming alarmed, I was startled one day to see Richard coming down the drive in his carriage.

I had been sitting in a chair next to the window, wrapped in a blanket that was long past requiring a washing, when I had to blink several times to understand exactly what I was seeing. Once I realized that it truly was him and not a hallucination borne of food deprivation, I stood, letting the ratty blanket fall to the ground. Against my own better senses, I quickly washed up and changed, and decided that if he offered for me again, I would accept him. Oh, yes, I was certain that I would fling myself from a window for Richard, if only he would ask.

He didn't ask. Instead, Richard approached me like a man determined to break a wild filly: gentle, wary, appraising me. With his gentle handling of me, we soon picked up where we had left off, as though the disastrous proposal had never occurred. I gained my figure again as Richard and I resumed our courtship at full speed. Mother was so pleased.

A year later, Richard gently suggested once more that I

might want to reconsider marriage to him, this time offering a specific promise that if I wished to serve as a nurse in people's homes or train other women in nursing work, he would stand behind me.

How tempting it was. Thoroughly unable to either refuse or accept him, I temporized and said I would think about it. I still shake my head in wonder at Richard's patience. Mother and Parthenope also tiptoed around me, alternately hopeful and despairing over what I might do.

And so it went until our entire relationship had reached an extraordinary span of nine years. On a frigid January night, as we sat companionably next to each other before a crackling fire while snow began to gently drift outside, Richard turned my face to his.

"My love," he began seriously. "I hope I have convinced you of my true and honorable intentions toward you and of my hope that you have come to trust me."

I froze, feeling myself to be that unbroken horse of years ago, ready to bolt. He sensed it and exhaled loudly in exasperation as he dropped his hand from my face. I suppose he had had a much longer and prettier speech to offer me, but instead he drove straight to his point. "Flo, I can do no more to gain your confidence. You yourself admit that you are not flourishing here, living under your mother's claw. I can offer you anything you could possibly want in life. Will you not become my wife?"

This time, my tarrying did not work. Richard slapped his knees in frustration and rose. "Very well," he said, seeming to accept the inevitable with a heavy sigh.

Once more, he plucked his hat off the stand and left. This

time it wasn't as a roaring lion but as a gentle lamb resigned to his slaughter. I once more stood at the window and watched him in the exterior torch lights as he waited for his carriage to be brought around. The swirling snow dusted his hat and broad shoulders, but he seemed to pay it no mind as he leapt into his carriage and slammed the door without even a glance back toward the house.

Even in that awful moment, I hadn't yet realized that Richard had asked me to marry him for the final time. I foolishly held out some hope that he might change his mind and venture into my world again without asking for my hand. It was a stupid and irrational thought on my part, but when are affairs of the heart ever anything but nonsensical?

Because I was more irrational than the first time Richard had left me, that foolish hope kept me buoyed for some weeks. Not even my mother's carping penetrated my shield of confidence that he would return at least one more time.

What bitter salt it was in my wound when Richard announced an engagement not three months later.

Even worse, I learned of it when Mother read it aloud from a newspaper article at the dinner table. She slapped the paper down and stared at me belligerently, as though I had arranged for him to do it. Despite the fact that my ears were pounding at the rush of blood through my head, I swallowed and smiled as bravely as I could. "How very nice for him," I managed.

With all of Mother's strangulated screeching and squeaking over the next few weeks, I was surprised she didn't develop black wings so that she could begin hanging from the ceiling. I was miserable enough myself that I would have happily turned into a moth so she could simply swallow me whole and satisfy her ravenous hunger.

I do credit Parthenope for recognizing how truly unhappy I was and making attempts to soothe me with little gifts and sweetmeats whenever Mother wasn't around. Eventually my mother forgave me, as she had little choice. As for me, I learned how to live with a heart that leaked a bit of sorrow each day, like the tears that trickled from me eyes and wet my pillow each night.

Now, two years later, I still think of Richard nearly every day, wondering about his health and happiness. He is at the top of my list of prayers each morning and night, and I will undoubtedly never get over him.

I left Nurse Hughes's room and closed the door behind me, wiping my hands against my skirts as if that would cleanse me of my foray into the past. Determined to focus strictly on the present, which was the only time period I could do anything about, I went to the rooms of Nurses Margery Frye and Clementina Harris.

Chapter 8

Nurse Frye and Nurse Harris may have been thrown together in close quarters only as part of their work, but they did seem to share much in common in terms of chaos. Upon opening their door, I felt as if I'd just walked into a Bethnal Green slum. My nerves thrummed as I took in the condition of the room, which was like the others except a little larger and with two painted, iron-posted bedsteads. Clothing and personal items were strewn all about, as if a violent storm had torn through the room. The room reeked to high heaven, almost as if there had been a corpse left to rot in it. Was there an old dish of food buried in here?

How could the inmates expect their conditions to be clean and safe when the nurses themselves lived no better than a pair of muck-rolling old sows? Frye and Harris had just catapulted themselves to the top of my list for hospital improvements, if my temper did not cause me to fire them outright.

Of course, I couldn't do that, could I? If I did, I was potentially turning a murderess out into the street, unpunished. In fact, all of my planned reforms would have to wait until the killer was brought to justice. The thought angered me even more.

At least I had no cause for concern that I was disturbing the premises with my search. I went to work, searching for anything that would give me insight into who my nurses were. Secreted in the back of the armoire the two women shared were two identical bottles of clear fluid labeled "Booth's Old Tom." One was unopened and the other was half finished. I pulled the cork on the opened one and took a whiff. The telltale odor of licorice-laced liquor was overwhelming.

I recorked it and set both bottles aside on their shared desk. So which of the two nurses was addicted to gin, the scourge of Great Britain? As with many medical practices, gin had been borne of the greatest of intentions and ended up ruining a large swath of London's populace. The British Army had encouraged the drinking of gin with tonic to ward off malaria in our growing empire, as the quinine in tonic acted as an antimalarial agent. Then the Navy had supported the drinking of gin and bitters, since the bitters alleviated seasickness. The unintended result was the establishment of numerous gin distilleries clustered in Clerkenwell, each spewing out bottles of drunkenness and despair on London's poor.

And apparently upon at least one of my nurses.

I put my sleeved arm over my nose and took a deep breath inside my elbow. The stench in here was awful. What was it? I tossed aside string-laced chemises, lurid penny dreadfuls, and broken hairpins as I searched for the source of the smell. How in heaven's name did they sleep in here?

I dropped to my knees to search under their beds. I saw a

strange shadow beneath the bed that was next to the window. Rising up once again, I grabbed the round, paint-chipped posts at either end of the foot of the bed and dragged the end of the bed to one side to inspect what was beneath it.

To my utter disgust, it was a dead rat. How had these two not been aware of a rotting rodent in their room? Clearly little Jasmine had not been doing her job very well either. Or maybe this was Jasmine's gift to the nurses. I covered my mouth and nose with my hand and bent over to take a closer look at the odious creature. He wasn't desiccated, so he hadn't been here too long, but certainly long enough to become offensive. Had he—

At that moment, one of the very nurses in question entered, grinning foolishly as she stared down at a piece of paper in her hand. That grin disappeared quickly when she saw me standing in the center of the room, my hands clasped primly in front of me. Her gaze darted over to where the one bed had been yanked away from the wall, and she looked back at me in silent confusion. I had not before paid much attention to Margery Frye's appearance, but now I saw the pouchy abdomen and the tiny broken blood vessels in her cheeks. I knew she was around my age, but her frizzed hair and stout frame made her look two decades older.

Frye's appearance was emblematic of all that was wrong with nursing. No wonder the public considered nursing the profession of thieves and drunkards. That was mostly what they were. I was determined to change that.

The nurse quickly folded her paper and shoved it deep into her dress pocket. "Something wrong, Miss?" she asked.

I hardly knew where to begin with the many things that

were wrong. "Yes. This room is appalling. You will take care of it immediately."

Frye's mouth gaped, and I got a glimpse of a few rotting molars. "But, Miss Nightingale, this isn't my mess. I've been trying to fix Clem's grubby self. It don't matter what I try, the room ends up like this."

I crooked my finger at her and led her to where the dead rat was. Pointing down, I said, "You hadn't noticed this or tried to fix it?"

She wrinkled her nose. "I stayed over at a friend's house the past couple of nights. Look at it all." She swept a hand out. "I have to get out to keep from going dotty, don't I? It must have happened while I was gone."

I grabbed the half-used liquor bottle and held it up, its clear contents splashing violently beneath the cork. "Does this also help you from going dotty?" I demanded.

That silenced her momentarily, but she quickly regained her footing. "That's awful, ma'am. I knew Clem had her secrets, but I didn't know she had a taste for spirits. A shame." Frye shook her head dolefully.

Brash and insipid, just like Nurse Wilmot. I wanted terribly to dismiss her from her post in that moment, as I was constitutionally unable to trust a woman I suspected of being too fond of drink. Not only for the good of the Establishment, but to serve as an example to the other nurses. I simply couldn't risk it, though, while I was seeking out a murderer in our midst.

I might not be able to fire her yet, but it didn't mean she wouldn't know the rod of discipline. "Watch your tongue, my girl. I won't tolerate a drunkard. And you will refer to her as Nurse Harris."

But almost as if she had insight into my very thoughts, Nurse Frye's lips curved into a secretive smile as she removed the gin bottle from my hands and set it on the desk. "I'll tell Clem you said so, Miss."

"You'll keep that lesson for yourself, Nurse, lest you find yourself working in the laundry." Perhaps I couldn't let her go outright, but I could make her life uneasy. A nurse's position in the Establishment was a comfortable one, much better than being locked away in the basement with one's arms soaked in dirty water up to the elbows all day.

She blinked several times and made a marginal step toward contrition. "You haven't been here long, Miss Nightingale, so I've been waiting for you to get all settled in before telling you that Clem—Nurse Harris—is a problem around here."

I paused, instantly alert. "What do you mean she's a problem?"

Frye pushed away items on the second unmade bed and sat down. It was more egregious behavior in my presence, but I wanted to hear what she had to say. So rather than chastising her for sitting down without being invited to do so in the presence of her superior, I followed her lead and sat across from her on the bed next to the dead rat. I was actually becoming used to the stink, which was not unlike a wound I had once treated on a villager who had had his leg gashed by a wild fox. The man had waited weeks before seeking help, and I had been the one asked to tend to his festering flesh. I suppose rotting meat smells like rotting meat, whether it belongs to human or beast.

"Nurse Harris isn't who she says she is, Miss," Nurse Frye

began mysteriously, as if she were a medium about to summon a spirit into the room.

"And who is Nurse Harris?" My patience was going to wear thin quickly if Nurse Frye was planning to shroud herself in dramatics.

The woman looked around as if to check whether anyone might be listening. More mystery for my benefit. However, what dropped out of her mouth next was truly shocking.

"She's here working as a nurse to hide her past," Frye said softly. "I think she killed her husband."

My mind warred with itself. It was difficult to believe this to be true, but it would not be the first unbelievable truth I had encountered over the past couple of days.

"Why do you think she killed her husband?" I asked.

"She has a mourning locket that she wears every day. She refuses to say who it's for, but she also wears a mourning brooch. There's hair done up to look like a basket's weave in it. That's for a man she lost. If she won't say who it is, it's probably because she feels guilt over it." Frye nodded knowingly.

Nurse Frye was proving to be very irritating. "How in heaven's name does a mourning locket prove that Nurse Harris murdered her husband? Or that she even had a husband?" I snapped. "We have experienced a tragic death in the hospital, and you are rattling on about an idea that is an invention of your mind?"

Frye was unperturbed. "Well, it's not like *I* killed Nurse Bellamy, is it? I hardly knew her. She must have been caught doing something. That's how most people meet bad ends, isn't it?"

I was not going to allow Frye to change the subject. "You haven't answered my question. Why are you convinced that Nurse Harris killed her husband?"

Frye knew I was a captive audience, though, and intended to torture me to the answer. "Because I'm a witness to things, aren't I?"

"What things?" I said in exasperation. "Speak plainly and quickly, Nurse Frye, or so help me, I'll—"

Frye held up a ragged-nailed hand. "You needn't make a fuss with me, Miss Nightingale. I'll tell you."

I felt my eyes narrowing at her insolence. She and Nurse Wilmot had a great deal to learn if they were going to remain here at the Establishment.

How had the previous superintendent ever considered these two for employment at an institution started by the esteemed Lady Canning? A blot on the Establishment was a blot on Lady Canning's reputation.

"Let me show you," Frye said, rising and digging around below the mattress beneath her. She withdrew a bone-handled carving knife with what appeared to be a rusted blade and held it up in the air. "Clem—Nurse Harris—doesn't know that I know this is here. Most likely her weapon, right?"

She lightly tapped the blade tip with her other hand. "This is blood, ma'am."

I had no choice but to agree with her assessment. But how did it follow that Harris had stabbed her husband with it, just because she had possession of it and she wore a mourning locket? I held out my hand, and Frye placed the knife handle in my palm. I curled my fingers around it in disbelief that I was potentially holding the weapon used in a murder associated with the Establishment. It simply could not be true.

That Nurse Frye was lying to me at some level, I had no doubt. But was it possible that she was telling the truth when she accused Nurse Harris of misdeeds?

As I took the gin bottles with me to dump into the sewer pipes, I realized that investigating the death of Nurse Bellamy permitted more probing questions of the staff than would normally be socially acceptable, with the side effect of a better opportunity for me to instill rigor and cleanliness in this place.

★　★　★

I found Clementina Harris in the basement of the Establishment, humming an unrecognizable tune as she folded sheets on the long table in the center of the linen room. The space was located next to the laundry room, and both were reached through a doorway at the far end of the kitchen. Shelves full of sheets, blankets, and pillowcases lined three of the upper walls of the linen room, which had previously been a butler's pantry. Running beneath the shelves were cabinets and drawers that had once held silverware and serving pieces but were now repositories for bandages, scissors, and other supplies. We even had a body thermometer, but it was a clumsy thing at nearly a foot long, and it took twenty minutes for it to obtain an accurate reading, so I discouraged its use.

She looked up and stopped humming as I entered.

"Nurse Harris," I began, facing her from the opposite side of the table where she was working. I held the knife behind my back.

"Most people call me Clem, Miss Nightingale," she said quietly. Harris was a stark contrast to the other nurses. She was tall for a woman, with an abundance of thick, auburn hair that I would venture to guess hadn't been cut in years. She wore it in long loops draped over her head and down her back. Unbraided, it must have reached her knees. She had green eyes that radiated intelligence, but there was a quiet reserve about her that I suspected would not be easily breached.

"Nurse Harris," I repeated firmly. If I did not instill proper forms of address among the staff, I would never be able to make any other progress with them.

Harris nodded respectfully. "Of course, Miss."

I pulled my hand from behind me and deliberately placed the knife down in the center of the table. It looked out of place atop a piece of muslin waiting for its turn to be sharply creased and folded into a square.

Several silent moments elapsed, during which I could hear a clock ticking from somewhere in Mrs. Roper's currently unoccupied kitchen.

"I see," she said. "You must have searched my room thoroughly for some reason to find that." She resumed her folding, but now her fingers trembled.

"Actually, Nurse Frye showed it to me."

Harris absorbed this quietly as she added her freshly folded sheet to a stack of completed ones. She lifted the knife and put it off to one side of the table as she picked up the bleached muslin beneath and began folding it as well.

"I guess I am not so clever then, am I?" she admitted.

Was she about to confess to a crime? I remained silent, waiting.

"I have kept this knife near my person for protection for quite some time, Miss Nightingale," Harris said, maintaining her calm composure. "I don't believe there is a law against it."

"Protection from whom?" I asked.

Harris shrugged as she dropped the folded muslin on her growing pile and picked up another piece of linen. She held it out and frowned at it, and I noticed, too, that part of the fabric was so weak that a hole was forming. She looked at me and I nodded in silent approval. She tossed the cloth to one end of the table and picked up another. I would have to speak to our outside laundress about being more careful to weed out linens that were no longer of use. Meanwhile, someone would need to figure out what could be done with the remaining part of the fabric that was still in good shape. It could be formed into napkins, bandages, or handkerchiefs.

"Miss Harris?" I prompted the nurse, who had not answered me.

She stopped what she was doing. "I come from Sussex, Miss, and don't know much about the city, except for the stories I've heard about the slums and workhouses. Terrible places inhabited by criminals and run by them, if the rumors are true. But I needed good work, and figured I could protect my person if I had a weapon with me most of the time. I don't carry it while I'm on the premises, I assure you."

Harris stared straight at me with those keen, sharp eyes, and I found that I believed her.

She resumed her work and said, "But what you really want to know is whether I murdered that poor Caroline Bellamy."

Actually, it was the possible victim of her knife that

interested me, but I agreed with her nonetheless. "Yes. Although Nurse Bellamy wasn't stabbed."

"Interesting that Marg—Nurse Frye was so anxious to show it to you. Did she tell you I had done in Nurse Bellamy?"

I considered whether or not to tell Harris exactly what Frye had said. Her curiosity was only natural if she was an innocent, but I wasn't keen on divulging everything the other woman had said. However, I did need to know more from Harris.

"No. She seemed to think that you had done in your husband." Harris visibly twitched as my statement crashed like a crystal glass on the table between us.

"My husband? How could she say such a thing?" She put a hand to her neck, and I realized she was reaching for a necklace that must have been hiding beneath her buttoned collar. "I would never have harmed Ralph." Tears gathered in the corners of her eyes and she quickly sniffed them away. "Please, it is too difficult to speak of him."

Now I was overwhelmed with sympathy that she had perhaps lost a great love. Strict I might be on nearly every aspect of behavior, but I had a soft spot for the brokenhearted.

"Very well. I have another question. Do the gin bottles in your room belong to you?"

"Found those, did you? Now I see why Nurse Frye produced my knife. What a grand distraction." Harris shook her head in disgust and reached for another linen to fold.

"Are you saying the gin is Nurse Frye's?" I asked. I had known in my heart that it was, anyway. Frye had all of the hallmarks of a drunkard, whereas Harris had none of them.

"She is often in her cups," Harris said. "I find she is much friendlier and easier to get along with when she is, so I take no exception to it. I doubt anyone else would wish to trade beds with me, anyway."

I doubted it, too. But there was still the matter of their shared quarters. "I must say, Nurse Harris, your room is in deplorable condition, particularly given that you've been here only about a week. You say you are frightened of the slum areas, but your living circumstances already resemble a tumbledown room in an East End rookery." I said this more gently than I might ordinarily, as there was something about her that suggested I was dealing with an equal. "Surely you noticed there was a dead rat in there."

She was stoic under my lecture, merely inclining her chin toward her shoulder in a submissive gesture and making no excuse for the room she shared with Nurse Frye. I knew there were better than even chances that the blight of her room was Frye's fault, so there was no point in thrusting my verbal spear any further into her heart.

With my lecture over, Harris looked me straight in the eye. "I imagine the rat was one of Nurse Frye's kills."

"One of her—kills? I don't understand," I said, openly puzzled. Did Frye make sport of them as men did pheasants?

"She tries out various powders on them, to see what most effectively kills them. She has a stash of potions from her time at Allen and Hanbury's."

I raised an eyebrow as I considered the implication of this. "Pardon me? Who are Allen and Hanbury?"

"They prepare physics. Pastilles for the throat, neuralgic treatments, and the like." Harris resumed her work with the linens. She was down to the last few sheets and blankets to be folded. "Supposedly they do a lot of work with the Americans, and they ship many of their pharmaceuticals to the West Indies."

"What did Nurse Frye have to do with them?" I couldn't imagine Frye in any sort of scientific endeavor. However, it certainly made sense that she might seek out employment as a nurse after having worked in a pharmaceutical factory.

Harris shrugged. "I think she was a packaging girl at their factory in Bethnal Green."

Bethnal Green was one of the shabby areas that Harris feared. "Do you know how she came to leave Allen and Hanbury?"

A tan wool blanket was tossed onto the completed pile. "Oh, yes, she was quite forward with me about it. She was caught stealing the company's products and instantly dismissed, but by then she had plenty of them stashed away in her personal belongings. That's why she has so many of them to try out on pests. She says that what might cure a person's cold might dispatch a rat, if administered in a large enough quantity."

Had inmate Alice Drayton been mistaken about which nurse had attempted to poison her? But why would Margery Frye harbor ill will against an innocuous, albeit garrulous, patient? Perhaps in her mental haze, Miss Drayton had mistaken Frye setting up a rat snare in her room for an attempt to poison her personally. Nevertheless, I had many more questions for Nurse Frye now, and at a minimum she would be made to produce whatever array of medical potions she possessed.

It seemed as though every time I interviewed someone, I discovered secrets about someone else. I felt some urgency to revisit Nurse Frye, but I still needed to probe Clementina Harris a bit more.

"Do you know if Nurse Frye was still associating with anyone from the pharmaceutical factory?"

Another shrug. "I can't say for sure, ma'am, but I do know she has a seemingly unending supply of medications."

"Where does she keep them?"

"I truly don't know. I don't believe she keeps them in our room, but whether she has a hiding hole here at the Establishment or has them secreted with a friend, I couldn't say."

It would seem I had reached the end of Nurse Harris's insight, but I had one more question. "This knife," I said, tapping the handle. "Perhaps you thought you might one day need your weapon against Nurse Frye?"

Harris pulled the final piece of linen toward her for folding. "I do not know her to be violent, but who can say whether I might one day need protection from her? I did not know her prior to coming to the Establishment, if that is your real question, madam."

The sound of Polly Roper shuffling into the kitchen and clanging about with pots and pans signaled that she was starting work on the evening's supper. The commotion gave Harris the opportunity to make an excuse about needing to prepare patients for their meals. She slipped away, leaving me in distracted thought until I heard Mrs. Roper cooing at Jasmine for having managed two more rat kills.

I picked up the knife and tucked the blade down into my dress pocket. I would decide later whether to return it to Nurse Harris or lock it up somewhere.

★ ★ ★

I went upstairs, intent on finding Nurse Frye again, but first came upon Nurse Marian Hughes inside a patient's room, straightening the covers over the sleeping woman. Hughes wore the same old lace-collared maid's uniform I had seen her in the day I found Nurse Bellamy. It reminded me again that I needed to have standardized nurses' uniforms made as soon as possible.

I asked Hughes to come to my study when she was finished, and within ten minutes she was before me, modest and quiet with her hands folded before her.

I invited her to sit down and she did so, again clasping her hands demurely in her lap as she gazed anxiously at me with those unnervingly pale eyes. She reminded me of a doe in the woods, ready to bolt if I inadvertently raised my voice or hand.

"Nurse," I said, my voice barely above a whisper. "As you are quite aware, I am investigating Nurse Bellamy's death. Let me be clear that I am not accusing you of any misdeeds."

At that, Hughes visibly relaxed and I resumed a normal speaking tone. "Right now, I'm simply trying to know the nurses and other staff in my charge, since I have been here such a short time. I was in your room earlier—"

Hughes stiffened again.

"—and I must say I found your button collection to be both peculiar and interesting." I lowered my voice once more, hoping she would stay still and not leap into the hallway as though I had a hunting rifle in my hands. "Why do you collect them?"

"I'm sorry, Miss," Hughes replied, her own voice a mere murmur. "I'll remove them if they offend you. I didn't mean—"

"They do not offend me; they are only buttons. I am merely curious as to why you have such a vast number of them." I folded my own hands on my desk, attempting to appear as nonthreatening as possible.

"They are pretty," she told me. "My first few buttons were from my mama's best dress."

"Is your mother in London?" I asked, trying to put her further at ease.

Hughes shook her head. "In heaven. With my papa."

It was, I thought, a very girlish way of explaining her mother's death, but there was nothing suspicious in it. "How long have you been with the Establishment?"

She bit her lip, thinking. "About a year, Miss."

I was ready to resume a normal voice again. "And how did you come here?"

She frowned, and I sensed that she didn't want to answer the question, particularly since she glanced sideways at the door, as if contemplating how many leaps it would take to pass through it. Apparently deciding against such an action, she finally looked at me again. "I was nurse to Mr. Benedict Maxwell in Southwark. He was Irish, come over because of the famine. But I didn't find the position to be to my liking."

That raised my curiosity. "Yet you took another nursing job here?"

"Yes, Miss. I didn't mind the nursing, only the patient."

She seemed disinclined to elaborate. "Was he aware of your extensive lot of buttons?"

Hughes nodded. Clearly she was not going to willingly

offer any more information, and I would have to dig for it as though I were seeking the end of an oak tree's tap root. I shifted the topic a little.

"Did you wear that—uniform—in your work with Mr. Maxwell?"

"Yes, Miss, it's nearly all I have, except for my buttons and a little bit of fabric that I keep down in the linen room."

I nodded. "I plan to have new uniforms made for all of the nurses here. Plain gray with white aprons, caps, and cuffs. I wish to have harmony in how you all look."

I noticed a faint spark in those colorless eyes. "Really? I-I'm fair handy with a needle. I'm very clean, too. I wouldn't dirty up any cotton or muslin for the trim pieces, Miss, if you would let me try to make the uniforms. Just a sketch is all I would need from you."

She sat back and waited for my reaction. It hadn't occurred to me that anyone on the premises might be talented enough to whip up a number of uniforms, and I wasn't entirely convinced that she was, either. "Did you sew the dress you are wearing now?"

She self-consciously fingered the lace at her neck. "I made changes to it, to try and make it more suitable for nursing work."

I noticed Hughes's own voice was gaining the slightest bit of confidence. Perhaps this was a good way to bolster her poise. I made an instant decision. "We will try it. I will give you a rough drawing, and you shall make a dress that fits your own frame. If I find it acceptable, you can make uniforms for the other nurses."

"Thank you, Miss. You won't regret it." Her cheeks

pinked with pleasure and all of a sudden she became much more talkative. "Nurse Bellamy admired my work, too. She was very nice to me and I was ever so sorry about her death."

"You say she was nice to you. Would you say you were friends?"

Again Hughes frowned and glanced at the door. "No. Nurse Bellamy was not the type to have many friends. She was very pleasant to me, but then, I never did pry into her business at all. She didn't like those who asked her lots of questions."

"Did many people ask her questions?"

"Only in the way that women do. No one meant her any harm, I don't think, but she was waspish if she believed that someone else was trying to learn too much about her."

If Bellamy had been that secretive, it might be difficult to truly discover who she had been. "Were there ever any gentleman callers coming and going?"

Hughes's hand flew to her neck again. "Miss! I would never presume to have men in my—"

How quickly this woman skittered into fright and fluster. I held up a hand. "Not you. I mean, did Nurse Bellamy have male visitors?"

"Oh." She calmed down, her hand settling back in her lap. "Not that I noticed, but I make it a point not to notice such activities. I do my work and keep to my room."

Her private room full of boxes stuffed with buttons. Hughes was an odd little thing, but I could find no fault in her, especially since she seemed eager to please.

I dismissed her, then retreated to the library to work on my chart detailing Caroline Bellamy's death before seeking out Margery Frye or anyone else. I tugged on the bell pull in the room that led to the kitchen and told Polly Roper when she appeared that I wished to have a pot of tea. I sat down with my charts, and in short order, there was a knock at the door. Instead of Mrs. Roper, however, it was someone who quickly made it clear that she desired nothing more than to see my goose cooked over a roaring fire.

CHAPTER 9

An auburn-haired woman stood before me. I estimated her to be in her late forties based on the tiny lines at the corners of her eyes and the subtle streaks of white in her hair. She wore a treasure chest of jewelry on her person, including rings on several fingers. The gold and gems were set perfectly against her emerald-and-black-striped dress, done suitably for elegant daywear with its high neck and long sleeves. She wore the jewelry with a studious air of boredom, matched by her tone when she said, "Do you know who I am?"

She was apparently someone I should be aware of through some clairvoyant process.

"My apologies, madam; have we met?"

She folded her hands in front of her waist. A ruby encircled by pearls glittered on her forefinger. "I am Lillian Alban."

Ah. Given how elegantly groomed Roderick Alban was, it made perfect sense that this was his spouse. They were like a matched set of Limoges vases, except I sensed that Mrs. Alban might have a hidden crack running down the back where no one could see it.

"How do you do?" I said politely, my curiosity regarding her visit now quite sharpened.

She made me wait for an answer, taking the time to glance around the room as if disinterested, but I sensed that she was secretly memorizing everything about the place. "I understand my husband recently made a visit to you."

I wondered whether Roderick Alban had actually told his wife of his visit or if she was merely probing me to find out. "Yes, that is true," I replied.

"What was the nature of your conversation?" she asked, absentmindedly twisting the ruby ring with the thumb and forefinger of her other hand.

A prickle of alarm ran up my spine. How much did Mrs. Alban know about the Establishment being home to a murder? Some husbands shared all with their wives; others considered very little to be their spouse's business.

"You may know that we had a death here . . ." I started, hoping she might pick up the thread and tell me what she knew.

"Hmm, yes, a maid or something," Mrs. Alban said with a dismissive hand wave.

"Actually, it was one of my nurses, Caroline Bellamy," I said. Somehow I felt insulted that she had referred to the young woman—albeit one I had hardly known—as a "maid or something."

Lillian Alban flicked away some invisible lint from her bodice. "Poor dear." She said this as if hearing about a dog's tail having been stepped on. "Why did my husband need to speak with you about it?"

I was growing irritated with this woman. I might be under her husband's oversight, but surely this woman realized I was of equal social stature to her. Her attitude suggested I were a mere chimney sweep, hardly worth a glance. I decided, however, to be diplomatic.

"I am the superintendent here, madam, and Nurse Bellamy was in my charge. As for Mr. Alban's visit to me . . ." I paused. His visit had occurred only the day before, and yet so much had happened. "He seemed most concerned about the reputation of the Establishment in light of the nurse's death. He has apparently been a great patron of the hospital."

She raised her chin. "Thus *we* have been great patrons."

"Of course, Mrs. Alban." I tried not to roll my eyes as the knot of irritation tightened inside me.

The knot began to choke me when she suddenly demanded, "Miss Nightingale, I would know the nature of your relationship with my husband."

"Relationship, madam?" I said, confused. "He is a member of the men's committee for the Establishment. I only first met him a few weeks ago before Lady Canning brought me in to run this hospital."

What was the woman implying? I had denied myself my greatest heart's desire in Richard, and she believed I would debase myself by—

"If not you, then who is it?" Mrs. Alban implored. "For I know it's someone here, and you are the most gentle-born of the staff. If a woman had the guile to lead my husband astray, surely it would not be some lowly maid."

Even Lillian Alban was unable to make such an accusation

with an air of boredom, and I heard the rising tone in her voice. Perhaps it wasn't that she had a hidden crack but that she was made of altogether brittle material.

"I will find it out, you know. Whether it is you or someone else. I will destroy her. I will personally snap her neck." Mrs. Alban twisted her balled fists in opposite directions to emphasize her intent. Her motions were incongruous with the elegance of the jewelry adorning her hands.

There was a light tap at the open door, followed by Mrs. Roper's entrance with a tea tray. "Here's your—" she began before glancing at Lillian Alban's wild expression. The cook blinked twice and hurriedly set down the tray on a table near me, then walked out as quickly as she could without breaking into an open run.

I used the interruption to calm Mrs. Alban down. "May I pour you a cup?" I asked. Although my instincts screamed that I should get her out of my presence as quickly as possible, my logical side whispered that Mrs. Alban might have information about the Establishment—or even my dead nurse—that I could glean from her.

She began winding her rings around her fingers again. "I don't believe I should."

Was that the tiniest bit of a waver in her voice? "Please, madam, it isn't likely that I shall drink the entire pot, and it would be a shame for it to get cold and go to waste."

In the time it took me to pour a cup for her, Lillian Alban had settled back into her bland, distracted persona. How much effort must be required for a woman to preserve her sanity against a wayward husband?

Unless, of course, the husband had a roving eye because of his wife's insanity.

We sat down, and I watched as my visitor raised her cup with trembling hands.

As she sipped and the warm beverage appeared to calm her agitation further, I said, "Mrs. Alban, you should know that I have a sacred trust with the inmates here, to keep their business private so that the world does not know of their afflictions and disfigurements. Although you do not have any disease to speak of, I believe your heart to be broken and ailing. I extend my same assurance of confidentiality to you if you wish to unburden yourself."

She set the cup and saucer in her lap and smiled grimly. "You see yourself as a priest in a confessional, Miss Nightingale?"

I hadn't intended to elevate myself in such a manner. "In no way, madam, but the scriptures do tell us to confess to and to encourage one another, even as we perform our primary duty of working for social good and lifting up the worth of every human being. I am happy to be of encouragement to you if I can be so."

I had made things worse. Mrs. Alban frowned in displeasure. "You sound like one of those Unitarians."

At least my words matched my inner beliefs in the eyes of others.

"Yes, well," I said, clearing my throat. "Mrs. Alban, what makes you believe that your husband is engaged in an, er, escapade? I am especially curious to know why you believe the woman is here at the Establishment."

Mrs. Alban was silent for several moments, tapping the side of her cup with a finely manicured nail. Finally, she sighed as if reaching a momentous decision. "Very well," she said, putting the cup aside on the table. She brought forward the ebony satin bag strapped to her wrist and reached in, withdrawing a folded piece of paper. Wordlessly, she passed it to me, and I read it.

My heart stopped, and not merely because of the contents.

Toonite at the usual place

It was in the exact same handwriting as the letter I had retrieved from Nurse Bellamy's room, and it also had no signature.

I carefully refolded it but kept it in my hand. "I certainly understand why your suspicions fell on the hospital, and particularly on me," I said. "But I assure you I am not this illiterate."

"That had occurred to me before I came here, but I needed to know," Mrs. Alban said. "The question remains, who wrote this to my husband?"

Wasn't that answer obvious? "I imagine your husband would be able to ascertain who the culprit is if you simply asked him."

Lillian Alban visibly shuddered. "No, no, I couldn't bear hearing it from his lips. I plan to discover who the harlot is, ruin her, and cause her to disappear from his life."

The words, stated with her now-resumed nonchalance, were more chilling than if she had spewed them in violent anger.

"Madam," I said, tapping the letter against my knee. "Might I keep this temporarily? I would like to see if I might figure out whose words these are."

She narrowed her eyes at me, probably still not entirely convinced I wasn't the enemy. "I suppose that would be all right."

"Thank you. And let me ask, how did this come into your possession?"

Mrs. Alban lifted a shoulder. "The usual way. I went through his jacket."

Clearly her husband didn't suspect her of such behavior or he wouldn't have left the note in a place where she might so easily find it.

However, the note itself did beg a comment. "May I suggest that this is not necessarily a love letter?" I said. "After all, it says very little and isn't overly romantic."

Mrs. Alban grimaced. "I found this in Roderick's overcoat last night, and it smelled quite distinctly of hyacinths. Assuredly, Roderick is strictly a bergamot man."

I lifted the paper to my nose and agreed that it carried the fading scent of hyacinths. I had to admit that was suggestive, but it wasn't conclusive. A woman with a headache doesn't necessarily have a tumor, after all, and women tend to scent everything, from handkerchiefs to gloves to hair pomades. In fact, whoever had written the note might simply have had a stack of stationery sprayed with her favorite perfume so that everyone she wrote received scented correspondence.

I started to say so, but she interrupted me. "Miss Nightingale, you are not married, correct?"

"No, I was unfortunate in—"

Mrs. Alban held up a hand to halt my explanation. A charm bracelet slid down her arm. "Then you cannot possibly understand a wife's instincts. They are infallible."

I did not think Mrs. Alban's instincts were necessarily infallible, but she had left me no room for argument. Despite her continued crass treatment of me, I attempted a conciliatory tone once more. "No doubt you know much more about our male counterparts than I do. How long have you and Mr. Alban been married?"

"Let me see." The manicured nail tapped the arm of her chair as she contemplated my question. "Daphne is twenty-one and Roddy is twenty-five, so it will be twenty-seven years next March."

"More than a quarter century," I murmured. "A long time." They had been married when I was a mere girl of six.

"Hence you understand when I say that I have certain *instincts* about my husband."

"Has your husband—did Mr. Alban ever—" I grasped about for the right words. "Is this the first time you have suspected your husband of infidelity?"

"Of course not. He is a fine specimen of a man, isn't he? The cut of his trousers, his confident stride. What woman wouldn't want him?" Mrs. Alban swallowed, as if regretting offering me such naked truth.

"He is a handsome gentleman," I agreed, unwilling to consider him favorably in any other way. "Has he admitted to infidelity?"

"No, he never does. He says I am unnecessarily jealous and lose all semblance of reason when I confront him over his peccadilloes. Then he disappears to his club for a few days.

For me to calm down and regain my senses, he says. But I can't really even know that he's ever where he says he is, can I? Perhaps he isn't at his club but off with Miss Illiterate Hyacinth or someone else entirely."

For the briefest moment, I had sympathy for what Roderick Alban must be enduring at home, for surely his wife was a bitter, volatile pill to swallow each day.

"How did your husband come to sit on the men's committee of the Establishment?" I asked.

"Oh, that." She was bored again. "I suppose Lady Canning knew of his work on the boards of the Charity for the Houseless Irish Poor and the Home for Incurable Children. Roderick is very charming and persuasive and is able to secure donors with a crook of his finger, so it is no wonder she asked him."

Presumably Mrs. Alban was not jealous of the vivacious Charlotte Canning. Of course, Lady Canning was renowned for her devotion to her own husband, Charles, as well as her devotion to Queen Victoria. Lady Canning had the honor of serving as a favored lady of the bedchamber to the queen, while her husband toiled ambitiously in Her Majesty's government as postmaster general.

Lillian Alban looked at me speculatively. "I should ask you the same question, Miss Nightingale. How did a gentle-born woman from a respectable family come to engage as a nurse, of all things? Is there something wrong with your person that you were unable to marry well?" She pointedly tapped the side of her head twice. "Did you bring shame to your family, necessitating that you leave home and make your own way in the world?" This time she put her hand to her stomach, spreading it for emphasis, which had the further effect of flashing an unusually large diamond ring at me.

How dare she suggest such a thing to me, even in private? I was at least as well born as she was, I was sure, and she was speaking to me as if I were a trollop or else thoroughly demented. She was, though, the wife of a committee member hand-selected by my employer, so I could not do what I truly wished to do: slap Mrs. Lillian Alban smartly across the face.

I took a deep breath and attempted to mold my features into neutrality, as she was so expert in doing. It did not come naturally to me, and I'm sure my grimace made me look as Jasmine might if she were being strangled.

"Nothing of the sort," I replied. "I *chose* this work, over the very vocal objections of my family. In fact, I refused more than one marriage proposal in hopes that I might one day end up in a situation such as this one."

Mrs. Alban's expression was incredulous. "You *wanted* this? When you could have had a husband, a home, a family? What manner of woman are you?"

There was no use in explaining my divine visit to her, nor my conviction that Christian principles must not just be argued but put into decisive action. Instead, I merely told her, "The sort of woman who would bring you back to health should you fall ill of a fever, madam."

Mrs. Alban responded with a laugh. "We have a doctor to tend to us in the event of sickness."

I clasped my hands in my lap and leaned forward, saying forcefully, "I have worked with many physicians while caring for friends, family, and villagers in the past. They are expert in prescribing physics, that is true. But when was the last time a doctor brought you a bowl of nourishing bone broth, or opened the window to provide you with fresh air, or changed your bed linens? Doctors prescribe, nurses care."

The struggle for control over my tongue was an eternal one. No doubt Mrs. Alban would return to her husband—who loathed me—with this bit of tattle, and he would go directly to Lady Canning and report me as insolent and undermining of Dr. Killigrew.

Well, I had uttered it and couldn't shove it all back into my mouth now. To be truthful, I felt a glow of satisfaction in having spoken my mind.

For her part, Lillian Alban stood, and I rose with her. "Miss Nightingale, it is obvious that you are mistaken in your impression of what I am capable of wreaking in your life. Have a care for your person."

She stalked out of the room, and I resisted the urge to slam the door behind her.

★ ★ ★

I still had so much to do—speak with Graham Morgan, interview Margery Frye again, and investigate who might have written the two letters I had read, even if only one was now in my possession. Moreover, since I still had to make headway on my improvement programs, I had no time to dwell on Mrs. Alban's unfortunate visit. But before I could start another endeavor, I was interrupted yet again by the arrival of Charlie Lewis.

"Miss Nightingale, I was outside and saw a carriage p-p-pull up. I'd say you have another i-i-inmate."

I frowned. Usually word was sent along that a woman

wished to enter the hospital, to ensure the availability of one of our rooms and so that the superintendent could review the case to be sure that the patient was a proper sort for the Establishment. Moreover, someone needed to be on hand to greet the new inmate.

"Very well," I said briskly. "I will need your help."

Charlie followed me to the front door of the building, where he easily loped down the steps to meet the woman who stood next to a trunk while a gentleman paid the hack driver. I stood on the stoop with my hands folded in front of me, waiting to greet them.

The pair ascended the steps while Charlie lifted the straps of the trunk to lug it around to the back of the building. I immediately realized this was not a new inmate. This was Hester Moore, accompanied by her brother, Dunstan. She had been discharged from the Establishment just a few days before, right before I had found Nurse Bellamy.

Dr. Killigrew had determined that Hester's melancholia was of her own devising and that no amount of physic in the world would help her, so we had summoned Dunstan to retrieve her.

As I have mentioned, I do not like to go against a doctor's orders, and I had obeyed Dr. Killigrew to the letter in the matter. However, Hester Moore had experienced a horse's kick to the head many years before while serving as a governess in Surrey. I thought that might explain why her brother had reported her to have these periodic bouts of low melancholia, as opposed to the idea that her condition was self-imposed and thus self-controllable.

"Miss Nightingale, we have returned, as you may have

expected." Dunstan's voice boomed inside the confined area under the portico. Perhaps he was partially deaf.

"Good afternoon, Mr. Moore. I confess I did not expect you. Mrs. Moore, how do you fare?" Hester Moore had never been married, but we extended the title to her as a courtesy, given her age and position.

Hester Moore glanced nervously at her brother. "I have not been myself lately," she said.

I should say not. She was practically trembling. "As luck would have it, your previous room is still open," I said. "Perhaps the familiar surroundings will be helpful for you." I led them into the Establishment's lobby, which had once been the previous owner's grand entrance hall.

By now, Charlie would have the trunk upstairs, and I hoped he had had the instinct to place it back in the room Mrs. Moore had just vacated.

Hester opened her mouth to respond, but her brother answered instead. "Yes, I like the idea of Hester having the same room. A nice window overlooking the courtyard, right?" He tucked his sister's arm in his own as he now walked past me, as if *he* were now leading *me* to the room.

"Yes, it is a pleasant view, and I encourage Mrs. Moore to sit in front of the open window, if not in the gardens themselves, as much as possible until Dr. Killi—"

"Here we are, dear sister," Dunstan said in an overly jovial tone as we reached her room. "Your trunk is already here and I'm sure Miss Nightingale will arrange for a vase of flowers and some books for you. You've always talked of learning to paint, haven't you? Miss Nightingale could probably hire an art tutor for you, as well."

Hester smiled wanly at her brother while I restrained my temper for the hundredth time in the past few days. Whatever Dunstan Moore might think, the Establishment was a hospital, not a finishing school for middle-aged women. There was no point in upsetting his sister, though, who reminded me of a fragile swallowtail butterfly with one shimmering blue wing about to break off.

Her health was of paramount concern, not the dressing down her overbearing brother so desperately needed.

He watched intently from the doorway as I helped Hester get herself situated in the room. Once that was done, I invited her to accompany me on a walk through the courtyard gardens. I did not believe that being shut away in a room—no matter how airy—was beneficial for her.

Once again, her gaze sought out her brother, who said, "My sister could use some rest. The journey was tiring for her. And I would like to speak to you in private, Miss Nightingale."

Hester Moore bobbed her head meekly up and down in agreement. The poor woman was so nondescript next to her brother that I was certain that the moment I walked away from her, I would forget what she looked like. Dunstan, however, filled the room with his swarthy features and full, dark, close-cropped hair and beard only mildly tinged with gray. The two siblings could not have been more different, either in personality or looks. Dunstan might have been an Arab and his sister from the far reaches of Norway, so opposite in complexion were they.

As he and I left the room together, I noticed Hester go to the partially raised window and lean her forehead against a pane of glass. I couldn't see her expression, but her resigned posture told me she was deeply unhappy.

Dunstan followed me down the corridor to the lobby and then up the stairs to where my study was. I sat behind my desk and invited him to sit across from me, but he instead chose to pace, reminding me of a prowling panther I had once seen in Regent's Park Zoo.

"Mr. Moore," I began. "Customarily we should have advance notice of an inmate's arrival."

He paused long enough to airily wave a hand. "My sister is well known to this place. She won't be any trouble for you. I need to go out of town for a short time and this is the best place to leave her to be cared for."

I stared at him open-mouthed. "Sir, do you believe the Establishment to be a nursery? Or an orphanage? If your sister is not genuinely ill, then I must insist that you—"

The hand flipped back and forth dismissively again. "Of course she is ill, Miss Nightingale. Has been for as long as I can remember. Hester was hardly cured when Dr. Killigrew sent her home last week, was she? She needs more care, and I was impressed with what I have seen since you have taken over the Establishment. So I decided to bring her back to see what you can do for her."

Silkily stated, I thought. He would pay the full going rate for his sister's stay. "Why did you wish to see me privately?"

Dunstan had moved over to the window of my study, which also overlooked the courtyard, and gazed out, his profile to me. Instead of sharing his sister's sad stance, though, he looked hungry and determined. He turned back to me and finally sat down in a chair across from me. "I chose to bring my sister back here for the reason I stated, but I do have some concerns. Specifically, I have heard about the death of one of your nurses."

I nodded. "Nurse Bellamy, yes. I can assure you, Mr. Moore, that her death was not related to the inmates here and was likely just a random—"

He waved his hand again. The motion was becoming irritating. "Did you find the body yourself?" he asked.

"Yes," I replied, suddenly wary of why he should ask.

He leaned forward. "What are your thoughts about her death? Suicide or murder?"

How bluntly queried. I cleared my throat and said tactfully, "The police believe it's a suicide."

He sat back, elbows on the chair's arms as he templed his fingers together. "So *you* believe she was killed. Do you have in mind a suspect?"

This was altogether uncomfortable. "Mr. Moore, again let me try to assure you that your sister is perfectly safe here. I hope the unfortunate incident will not shake your faith in the Establishment."

"Would I have brought her back if I thought you incapable of nursing her?" He rose and began his feral pacing again. "What I wish to know is whether you have any idea who might have done it. Man or woman? A stranger or friend?"

I was quiet as I puzzled out what the man's interest was. I sat back in my chair. The seat creaked in the silence.

"Are you a detective, sir?" I asked.

He looked at me quizzically. "You know that I am working with Brunel on the Leviathan."

Ah, yes. I had forgotten that he was a mechanical engineer in the employ of Isambard Kingdom Brunel. If he was deaf, it was probably because he had spent too much time in locomotive yards and on shipbuilding docks, having his hearing assailed by the screeching, clanging, and banging that accompany such monumental endeavors.

Brunel was currently constructing an enormous ship, which would reputedly carry four thousand passengers to places as far-flung as India and Australia and back without having to stop to take on more coal reserves. The ship's design had been mocked in the papers, what with its extravagant cabin appointments. What society man or woman, they said, would be satisfied being trapped on a three-month voyage without ever stopping at points traditionally visited on the Grand Tour? Brunel was merely creating a luxurious cargo ship and it was certain to fail.

"I did not recall that you were working on such an immense project," I said.

"Problems have arisen with the new double-hull system Brunel has developed, so we will spend some time at Napier Yard overseeing construction."

Napier Yard? "Isn't that here in London, on the Isle of Dogs?" I asked.

"Yes, but I cannot be distracted by Hester's hysterias. My mind will be set at ease if she's here."

I sighed. "Mr. Moore, I will allow it this time, but you cannot simply deposit your sister here each time you find her inconvenient. You can hire a private nurse or companion for her."

"No, she must stay here." He reached into his jacket, pulled out a cigar, and held it up to me. "Do you mind?"

"In fact, I do." It was time to end this conversation. I didn't want him lingering for the time it would take him to smoke the roll of tobacco.

He grunted and put it away. "I'll go say good-bye to my sister, then."

I was glad the odd conversation was at an end. I was beginning to think there was almost no one associated with the Establishment who wasn't peculiar in one way or another.

"By the way," Dunstan said casually as he put his hand to the door latch. "I remember Caroline Bellamy."

"Yes?" I said. Perhaps Nurse Bellamy had served his sister in his presence. I couldn't remember.

He nodded. "It's hard to forget a girl dressed in hand-me-downs who claims she is on the verge of becoming wealthy."

I paused, all of a sudden not as eager to see him leave. "Pardon me? How did she claim she was to acquire this wealth?"

Moore grinned, and I didn't care for how self-satisfied his expression was. "Nurse Bellamy said that she wouldn't be a nurse much longer. She said that she would soon be in much better circumstances, thanks to her own clever planning."

That could mean anything. "She didn't tell you what she had planned?"

He shook his head. "At first, I took it as just the bragging of a young woman disenchanted with her lot in life. After she died, though, it seemed to me that whatever plans she had made were perhaps not so clever after all."

That, or someone else was far *more* clever.

★ ★ ★

I was reeling from one shocking pronouncement to another at this point. I retreated to the library with some of my papers for peace and quiet. Ivy Stoke was there, sitting in a chair in a corner. In her lap, a book lay open atop a blanket that reached down to the floor. Jasmine was curled up on top of the book, so I figured it must be the cat who was reading, not Ivy. I nodded absently to the inmate, not willing to engage in chatting while I needed to empty my mind of all that was racing through it.

As my first task, I sketched out the design for a nurse's uniform. The result was a plain dress in drab gray containing two deep pockets for carrying around bandages, scissors, and other common supplies. I drew it topped with a bleached white apron and accompanied by a close-fitting white cap, under which all of a nurse's hair—even Nurse Harris's—would fit. I would want two versions, one in wool and another in a lighter fabric for summer wear. Nurse Hughes could select it.

Satisfied, I moved on to my chart that I had started regarding Nurse Bellamy's murder and added in what little new information I had gleaned in my conversations with Lillian Alban, Dunstan Moore, and my nurses.

I admit my own chart was becoming complex and confusing, so I decided to reduce it to what statements I could make about Nurse Bellamy, although most of it was simply hearsay from others.

> Nurse B— was seen by Nurse W— with a gentleman friend (or friends?)
> D— M— says Nurse B— claimed to be about to come into money
> Someone paid for Nurse B—'s funeral.

L— A— suspects her husband of infidelity
Nurse F— believes Nurse H— to have murdered her
　　husband
A—D— certain Nurse B— trying to poison her. Reliable?

What leapt out at me as the most definitive truth was Nurse Bellamy's funeral having been paid for by some unknown person. I should be able to resolve that with a quick visit to Morgan Undertaking, and then I would—

My thoughts were interrupted by the sound of Miss Stoke's book sliding to the floor and landing with a thump. I checked on her and saw her head lolled back in the chair, her mouth agape as she snored gently. Jasmine was simply repositioning herself in the woman's lap.

I woke Ivy and escorted her back to her room, with Jasmine meandering behind us. Then I dropped my sketches off to Nurse Hughes, whose gratitude for the project was almost cloying.

I checked on Hester Moore and discovered her brother in her room, breezily pacing around and smoking his cigar. Hester was smiling at whatever he was saying. I greeted her, ensured she required no immediate assistance from me, then dropped instructions with the other nurses before heading out to see the undertaker.

★　★　★

My hope was that finding out who had paid for the funeral might be a clue as to who Bellamy really was and with whom she was associated. I hired a taxi to take me to Morgan Undertaking in Queen's Road. For the first time in several days, I found myself actually relaxing. Despite the torn, tufted-leather seats and the jarring, noisy ride of the conveyance, which seemed to have no springs whatsoever, I enjoyed the time alone.

The hack pulled up to a brick building with wide windows on either side of the deep-green front door. The windows were topped with a glossy black sign with gold lettering. I tried not to be disturbed by the elaborate coffin displays behind the glass. It was certainly a depressing fact that as hard as I might try to bring someone to health, it was ultimately in God's hands, and many of my patients would need the Morgans' services.

The Nightingales had known the Morgan family since before Graham's grandfather had gone off to fight against the Americans in the second skirmish between our two nations. When old Mr. Morgan had returned and decided to make a fresh start with his business in London, my family had retained his family's services.

Graham Morgan's young wife greeted me, emerging from behind a counter to do so.

"Miss Nightingale, this is a pleasant surprise. How may I be of service?" Violet Morgan's tone was mature beyond her years. I felt that sickening, jealous twinge again as I recalled how enamored she and her husband were of each other.

"Your husband conducted the funeral for my nurse, Caroline Bellamy."

Violet nodded her head in agreement.

"I would like to know who provided the money for it. Can you tell me who it was?" I asked.

"Let me see." Mrs. Morgan returned behind the counter,

which was full of miniature coffin samples, brass coffin plates, and thick-bordered mourning stationery. She pulled open a drawer in a secretary standing against the wall behind her. From the drawer she withdrew a large, leather-bound ledger. It was enormous in her hands, but she hefted it onto the counter as if it were no more than a gossamer-light shroud.

Flipping back a page in her ledger, she ran her finger down the entries. "Hmm," she said, frowning. "This says 'Twelve guineas, paid anonymously, see receipts.' Let me check the receipts."

This sent Mrs. Morgan to another drawer in the secretary, from which she pulled out a lidded box. She went through the box until she exclaimed, "Aha!" and picked out a piece of paper, which she lay on the counter facing me so I could read it. It was plain, with no engraving or identifying markings.

Please accept this as payment for a decent funeral for Miss Caro. Bellamy. She deserves the best, but I cannot give it to her.

It was unsigned. Was this from her mysterious gentleman friend?

"I remember now," Mrs. Morgan said. "Graham told me he had heard the door's bells jangle from the back room, and when he came out, no one was here. But this note, in an envelope along with the money, was on the floor. As if someone had opened the door, tossed the envelope in, and run off. I'm sure my husband will return soon if you'd like to wait for him. He can answer any other questions you might have."

I shook my head. I had obtained as much information here as I thought possible, which was to say not much.

It was oddly comforting to know that Caroline Bellamy had had someone who cared enough about her to pay for her funeral, but why did it have to be done in secret?

Mrs. Alban's recent accusations rose up in my mind, and I wondered if the proper victim for her wrath was perhaps a young woman who was already dead.

CHAPTER 10

I passed another fitful night of sleep. In the morning, I resigned myself to working at the desk in my room for a couple of early-morning hours before assembling Wilmot, Hughes, Frye, and Harris to discuss the day's plan. As I mentally planned the day's schedule, there was a soft knock on my door.

I hurriedly threw a wrapper around my nightdress and opened the door. It was Charlie, who turned red as a strawberry at my dishabille. I was a bit nonplussed myself.

"Begging your p-p-pardon, ma'am," he said, turning around so as not to look at me. "This just arrived, and the b-b-boy says he is to wait for an answer from you."

Charlie held up an envelope behind his back. I would have laughed, except I was becoming entirely distrustful of what lay inside any sheet of stationery that fell into my hands of late.

Unfortunately, this missive was no different. It was from Lady Canning and was a summons to meet with her, Roderick Alban, and Cyril Matthews at ten o'clock in Mr. Alban's offices. The meeting regarded "the recent events."

Cyril Matthews sat on the men's committee with Roder-ick Alban. Was I about to be removed from my position? Alban had made serious threats against me. Perhaps he had followed through on them.

I scratched out a note of assent and gave it to Charlie, then began preparing myself for what I was sure would feel like a trip to the gallows. After donning the same cranberry-and-gold plaid ensemble I had worn to see Elizabeth Herbert, I assembled my nurses. I gave instructions for the day—with a restrained admonishment for Nurse Frye's unkempt hair— and set off for the address provided in Lady Canning's mis-sive. Was it intuition that caused me to tuck my prepared chart and list inside my reticule?

Mr. Alban's rooms inside the walls of the City were inside the Royal Exchange. The hack dropped me off at the taxi stand at the corner of Princes and Threadneedle Streets, and I admired the impressively built stone edifice. The front con-tained an expanse of eight Corinthian columns topped by a pediment with an elaborate, sculptured frieze running across it. Beneath the frieze was some easily translatable Latin, stat-ing that the Exchange had been founded in Queen Elizabeth's thirteenth year and restored in the seventh year of Queen Victoria. Two previous iterations had burned down—one in the Great Fire and the second in 1838—and it had been rebuilt yet again a decade ago.

The Exchange was rumored to have a glass-covered court-yard inside where merchants could do business, although pre-sumably the seventeenth-century version had not had such a modern covering. I entered the building only to gasp—my imminent rendezvous with doom momentarily forgotten—as

I absorbed the spectacular, paned-glass canopy that illuminated the three stories of column-lined arched windows and doorways beneath it. The sound was cacophonous as hundreds of men in finely finished morning coats shook hands, argued, and shook hands again. I was one of few women here, and although no one even noticed my presence, I felt as though I were invading some private, inner male sanctum. I made my way to a staircase that would take me to Roderick Alban's suite of rooms on the top floor.

I was out of breath by the time my sturdy boots clacked their way up so many stairs, and I paused outside the paneled wood door that had Mr. Alban's name etched in black in a glass inset to calm my breathing. I whispered a quick prayer that I would have the strength to respond gracefully if I was to be instantly dismissed. The thought of my mother's flapping and screeching "I told you so!" was worse than the idea of actually being ousted from my position.

With the prayer sent up fortifying me as well as could be, I knocked twice on the door, then entered. Inside, I found three joyless pairs of eyes staring at me.

At least Charlotte Canning offered me a wan smile from where they all sat behind the table. She rose to greet me with a dry kiss to the cheek. She introduced me to the two men, who remained seated. Of course I already knew Alban, who was in the middle chair.

On the left was Cyril Matthews. He looked older and harder than Alban, with his balding head framed on the sides by wiry silver hair just above his ears. That hair led to a closely cropped beard and mustache that did much to cover his pale, pitted skin. His eyes, though, were as light a blue as an unclouded sky. They stared at me now in open—but I hoped not hostile—curiosity. Her wore an unusual jacket, sharply cut, in a tight brown-and-gold-checked pattern. It seemed to me that time had been unkind to Cyril Matthews, while it had blessed Roderick Alban.

Mr. Matthews's appearance, though, was inconsequential compared to the room in which I now stood. The exterior and public interior spaces of the Exchange were impressive. Mr. Alban's rooms were . . . fascinating. The walls were papered in a busy swirl pattern of dark moss green, and the draperies covering a window that—if my bearings were correct—looked out over the courtyard were made of green velvet a shade deeper than the walls. The hissing chandelier above us illuminated the chair placed on the other side of the table that I was obviously to occupy. It, too, was overwhelming in alternating olive and mint stripes.

At the sound of a masculine throat clearing from Roderick Alban, Lady Canning squeezed my hand and returned to the right-hand seat behind the table. The three chairs behind the table matched my own, but at least the bodies in them blocked the gaudy fabric upon which they sat. She invited me to sit down, but I hesitated. It seemed as though it would put me at a terrible disadvantage to be seated there while the three of them sat like vultures on a branch across from me, hoping my flesh would begin rotting before them.

"Don't worry, Miss Nightingale, we won't eat your head off," Matthews said mildly, as if he were reading my soul. A faint Welsh accent tinted his speech, softening his severe expression.

I sat down, hoping my hands didn't tremble as I arranged

my skirts. I folded them in my lap and lifted my straight-forward gaze to theirs. Lady Canning's own gaze had become sympathetic, Matthews's was curious, but Alban looked as though he would happily break my neck.

What had his wife told him about our meeting?

"You are looking well, Miss Nightingale," Lady Canning said. "I am glad to see it, considering the difficulties—"

Alban interrupted her. "Yes, considering the difficulties the Establishment is now experiencing. Thus far it's been kept out of the papers, but it's only a matter of days before *The Illustrated London News* or some other tripe rag grabs hold of it."

I wondered whether I should just resign now to save us all the trouble. But then I remembered Nurse Bellamy slowly twirling at the end of a rope. I remembered her swollen face and cut wrists. I thought of how she seemingly had no one in the world except an anonymous donor who was also perhaps her anonymous lover. I thought of how she would have absolutely no one seeking justice for her if I left the hospital. It was enough to strengthen my resolve, and I decided that if I was going to be terminated, it would be with good cause and not with me weakly protesting my innocence.

I kept my hands folded and stared directly at Alban. "Well, sir, if they 'grab hold of it,' as you say, it will at least prove that someone in London actually cares about that poor girl's death other than me."

Alban glared at me, but I refused to look away, even though I thought he might have the power to fry me where I sat, like a magnifying glass over a black garden ant. It helped to see Cyril Matthews out of the corner of my eye, a balled fist over his mouth to conceal a smile.

Alban quickly regained his footing. "We wish to know what progress you have made in discovering who may have harmed the girl, this Caroline Bellamy."

I maintained my level gaze. "It has been reported to me that Nurse Bellamy may have had a gentleman caller at inappropriate moments."

"Dear girl," Lady Canning said, an eyebrow arched. "There is no appropriate moment for the nurses to be visited by men."

I felt heat creeping up my neck, as the underlying comment was that I had not gained control of my staff in the short time I had been there. "Yes, madam, although I have this on the hearsay of another nurse and did not witness it for myself."

A few silent moments ticked by, and then Matthews asked quietly, "Is that all?" He put his elbow on the table and rubbed his temple with two fingers. I thought it might be exasperation with me, but he closed his eyes briefly and I realized he must have a headache.

"Well, no, but I don't know how significant anything is because, quite truthfully, I know so little about the young woman. Perhaps, Lady Canning, you can tell me how Nurse Bellamy came to be hired at the Establishment."

"Hmm," Lady Canning murmured, tapping a finger on the table. "I seem to recall that hers was a sad story. She was running away from an abusive husband. I thought it might be trouble to bring in a nurse who might be visited by a jealous or unruly spouse, but the superintendent then didn't think he would find her."

"Perhaps he did," I said, wondering why my employer hadn't gotten word to me about this important piece of information sooner. It was knowledge to add to my growing list of seemingly unrelated facts.

"I have been gathering as much information about her as I can." I reached into my reticule and retrieved my folded papers. I unfolded them slowly and deliberately in my lap, so that they might all see that I had been working diligently. On one hand I ticked off the seemingly unrelated and inconsequential events that had occurred since Bellamy's death: the anonymous donation to her funeral, Alice Drayton's accusation that Bellamy was trying to poison her, Nurse Wilmot's claim that Bellamy had secret gentleman callers, and so forth. I omitted the strained and awkward visit from Mr. Alban's wife.

I folded my papers and put them away. From three stories below, a roar of laughter rose up and penetrated through the window. Nothing inside the room was particularly amusing, though, and the onslaught of green covering every surface was beginning to nauseate me.

To the unasked question hanging in the air, I said, "Thus far, I see very little that links these disparate facts and claims together."

"Perhaps there is some way in which we can assist you in the matter, Miss Nightingale?" Matthews asked, now steepling his hands on the table.

Before I could respond, Alban jumped in with outrage. "We cannot possibly sully our hands in this, Cyril! Can you imagine the damage to our reputations if we allow ourselves to be involved? I have banking interests, and you have your own business concerns, as you well know. No, the superintendent must solve this matter on her own. I suggested to Charlotte that we should simply dismiss Miss Nightingale, replace her with someone new, and forget about the unfortunate death, but she is adamant."

Lady Canning nodded at me. "As I said, Roderick, I selected Miss Nightingale myself upon Mrs. Herbert's recommendation, and I'm not about to throw her in the rubbish bin only a week after she's arrived. Besides, you offer no logical reasoning for why replacing her would somehow save the Establishment's reputation. I would think that if she got to the bottom of the matter, that would rescue any damage done. 'Hospital's superintendent solves murder.' It would enhance our standing in the community, I would think."

"Not only that," Matthews said. "There is the moral absolute of the poor little bird requiring justice."

Finally. Someone who understood. I was warming up to the Welshman. "Thank you, sir, yes."

He smiled at me. The smile was avuncular and welcoming. "Despite this puss face's complaining"—he cut his gaze over to Alban briefly—"you should know that your reputation preceded you into the Establishment, thanks to Mrs. Herbert's glowing recommendation. We all readily agreed to your appointment when Charlotte suggested it. Even Roderick."

Lady Canning nodded again, while Alban sat stone-faced.

"I find your idea of changing the status of nurses quite compelling," Matthews continued. "May I ask what you have implemented?" He leaned forward in interest, and I noticed he was rubbing his temple again.

"Well, sir," I began. "I was present only a short time before—"

He held up the hand that had been massaging his head. "Of course, of course. What was I thinking? I would be most curious to hear of your progress in this area as it occurs."

"Naturally you would be interested, Cyril," Alban spat scathingly.

Matthews ignored him. "Roderick very generously allows me to use his office space for conducting some of my own business until the rooms I wish to use are vacated by the current tenant. I do find, though, that Roderick tends to not spend much time here anymore."

Alban's expression suggested he wasn't much enjoying sharing his space. Why, then, did he do so?

"Perhaps, Miss Nightingale, you might return in, say, two weeks? Once you have cleared up this other sorrowful matter. I wish to know how you envision nursing in the future, and what specifically you are doing to see your vision through. I might be able to assist you."

He raised those dark eyebrows in question, and I happily accepted his offer.

Alban hadn't finished his grumbling, but now he directed it at Lady Canning. "He gets a minor post on the stock exchange and he believes he is the Lord Almighty himself."

But Charlotte Canning was becoming irritated herself. "Roderick, why so much invective, both at Cyril and Miss Nightingale? If I didn't know better, I would think you to be a jealous suitor."

Another thick, uncomfortable silence descended over the room, while more laughter floated up from the Exchange floor.

I cleared my throat. "Mr. Alban, sir, your rooms here are decorated very . . . unusually. Did your wife do it?"

"Er, no," he replied, and I thought he was being evasive. "I had them redone recently by a . . . er, friend . . . of some talent who wished to experiment in the latest colors. I like to stay on top of such things," he added, as though that explained it.

"The color selection is certainly the most unique I've ever seen," I said, hoping he might soften a little more.

Instead, Cyril Matthews laughed softly. "Dear lady, 'unique' and 'unusual' are very diplomatic terms. You should consider a career in ambassadorial service instead of nursing."

Alban harrumphed. "As I said, the Lord Almighty himself, bestowing positions and titles. They call it Schweinfurt Green, Miss Nightingale. With the bright light of kerosene and gas lamps becoming commonplace, we don't need all of those drab, pale wallpapers anymore to reflect candlelight. The most fashionable homes and buildings are using dark wallpapers now, I am told." I couldn't tell if he genuinely believed it or had simply wanted to please whoever had done this to his rooms.

Matthews clapped Alban on the shoulder. "Be of good cheer, Roderick. No one challenges your status in society . . . nor on the men's committee."

Charlotte Canning sighed and rose to conclude the meeting. "Miss Nightingale, thank you for coming. We will be checking in on you prior to your meeting with Cyril to be sure you are making progress on hospital improvements. This is, after all, what you were hired to do. I am inclined to give you as much time as you think necessary, but not everyone on the women's and men's committees is as generous. It is imperative that you determine quickly what has happened, else I fear the committees will become . . . restless . . . about your position." She offered me a sympathetic look.

I kept my expression neutral at this pronouncement, although I was actually relieved not to be dismissed outright.

Of course, that relief lasted only as long as it took to return to the hospital, where I had terrible news waiting for me.

★　★　★

At this point, I should have known to simply not open any letters proffered to me. But this one was accompanied by a mousy, older woman whom I vaguely remembered from Holloway, Derbyshire, where my family's first home, Lea Hurst, was, although I couldn't quite place her.

We sat together in the library, the woman occupying the chair so recently vacated by Mrs. Alban. She said she had arrived at the behest of my parents, who now believed I needed a companion, and then introduced herself as Mary Clarke. "You do remember me, don't you, Miss Florence?" The wire-rimmed glasses she wore slid down her nose, and she pushed them back up again.

I ignored her question and opened the missive, written in my father's precise script.

> *Darling Flo,*
> *I am sorry to tell you that your grandmama, Mary Shore, has died. It was with a minimum of fuss, so you need not think your absence in her care led to her downfall. She was, after all, 95 years of age.*

The thought of Grandmother Shore brought back bitter-sweet memories. Grandmama had been fierce in her opinions, whether on parliamentary reforms or the proper flowers to plant in the garden. She would argue to the death like a gladiator in the arena over either one, too. Being right was paramount to her.

I have waited to send you this notice, and forbade Parthenope from writing to you, until my mother was in the family plot. After you had finally escaped us, I did not want you to feel obligated to return so soon to attend her funeral. Besides, your mother and sister might have physically restrained you from leaving again, eh?

I would eventually have to return for a visit though, wouldn't I? The idea was almost appealing at the moment, what with events seeming to bear down on me, ready to crush me on both sides as though I were a sea urchin in the claw of a lobster. But Papa was right, I had to remain here and figure out how to solve Nurse Bellamy's death without my family finding out about it. If my mother knew, it would surely result in her dashing to London to yank me back to Embley Park like a lioness dragging her cub to safety.

You will remember Mary Clarke's husband, Milo, as tutor to you and Parthenope for a short time until I took over your education myself.

Ah, now it came back to me.

Milo has recently died from some sort of stomach obstruction, although he had been suffering from other ailments for quite some time. Mary has no family here, what with her son serving the East India Company off the coast of Burma. Your mother thought Mary would be well occupied—and you well served—if Mary were put into place as your companion.

Can you find a place for her to sleep in your lodgings? I am sure you can find use for her at the hospital. It would ease your mother's mind to know that you have a companion to add respectability to your position there.

It would also ease my father's mind not to have my mother constantly carping at him about me.

However, I had no desire whatsoever for the suffocation caused by a companion in my parents' employ and was tempted to turn her out with a scathing note back to my mother. Then I thought of what my poor father would endure when my mother found Mrs. Clarke on her doorstep, and it made me hesitate.

Mary Clarke looked at me hopefully. Her glasses fell again and she pushed them back up, blinking owlishly at me.

"It would seem you come highly recommended as a companion, Mrs. Clarke," I said, trying to figure out what in the world to do with her. I had so much already occupying my mind and time without having to come up with busywork for a widow.

"Have you any nursing experience?" I asked. Now it was my turn to be hopeful.

"I was at my darling Milo's side when he went on, Miss. Such a good man, and I long for his presence every day. You do remember his trying to teach you mathematics? You were ever so much more willful than your sister, he said, but ever so much brighter. He never did have such an unusual child as you for a pupil, and he had taught for many prominent Derbyshire families. Why, I remember Milo once said—"

Mrs. Clarke prattled on about her husband for several minutes while I pretended to have a modicum of interest. My mind was occupied with determining what to do with the woman who sat before me. I hardly remembered her from my girlhood days, as, I suppose, I had met her on only a couple of occasions. I guessed Mrs. Clarke to be in her early fifties. Her hair, still dark despite her age, was pulled severely back from her face with what must have been a myriad of hidden pins. The only break in the severity was a coiled loop at her neck. The black widow's weeds covering her stout frame were plain but neat.

As I recalled, Mr. Clarke had been a kindly tutor, if so nearsighted that he could hardly read any assignments I put before him. The poor bespectacled man hadn't lasted long under my constant, if innocent, questioning about polynomial equations and the measurement of planets. When Papa saw that I was mentally torturing the man, he had gently dismissed Clarke with a superb character reference. I vaguely remember Papa talking at the dinner table of Clarke's next position with a family of greater note than ours.

Mary Clarke certainly presented herself modestly, as if my mother had hand-selected her to watch over me instead of her merely being a widow at loose ends. I interrupted her description of a book her husband had been working on when he fell ill.

"Mrs. Clarke, have you any talent at correspondence? Caring for a wardrobe? Housekeeping?"

Her expression became increasingly more worried with each skill I proposed. "Mrs. Nightingale said I was just to be a companion to you, Miss. Read to you, go with you when you go into town, and the like. She didn't say anything about my being housekeeper, or lady's maid, or personal secretary."

So my mother had sent me someone respectable but use-less? I shook away the irritation. It would serve no purpose to take out my frustration on this poor innocent woman. I studied her further, and I sensed how uneasy she was under my scrutiny. However, an idea was forming in my mind. I wondered if perhaps she could be of some use to me in my investigation.

"Can you keep secrets?" I asked abruptly.

She looked at me in surprise and reached out a hand to me. "Why, Miss Florence, don't you remember the time you told your parents you were coming into the village to pick up a book on trigonometry, and I found you at the village green? You asked me not to tell, and I never did. I never even told Milo. Not that he was untrustworthy, bless his soul, but because you asked me not to do it."

The memory of Mrs. Clarke came back in a rush. I did recall that day. I had probably been ten years old, and I was bored of Milo Clarke's lecture on the Greek mathematician, Pythagoras. Professing myself to be so enamored of the topic that I needed an additional book on it, I had escaped into town for a couple of hours. I had truly intended to find a book at the subscription library where my father belonged but got distracted by some younger girls skipping rope on the green. I then stumbled upon a poor rabbit who was injured and bleeding. It seemed to me that he had been hit by a sharp stone, probably thrown by some obnoxious little urchin.

I had carried the creature in my skirts to one of the benches along the green's perimeter and was attempting to nurse the poor thing—who didn't long survive my ministrations—when Mrs. Clarke came up to me. She carried a twine-wrapped butcher's package in her arms and innocently asked what I was doing.

With a bloodied, squeaking, dying rabbit in my lap, I couldn't very well claim that I was in the midst of signing out a book. In my panic, I blurted out the truth and begged her not to repeat it to her husband.

Now that I thought about it, I never had gotten in trouble for it, despite arriving home disheveled with my clothes bloodstained and no book in sight.

"Well, Mrs. Clarke," I said now. "It seems you do indeed have a talent for secret-keeping. That is what I can use here at the Establishment."

Mary Clarke nodded sagely. "To keep confidential the conditions of the patients here."

I smiled thinly. "Actually, no. I have something else in mind for you. But first we need to fix where you will reside."

Mrs. Clarke's relief at my acceptance was palpable, as if she didn't realize I had little choice in the matter if I wanted to keep peace within my family.

I escorted her to my rarely used lodgings in Wimple Street so that she could unpack the small bag she had brought with her. She said she would send for her other belongings. Having her in my lodgings would ensure that Mother would be satisfied that Mrs. Clarke could keep an eye on me, but provided me with space to breathe. I could remove her from my person each evening, like unhooking a tight-fitting corset. Yet during the day I would have the advantage of her assisting me in maintaining the form and posture my mother wished everyone to see.

"Now we will return to the Establishment so you can perform your first task," I said.

"Shall I make you a nice pot of tea, then?" she asked brightly.

"Hardly," I replied. "You will take notes while I interview a woman who might be a murderess."

Poor Mrs. Clarke. I know it took all of her intestinal fortitude not to collapse in a faint on the floor at my pronouncement.

Was it too terrible of me to be a little pleased that I had so shocked my mother's dictated companion for me? The unfortunate woman had yet to hear the sordid tale of Nurse Bellamy.

★　★　★

As soon as we were back at the Establishment, I issued an instruction for someone to find Nurse Margery Frye and send her to my study. Before Frye arrived, I already had Mrs. Clarke perched on a wood chair in a corner with a notebook and freshly dipped ink pen in her lap.

Frye frowned at seeing a stranger in my study and seemed even further irritated that not only did I not introduce Mrs. Clarke, but the older woman remained hunched over her notebook and did not make eye contact with her.

I could see that Frye desperately wanted to know who

Mrs. Clarke was but didn't have the nerve to ask. All of a sudden, out of the comfort of her own room, Nurse Frye wasn't so confident, and was in fact disconcerted. I was learning that picking your own battlefield was helpful in winning a war, if it could be said that I was at war with my own staff.

"Nurse, please sit down," I said, extending my hand to the chair across from me. Frye sat slowly, giving Mrs. Clarke a final dubious glance before fully concentrating on me.

"Yes, Miss Nightingale," she said dutifully.

"I understand you once worked for Allen and Hanbury's."

Frye's eyes narrowed. "How did you come to know that? Did Polly tell you?"

Was Polly Roper her confidante? That was interesting. I hoped Mrs. Clarke was making note of it. The pen was in her hand, flying across the page, so I had to assume she was.

"It is of no matter who told me. What *is* of concern is that you apparently had access to all manner of pharmaceuticals. Did you by chance handle arsenic?"

"You mean rat poison? Like what ol' Charlie uses around the edges of the building to control vermin? Sure," she shrugged. "Caught my own rat that way, didn't I?"

I remembered the dead rat in her room. Why hadn't she told me then that she had killed the creature?

"Where do you keep it? In fact, where do you keep all of the medicinal supplies you possess?"

She shrugged. "Here and there. Some down in the kitchens."

Polly Roper's domain.

"A bit tucked away in my pillowcase. A few hidey-holes I've found. I've given some to Charlie."

Her answer suggested that she held it all so loosely that anyone in the building might have access to it. So was it possible that it actually *was* Nurse Bellamy who had attempted to poison Alice Drayton? Or was that idea still borne out of Miss Drayton's confusion?

"You will look among your 'hidey-holes' and in your pillowcase and wherever else you have put them and bring them to me for safekeeping until the matter with Nurse Bellamy is sorted out."

Frye's jaw dropped. I really disliked viewing the rotting interior of her mouth.

"But they are mine, Miss Nightingale. I risked a lot to get them."

"Yes, undoubtedly," I said dryly, but Frye did not catch my sarcasm. "Mrs. Clarke here will accompany you as you gather them up."

Now Mary Clarke's expression was one of surprise as she looked up from her scribbling, but she didn't challenge me.

"While you're at it, give Mrs. Clarke any other gin bottles, too," I added.

"But Miss Nightingale, I told you they belonged to Clem—"

"Nurse Harris. Yes, I know you did. And do you know"—I leaned forward—"*I don't believe you.*"

She continued to protest. "I showed you her murder weapon. You should be after her, not persecuting me."

I almost felt sorry for Mrs. Clarke, who was swallowing repeatedly as her complexion turned pale. Still, she did not speak up to refuse the task. I confess I was pleased.

Margery Frye, however, was not so pleased. "I'll not be treated like a mangy cur, kicked in my hindquarters by a mean master. You can't—"

I held up a hand to stop her, as Cyril Matthews had recently done to me. "I am not kicking you, Nurse. I, as superintendent, simply won't allow you to have your own supply of medicines inside the Establishment. Particularly while I am investigating Nurse Bellamy's death."

I was even more determined now because of her defiant attitude to make sure those medicines were off the property. I would store them at my off-premise lodgings that Mary now occupied so as to prevent any theft of them from the Establishment.

Frye crossed her arms and leaned back, sulky now. "The other superintendent didn't mind."

"The other superintendent is no longer here. *I am*."

Frye blinked several times at my pronouncement, then tried another approach. "I told you about Nurse Harris and her husband. You should have her arrested. If anyone would be guilty of a murder, it would be her. Instead you go after poor innocent women like me."

Once more the urge to dismiss the insolent harpy was overpowering. *Not yet*, I counseled myself. "I will worry about Nurse Harris. For now, you should be concerned only with yourself and how you measure against the standard I am setting."

I released her from the room and nodded my head to Mrs. Clarke that she should follow the nurse. My new companion scuttled out behind Frye, her notebook tucked under her arm. She reminded me of a goose who willingly follows the farmer to the block, even knowing what will happen next.

Poor Mrs. Clarke would have to learn quickly that being at the Establishment meant enduring many such awkward, uncomfortable moments, particularly as the rank and file were brought in line.

★ ★ ★

While Mary followed Margery Frye around to collect the nurse's potions and powders, I decided to check on my nurses. My hope was that they were tending to patients.

I found Nurse Wilmot on her hands and knees in Ivy Stoke's room, reaching one arm under the bed while Mrs. Stoke crouched behind her, offering encouragement.

"What in heaven's name are you doing?" I asked.

Wilmot froze, her rump no longer wriggling as she reached for an unseen object, while Mrs. Stoke jerked up in surprise at my appearance.

"Miss Nightingale!" the patient exclaimed. "This nurse is helping me capture Jasmine. My sweet girl got spooked by something and flew in here, racing right under the bed."

I reminded Wilmot that Ivy Stoke would need to smoke one of Dr. Killigrew's new cigarette blends, then shook my head and left them to what they were doing.

I nearly bumped into Nurse Hughes, who was carrying a stack of linens into Alice Drayton's room. Atop the sheets and blankets was a precariously placed tray containing a steaming teapot, cup and saucer, and the other makings for proper tea. After placing the linens at the foot of the bed and the tea tray on the desk, Hughes helped Alice from the bed to the chair so she could change the bed linens.

While she did so, I held my breath and examined Alice's throat. To my utter surprise, Dr. Killigrew's cure actually seemed to be working. The ulcers had clearly diminished. Remarkable.

I continued to check on the inmates, raising windows, opening doors, and flapping sheets wherever I could to stimulate fresh air.

I reached the end of the hospital's modest ward, satisfied that all was well, and made my way to the library to wait for Mary to return with Margery Frye's medicine collection.

As I reentered the main hall, it occurred to me that I should talk to Polly Roper once more to question her about her relationship with Nurse Frye.

I headed to the rear of the building to use the servants' staircase. There was a window providing light to the narrow, winding stairwell, but the day had grown overcast, so the light was minimal against the yellow walls. At least Lady Canning had had the foresight to have a rail installed. At Embley Park, my parents had no such bar for servants to hold, as such extravagances were usually reserved for the resident family and the main staircase. Nurses and other staff alike had cause to come down this way to the kitchens, so the rail was beneficial to all.

I took the rail in my right hand and my skirts in my left, feeling my way onto the first creaking oak step. I wished I had thought to bring a lantern along with me. Perhaps I needed to return to—

I heard the briefest scuffling behind me, but before I could turn to see who was there, the shadowy form of a hand appeared in front of my face and I felt a cloth pressed against my nose and mouth. The sharp, sickly sweet smell of chloroform was overpowering. What was happening?

I instinctively grabbed at the hand holding the cloth over me, but whoever it was had a tight grip on me. I had no idea if it was a man or woman who clutched me so tightly, but the hold was firm enough that I couldn't manage to effectively claw or bite my way out of his—or her—control.

It is strange how in the panic of looming death, one can have a plethora of unrelated thoughts in the space of mere seconds, none of which have anything to do with recapturing life.

I thought about the queen, who had delivered her eighth child, Leopold, back in April, with the use of chloroform. Prince Albert had thoroughly interrogated the doctor proposing its use before permitting it to be used on his wife. What a kind husband.

I thought about Polly Roper finding my lifeless body at the foot of the staircase and how inconvenient it would be for the inmates' dinner preparations.

I thought of poor Mary Clarke, here for only a few hours and already facing tragedy.

Nurse Bellamy's revolving corpse rose up in my mind, with the realization that no one in the world—except for perhaps Cyril Matthews—cared about justice for her, and so my death would end the pursuit for her killer.

Urgent whispering from somewhere behind me caused my attacker to release me, then push me forcefully between my shoulder blades. In my drugged state, I was unable to find the rail, and I pitched forward in an ungainly manner as my skirts tangled beneath me. As I plunged downward along the stone steps, with justice for Nurse Bellamy still on my mind, I knew exactly why I was being murdered.

I had somehow stumbled into knowledge about the murder of my nurse, even though I did not yet realize what it was.

CHAPTER 11

I awoke to a distant buzzing, as if I were near a beehive. No, that wasn't it. I strained to listen more closely to determine what was humming in the room. The effort made me realize how terribly my head was pounding. It didn't help that the ground beneath me was so hard.

I was also thirsty, as if I had gone days without water. I tried to swallow, but my tongue felt like a gigantic obstacle in my mouth. Had I survived an attempted murder only to be perishing of dehydration?

The buzzing was now splintering into distinct sounds, and it wasn't long before I realized that I was hearing voices.

Were they imaginary? Was I insensible?

I felt light against my eyelids and attempted to open my eyes. I barely managed to flutter my lashes, but in that moment caught sight of someone leaning over me as if waiting for me to speak.

Then all was black again.

★　★　★

The next time I awoke, my mind was a little clearer, and I knew I was somewhere else. The ground was softer and the air was quiet, no longer full of irritating buzzing.

I felt a moist cloth pressed against my forehead and then against my lips. I jerked my head away, terrified that I was under attack again, although I didn't smell chloroform this time.

"Are you awake, Miss?" came a female voice from above me. "You took quite a fall. Dr. Killigrew is here and wanted to be notified immediately when you awoke. You are awake, aren't you?"

I slowly opened my eyes and peered through the slits that formed. "Nurse Harris?" I asked. My voice was but a croak.

Harris came back into view again. Her expression was somber and her green eyes were full of worry. "Indeed. Wait here while I fetch Dr. Killigrew."

Where did she believe I was going? I attempted to arise after she left the room. I managed to struggle into a seated position. I was worn out from my efforts but at least better understood my location, which was a patient room. The room had a faded oval on the red toile wallpaper, where a portrait of a long-dead family patriarch had likely once hung. There was also a large, jagged-edged scorch mark on the wood flooring in front of the fire grate, no doubt the result of a clumsy ash-clearing in the past. It was difficult to shake the feeling that this was still a living, breathing family home, despite the age-old decay that remained.

This room was at the end of the ward and had not been used since my arrival as superintendent. How ironic that I was to be its first occupant.

I looked down at myself. I was covered loosely with a sheet and still wore my day clothes. Did that mean I had been unconscious only a short time? In truth, I was glad my nurses had not attempted to change my clothes. I wasn't sure I entirely trusted all of them with touching my person.

What a horrid thought. But I suppose truth can be a horrid thing, raw and ugly and showing no pity for the weak or unaware.

Once more I remembered how thirsty I was. I noticed a glass and full water pitcher on the room's desk. I made mental approval of Nurse Harris's attention to detail.

As I made the decision to attempt to go to the desk, Nurse Harris returned with Dr. Killigrew. The good doctor wore his usual beaming smile, although I found it a little forced in my presence. My status as a patient probably unnerved him as much as it did me.

"It is splendid to see you alert, Miss Nightingale," he boomed, while Nurse Harris—bless her—instinctively poured a cup of water for me.

She held the cup to my lips and I drank like a greedy child, both of my hands covering hers. She removed the empty glass from my lips and I felt rejuvenated. It was extraordinary what a bit of liquid could do for one's mental and physical states.

"Nurse, I should like to have—" I began.

"A bowl of bone broth. Yes, Miss, I will tell Mrs. Roper immediately." Having thus peered into my mind once again, Harris returned the glass to the desk and left the room.

Killigrew watched her retreating figure, then turned back to me. "Quiet, that one, but competent, eh?"

Yes, she was.

I found myself yawning and covered my rudely gaping mouth with a fist. I felt better, but achy and exhausted.

"You took quite a tumble down into the kitchens," Killigrew said, sitting down in the room's chair. "The staff weren't sure if you might be dead, but fortunately they sent your boy to fetch me, and I had you removed from the floor up to a proper bed."

I wondered if anyone had thought to give John Wesley a penny or two. I nodded my thanks to Killigrew, who pulled the desk's chair around so that it was positioned next to the bed, facing me. He sat down heavily, his smiling expression mixed with concern.

"Tell me of any symptoms you believe you have," he said.

I told him of my powerful but recently sated thirst as well as my overall soreness.

"Minor afflictions given that you might easily have broken your neck," he said. "I suggest not looking in the mirror for the next few days. You face absorbed a lot of the shock, I'm afraid. Your Nurse Harris was very insistent that she be your sole attendant up here. I don't believe she left the room for hours. It would seem that she is at least somewhat responsible for your good recovery thus far."

Until this moment, Dr. Killigrew had not enthused over any of my nurses.

"I shall inform her of your praise," I said. Perhaps she would be a motivating example to the others.

He nodded. "She will want to know that she is esteemed. Now," he said, slapping his hands on his knees. "Can you tell me what caused you to fall? You don't strike me as ungainly in your movements, and surely you were holding the rail as you went down."

I was torn. Should I tell Dr. Killigrew what had happened, thus bringing him into my confidence? Was it a matter better left for the police? Or perhaps I would risk telling no one as I continued to ferret out who Nurse Bellamy's killer was. Clearly I had come close to the answer, else I wouldn't have been attacked.

I wasn't sure why I was reluctant to be open and honest with the doctor. He was kind and intelligent, if a bit exasperating with his constant puns and riddles. Perhaps I was just becoming a lunatic.

"I can't imagine," I said. "One moment I was casually stepping downstairs, the next I must have gotten caught up in my skirts. As though I had just today become a child on unsteady feet, I suppose, and taken a toddler's tumble." I smiled weakly again.

"Hmm," the doctor said, his expression becoming the most serious that I had ever seen. "You didn't see a mouse that might have startled you? Or, perhaps, you heard something that gave you a fright?"

It was clear that he didn't believe my explanation. "Not that I recall. The stairwell is very dark."

He studied me silently for several moments, which unnerved me to no end. Finally he said, "Although you are dented and bruised, you have no broken bones. You were quite fortunate, don't you think?"

"I suspect I am quite fortunate to be alive at all," I replied in jest, but Dr. Killigrew was not amused.

His scrutiny was transforming him from jovial jester into

probing inquisitor. "I have had patients before who, lacking the sort of attention they want—or trying to deflect attention away from misdeeds—have injured themselves to acquire sympathy and thus eliminate careful examination of their condition."

I was aghast at his insinuation. "Are you suggesting that I purposely fell down the stairs to deflect attention away from Nurse Bellamy's death?"

Dr. Killigrew stood and returned the chair to its place. Then he turned to face me again. "I do not suggest anything, madam. I only explore all possibilities. Lady Canning informs me that the committees are concerned about your . . . stability . . . here given what has happened."

My stomach was working into a furious knot. Why was my employer talking to the Establishment's doctor about such things, particularly when she had seemed so supportive of me when we had previously met? On the other hand, why would I think she wouldn't do so? If Charlotte Canning, seemingly one of my only advocates, was gossiping with Dr. Killigrew, I could only imagine what braying and grousing committee members like Roderick Alban were doing.

Now I was caught. If I proceeded to tell Dr. Killigrew that I had been pushed down the stairs, it would seem I was making it up in the moment to justify myself. If only I had made a wiser choice two minutes before.

Yet now I knew with certainty that if I shared anything with him, it would be deposited straight into my employer's ear like a love-starved girl's penny into a wishing well. I had to maintain a confident front.

"The committees' concerns are appreciated, but I assure you that even a hospital superintendent can experience an accident. I already feel better and will be back to work in short order." I said this decisively, and it seemed to have the right effect on the doctor, for he smiled once again. "That's the woman I know. Tough as ten-year-old mutton. I may as well go check on the other inmates while I'm here; then I'll check on you again during my regular visit next Tuesday. That reminds me, what is the difference between a tube and a foolish Dutchman?"

I shook my head. "I do not know."

"One is a hollow cylinder and the other is a silly Hollander." With that, he burst into laughter. I smiled wanly in response.

I was both glad to see Dr. Killigrew leave and thoroughly unsettled by his visit.

★ ★ ★

I refused all other visitors except Mary Clarke and, of course, Nurse Harris. Harris was dedicated in ensuring I had plenty to drink and in applying salves to my various bruises.

Mary presented the collection of Nurse Frye's pharmaceuticals. The crate was heaped with bottles and boxes, an impressive haul.

I sent Mary back to the lodgings with instructions to hide the crate in my rooms and return immediately thereafter.

For it had occurred to me that my attacker had not finished his job and might seek to do so during the night.

I had Nurse Harris bring in a cot for Mary. The room became awkward for Harris to maneuver in, but it was the least of my concerns. For the moment, I believed Mary to be the only person I could trust without reserve, given that she was a complete stranger to the Establishment and could have no possible agenda or motives for any damage befalling the hospital.

How had I gone from resenting her presence to craving it in the space of a half day?

Mary returned after dark and accepted the cot in my cramped room over a comfortable bed in my lodgings without complaint.

We shared a silent supper together, and then she retrieved nightclothes for me from my room and helped me change. Even in the dim lamplight, I could see how bruised I was. Raising my arms over my head was painful, but I gritted my teeth and pretended I was fine.

I had to be fine, as wasting this many hours was quite enough. After tonight, I had to return to getting the hospital in order and continuing my investigations.

* * *

In the morning, Mary Clarke helped me rise and change into day clothes. I felt immensely better after a night of sleep, even though the previous day's cloudiness had turned into pouring rain overnight. The constant patter was rhythmic and comforting.

I instructed Nurse Harris to have breakfast brought to Mary and me in the library. I planned to work there while recuperating. The sight and smell of books would no doubt encourage my recovery.

As we finished up our deviled kidneys on toast, served in lap trays at the far end of the library, Persimmon Jarrett entered, humming as she unpinned her bonnet and tossed it onto her desk near the door. She smoothed her pinned hair back with one had as she turned in our direction.

Jarrett squeaked at the sight of me. "Miss Nightingale, you gave me a scare! I didn't realize you would be here. I thought you were—" She stopped, looking perplexed.

Even from my distance, I saw that she held a butter biscuit in her other hand. I arched an eyebrow. "I see you visited Mrs. Roper on your way in, Miss Jarrett."

Like a young child making an obvious attempt to hide a wrongdoing, she put her hand behind her back.

I ignored it. I wasn't ready to war with the librarian over her indulgences when I had literal life-or-death matters at hand.

"This is Mary Clarke," I said, nodding at Mary. "She is my new companion here at the Establishment."

Jarrett's expression became even more confused. But as she neared us, she offered Mary a "Pleased to meet you," and they exchanged pleasantries.

"Mrs. Clarke and I will be working on some papers," I told Jarrett, who took her cue and retreated to her desk.

I believed the librarian to be far enough away that she couldn't overhear a murmured conversation with Mary. I quickly explained to my new companion what had happened in the servants' stairwell.

Mary wrung her hands together nervously. "Oh, Miss Florence, the danger you're in. What will your parents say?"

I gazed steadily at her. I had not considered the fact that my parents—well, my mother—might expect Mary to report on me. Was there really no one at all neutral enough for me to talk to?

"Tell me, Mrs. Clarke, would it be necessary for my parents to know? Why would we upset them without cause?"

She withered under my stare. "Oh, dear," she fretted. "Oh, in the name of Peter and Paul." The literal hand-wringing continued.

It was obvious to me that Mrs. Clarke was trying to sort through where her loyalty lay: with the people who were paying her or with the girl to whom she had been loyal all those years ago.

"I suppose there is no harm in remaining quiet for now," she said slowly, nodding. "To not upset them unnecessarily, as you say."

I smiled to encourage her. "Perhaps this will be resolved in just a few days' time, and then you can send the Nightingales a glowing report of what has happened here . . . including your part as my assistant."

Mrs. Clarke blushed in pleasure at being called my assistant, and I knew I had won her to my side.

She sat up a bit taller in her seat and removed her breakfast tray from her lap, setting it on an armless old Chippendale chair next to her. "What would you have me do, Miss?"

"Well, Mrs. Clarke—" I began.

"No, Miss Florence, you must call me Mary. I insist."

"Very well . . . Mary. I have started a series of charts and notes that are in my study. Perhaps you could . . ."

"Right away," she said, rising and leaving to retrieve my documents.

I, too, was tired of my lap tray and was in the middle of moving it over to a table when Miss Jarrett came scurrying back to talk to me, a pencil drawing of some sort in her hand.

It dangled to her side in her left hand as she stood before me, breathless from rushing to the rear of the library. She really needed to spend time taking walks to increase her lung capacity.

"Miss Nightingale, if I may . . ." she began.

I nodded at her, and Jarrett turned back toward the door to be sure we were still the only ones there.

"That Mrs. Clarke who was here, is she to be an inmate?" Was that panic in her eyes?

"Mrs. Clarke is going to be attending me."

"Like . . . your maid?"

"No, Miss Jarrett," I said patiently. "She will attend to my personal affairs."

"So, your personal secretary?" The woman was clearly struggling to understand.

"Does it matter? Does the idea displease you?" I asked, wearying of this line of conversation.

"Ah—no. No, ma'am. I just didn't know if she was someone to be trusted."

How did such a thing affect Persimmon Jarrett? "What are you getting at? What sort of trust do you believe I should— or should not—place in her?"

Jarrett glanced furtively at the door again and dropped her voice. "Miss Nightingale, when I heard you fell down the stairs yesterday, I had my suspicions. I think you may have been pushed or tripped. Someone tried to harm you."

How did she know? I replied to her in a carefully measured tone. "How did you come to this conclusion?"

"I-I-hope you won't be too angry with me, ma'am, but ever since Nurse Bellamy's . . . well, you know . . . ever since then I have felt evil in this place. There are very bad spirits at work, but I don't know if they are attached to living beings or not."

I knew any evil in this place was most definitely living.

Jarrett's words now came out in a tumble. "The police never came back, and I saw that you were taking on the investigation by yourself, and so, begging your pardon, I thought maybe I could quietly do some investigating for you on my own. Especially since the tragedy happened here in this room." She shuddered. "I didn't want to bother you with it in case I wasn't up to snuff and would have no result."

Poor Jarrett was breathing heavily again.

"I presume, then, that you have a result, else why would you be mentioning it to me?" I said.

"Yes." She produced the pencil drawing for me to see.

I laid it on my lap and realized that it was a crude sketch of the Establishment's layout, including the back gardens.

"Did you do this?" I asked.

"Yes." She bowed her head. "I like being the librarian here because I like books. And maps. And drawings. Making drawings myself is just a foolish hobby, but I thought a sketch of the hospital might somehow help."

I looked back down at her drawing again. Though crude, it certainly showed the rooms of all three floors in fair proportion to one another. She had even drawn in all of the staircases, including the servants' stairs I had so recently fallen down.

"What are these arrows?" I said, pointing to lines that seemed to mark routings through the building.

Jarrett beamed. "I paced out possible entry and exit ways.

I heard Nurse Wilmot complaining about Nurse Bellamy's night visitors to Mrs. Roper and thought maybe I could figure out where they might be entering and leaving so as not to arouse anyone's notice. As you can see," she said, tracing a specific set of arrows on the paper, "a path from the attic stairs down to the rear of the entry hall, followed by the servants' staircase down through the kitchens and out to the rear of the building, is one to which almost no one would pay attention."

I traced it myself. What Jarrett said was true. But how was it helpful to know the escape route of Bellamy's paramours? "What are the filled-in circles drawn in some of the rooms?" I asked.

"Oh." Jarrett hesitated. "As part of my travels through the building, I noted rooms that had at least two doors leading in and out. I thought those likely rooms for trysts, since flight from them is so much simpler."

I examined these rooms. Only one patient room had two doorways in it, that of Alice Drayton, who had claimed Bellamy had tried to poison her. Now I wasn't sure at all that the inmate was confused, although surely Bellamy was not meeting a man in an inmate's room? Unless Miss Drayton had been out of the room and come back unexpectedly. Perhaps I needed to question her again.

"I don't know if this diagram has been helpful or not," I said to the librarian as I handed it back to her. "But thank you for showing it to me."

"Yes, ma'am. I'm glad you aren't angry with me for taking it upon myself and all to do this. It was just me wanting to help."

"I understand," I said, already becoming distracted as I wondered what was keeping Mary.

Jarrett continued to stand there, rocking back and forth like a puppy who needed to go outside to relieve itself but didn't know how to communicate its urgency.

"Is that all?" I asked, knowing it wasn't. "Why don't you sit down?"

Jarrett sat down in Mary's chair and sat back, hugging herself at the elbows. "I've been at my wit's end over whether to tell you this, Miss Nightingale, as I think I could be very seriously hurt—or worse—for telling you. You know I said I thought you were pushed down the stairs because of evil in the hospital?"

"Yes." I felt growing dread over what she might be about to say.

"When I told you I overheard Nurse Wilmot talking to Mrs. Roper about Nurse Bellamy's male visitors . . ." Jarrett trailed off, the fierce red blush of embarrassment creeping up her face.

"Did you overhear something else? Do not be afraid to tell me," I said.

Jarrett took a deep breath. "I also heard Nurse Wilmot ask Mrs. Roper if she wanted to be included in a scheme she had started with Nurse Harris."

"Nurse Harris?" I repeated in disbelief. "What sort of scheme?"

She shook her head. "I'm not quite sure. Something to do with becoming rich without anyone knowing about it. Charlie Lewis came downstairs about that time and I didn't want him to catch me in a bad position, you understand."

"Why did you not tell me this sooner?" I demanded in complete frustration. "Why would you keep such important information to yourself?"

"I-I-I—" She was becoming nervous again. "I thought perhaps if I could figure it out on my own—"

"Then you could be the heroine of your own novel: saving me, saving other staff, and saving the Establishment's reputation," I finished tartly for her.

"Well—I—well, I didn't mean to—" Jarrett was on the verge of tears.

I sighed. "Very well. You did the proper thing by at least *finally* coming to me. You will speak of this to no one else, is that clear?" I rose to end the conversation.

Jarrett bobbed her head up and down as she also stood. "No, madam. I mean, yes, of course, madam. But . . . is there any other way I can help?"

I paused. I had only just decided to trust no one other than Mary, who was known to me but was a stranger to the Establishment. I wasn't sure I was ready to fully extend my confidence elsewhere. "I appreciate your enthusiasm. If you happen to witness or overhear anything, tell me immediately. But"—I frowned to emphasize how much I meant this—"do *not* listen at doors or question anyone or do *anything* remotely investigative. Do you understand?"

Jarrett nodded, but I had the feeling she would be crouched down, peering through a keyhole, in no time. Should I worry that she might also be knocked down a flight of stairs?

Jarrett bobbed a curtsy and returned to her desk with her floor plan, humming happily once more as she folded it. As I left the library myself, I watched as she locked the floor plan away in a drawer as though it were a secret treasure.

I was developing a bad feeling about Persimmon Jarrett's future health and well-being.

★ ★ ★

In the corridor, I nearly collided with a confused Mary Clarke, who carried her writing notebook as well as the papers I had asked her to retrieve.

"Miss Florence, I thought you wished to—"

"What kept you?" I snapped, much more harshly than I had intended.

"My apologies. I misplaced my notebook. I could have sworn I put it on a bookshelf in your study, but it wasn't there. I found it on the table in the entry hall. I don't remember dropping it there."

I doubted she had been forgetful, but why would someone have moved it? "Let's return to my study," I said. There was no question that Jarrett's ears would be perked up like a terrier's if we remained in the library. My study was probably the only safe place in the building to talk.

Once we reached it, I firmly shut the door and turned the key in the lock. No need to risk it accidentally drifting open.

Mary watched me with a growing expression of concern.

I ignored the look and dragged my desk chair around until I was seated next to her. "Mary," I said. "It's time for you to hear a story . . ."

I spent the next half hour recounting the past few days to her, from the moment I had found Nurse Bellamy to the conversation I had just had with Persimmon Jarrett. I nearly wore myself out reliving the encounters with Roderick Alban, Lillian Alban, Nurse Wilmot, and Nurse Frye, not to mention my near brush with death the day before.

Mary stayed silent through my epic tale, the only signs of her distress the occasional hand-wringing, swallowing, and lips pursed into an O. She really was like a nervous little goose.

I actually found myself amused by it.

"The information I am missing is what happened with Nurse Frye when you retrieved all of her pharmaceuticals," I said.

"Well, I must say she was quite rude and stinks of gin," Mary declared huffily.

I smiled. "She is not as gently born as you. Few women who take up nursing are."

"Well," Mary repeated, "she killed me many times over with the daggers stabbing out from her eyes. I had to say, 'Is that all?' at least four times in order for her to show me all of her hidey-holes. At least I think we got to them all. Her hiding places were behind furniture, under floorboards, and in cupboards. A dreadful woman, Miss Florence." She made the pronouncement primly, and I smiled again.

"Tell me what you wrote up while I interviewed Nurse Frye," I said. I wanted to see if Mary's note-taking was thorough.

"Of course." Mary brought the notebook to the top of the paper pile in her lap. I should have had Jarrett give me the map to add to the growing list of documents pertaining to the investigation. I made a mental note to ask her for it.

"I don't understand," Mary said, frowning in puzzlement as she flipped back and forth between two pages. "Half of it is gone."

"Gone? What do you mean?" I said in disbelief as I held out my hand for the journal, and she passed it over willingly. I examined the internal sew seam. Someone had carefully torn out one of the pages upon which Mary had taken notes about my interview with Frye. Just a tiny shred of paper remained inside the binding to show that it had been torn out.

Someone had stolen the notebook to rip out this specific page. Was it Nurse Frye herself? Or could it have been Nurse Harris—which I could hardly countenance? Who else had an interest in that conversation?

It seemed I never had time to address one event before another crisis arose to take its place.

"Mary, we must think this through logically. To do so, we must add our new information to the list about Nurse Bellamy and my chart of people."

She nodded in agreement, and we spent an intense hour at it.

By the end, we had added the Moores, Cyril Matthews, and Lady Canning to my chart, and notes about all of the conversations I had had since I had last written anything down.

Although I typically found my medical graphs and charts a good method for thinking through the commonalities and causes of diseases, this was not the case here. I had to finally admit that with every update I made to my murder investigation charts, I was left more and more baffled.

Mary broke into my brooding thoughts. "Miss Florence, I

believe we know now the most important thing on which to focus."

"What is that?" I asked, willing to follow almost any rabbit trail.

"We need to know right away who attempted to kill you. And I believe I know who it was."

"You do?" I was amazed. Our discussion hadn't revealed any one suspect who stood out over another. Mostly it seemed as though nearly everyone *could* be guilty, while no one clearly *was* the perpetrator.

Mary nodded, as confident as I was indecisive for once. "Without question it was Lillian Alban."

Because I was still completely unsure of things myself, I could neither support nor ridicule her assertion. "Why her?" I simply said.

"It's obvious, isn't it? 'Hell hath no fury like a woman scorned,' that Mr. Congreve said. Mrs. Alban has been cast aside by her husband and believes you to be the reason." Mary pushed her glasses up her nose, presumably to better catch my reaction.

I stubbornly shook my head. "But I am certain I convinced her that I have had no dealings with Mr. Alban."

Mary smiled as one having to instruct a child. "Miss Florence, you said yourself that you weren't certain of the lady's stability. I remember when my darling Milo was courting me. It was back in, oh, '20 or '22. His parents wanted him to marry Grace Saintjohn, but he had met me at a Christmas market in Matlock and we fell so deeply in love."

Mary sighed and gazed off in the distance.

"Milo wanted to please his parents but was constantly

slipping away to meet me at tearooms, parks, and fairs. Eventually, Grace found out about it and they had a terrible row. Determined to keep hold of Milo, she decided to wreak havoc in my life. She may not have pushed me down a staircase, but she sent me vile letters and showed up wherever I went. After Milo and I married, she did a spell in the Derby lunatic asylum. Her parents moved away with her a couple of years later."

A romantic tragedy to be sure, but I didn't see how it was relevant to my own situation with the Albans. I said so, and then asked, "So what point are you making?"

Another sigh.

"You have so little experience in the matters of love, so you don't know what women in competition for affection are capable of doing, Miss Florence. You may know you have no interest in her husband, but Lillian Alban isn't necessarily convinced of that and might go to great lengths to eliminate a competitor."

The second part of what Mary said might be true, but she had not been witness to my agony with Richard. How easily I might have ended up as Grace Saintjohn, when Richard came to me to let me know in person that he had offered for the hand of Annabella Crewe. Only weeks had passed since my final rejection of him, making me wonder if he hadn't already been eyeing the lovely Annabella when he proposed to me that last time. As if meeting with me was sort of a final confirmation that he was free to do as he pleased.

Annabella was a brilliant match for Richard, even if her father, the Baron Crewe, was completely batty. He had contracted a second, bigamous marriage when Annabella and her siblings had been young children. It was an enormous scandal in Cheshire, but Annabella Crewe had not suffered socially for it.

No doubt the palatial, Jacobean-era-built Crewe Hall, a sign of the Baron's substantial wealth that had increased tenfold with the addition of his legal wife's Barbados sugar plantations, curbed what might have been total social castigation.

Certainly, the Crewes were better placed than the Nightingales, so how could I have complained, particularly since I was adamant about not entering a marriage contract myself?

I will never forget Richard's expression when he came to tell me. I knew in that moment that I merely needed to plead with him not to do it, not to abandon my distant affections, and he would return to me.

But I couldn't. I knew I had a solitary path to follow, one that didn't include Richard, so I impaled myself on a sword honed and gleaming from years of self-denial. I smiled tremulously and congratulated him, wishing him many years of marital felicity and a bevy of children.

The thought of Annabella Crewe bearing Richard's children was completely revolting, but I slammed the door shut on the idea.

I believe Richard died a little in that moment, much as I withered away myself. But he accepted it with a man's intestinal fortitude, kissed my cheek, and left.

That had been two years ago. I surreptitiously followed the society papers, and there had been no announcement yet of a child. In my darkest moments, I envisioned Richard and Annabella as estranged already. But it was as far as my imagination carried me. I would never intrude upon their marriage—nor impugn my own reputation—with silly threats or letters.

I shook my head. Now who was the one wrapped up in far-off wistfulness?

"Mary, I have experienced the mentally unstable and understand what you are trying to tell me. However, I don't think that every woman who is scorned becomes a raving lunatic."

"As you wish, Miss Florence," Mary said, bowing her head.

I could see that I had hurt her feelings, as she had been proud of her theory. It was an enormous failing, this temper and sharp tongue of mine.

I tried to rectify it. "However, I believe you are correct that there is someone mentally unbalanced in the Establishment. We need to discover who it is."

Mary raised her head. "It is Lillian Alban," she insisted.

I had to give my companion credit for sticking to her theory. "Perhaps," I said, noncommittally. "Let's add that to the chart next to Mrs. Alban's name."

I checked the watch pinned to my bodice. It was already nearly lunchtime and I hadn't checked on a single inmate, or on what my nurses were doing, or . . .

I was suddenly very tired and stifled a yawn.

"Miss Florence?" Mary said, concerned. "I don't think you are ready for this much strenuous activity. You need rest." She rose and offered an arm to help me up. I accepted it gratefully, as my aches and sores reminded me of my recent tumble.

As she escorted me to my own room for a nap, I mumbled,

"You are such a silly goose, Mary, but perhaps you are laying golden eggs for me that I have not yet found."

"Yes, Miss Florence," she replied patiently to my nattering.

I was soon changed and under my bed coverings, drifting off into a long, dreamless sleep.

I awoke in the early morning hours, sweating and shaking, to the sound of wounded-animal screaming.

CHAPTER 12

My body was still sore, but my mind was instantly alert as I listened to the scuffling and cries of pain below me. I rose as quickly as I could, one hand pressed to my temple to quell an oncoming headache. I dressed faster than I ever had in my life and hastened down the staircase.

It seemed that everyone else was awake, too, and crowded around a prone figure in the entry hall. The dawning sun, uninhibited by yesterday's clouds, which had dissipated, filtered through the windows and door transom and illuminated who lay there in an almost ethereal halo.

John Wesley.

"What has happened here?" I demanded.

John Wesley turned to face me. He clutched one knee. "Miss Nightingale, I'm sorry to wake you. Please don't send me away."

I moved toward the boy, and the others stepped back to give me room. I noticed Mary was part of the assembly. Why wasn't she back at the lodgings?

I knelt next to John Wesley and saw there was blood

seeping through his fingers as he maintained a grip on his knee. The poor boy's ashen face glistened with sweat.

"No one is sending you away," I said in a soothing tone. "We are going to help you."

I looked up. The nearest nurse to me was Nan Wilmot. "Make sure the inmate room I was just in is clean. Go now," I snapped, when she continued to stare down dumbly at the injured boy.

She certainly wasn't my first choice for anything, but preparing a room wasn't that difficult. Of course, for someone as sloppy as Wilmot, it might be. My regret doubled as I watched her saunter down the corridor of rooms with no urgency at all in her steps.

I pointed to Charlie Lewis. "Go fetch Dr. Killigrew."

I turned my attention to Polly Roper. "A nice big bowl of bone broth right away, if you please."

To the other nurses I gave instruction to check in on the inmates to calm anyone who might be upset. If John Wesley's pained yelling had awoken me with a start, I could only imagine how terrified the patients might be.

Nurses Hughes, Frye, and Harris moved off to do my bidding, but on impulse I stopped Harris. "You will help me move John Wesley," I instructed her.

Harris nodded in that reserved way she had and wordlessly knelt to assist me with the boy. I couldn't help but admire his courage, since it was obvious he was in great pain, and just as obvious that he didn't want to cry out in front of me.

Mary also remained in the entry hall, looking unsure of herself. Had she not ever gone to her bed, or had she returned here for some reason? Surely not—the streets of London were no place for a woman to traverse in the pre-dawn light.

"Mary," I said. "Get your notebook. You will need to record my questioning of John Wesley." I figured anything unusual that happened inside the walls should be noted, even if it was as inconsequential as a boy banging up his knee. Secretly, though, I intended for her to take notes as I questioned Nurse Harris.

That moved her to action, and within a few minutes, Harris and I somehow managed to transfer John Wesley to a sitting position in the bed while he grunted and clutched his knee. Mary sat in a corner with pen, ink, and notebook.

It was then that I noticed how green she looked, like the sky before a turbulent storm. I hoped she did not intend to be sick, for I was dealing with quite enough at the moment and was not entirely well myself.

With John Wesley lying atop the bed, I convinced him to let me examine his knee, which he did reluctantly. It was clearly fractured and devastatingly so. It was an open fracture, so there were bone fragments that had penetrated the skin. The area was a frightful wreckage of dirt, pulp, and sharp-edged cartilage.

The child must have been in extraordinary pain.

Moreover, I was gravely concerned about the fracture itself. With the skin broken, there was a very high risk for infection, both in the wound and of the bone itself.

"John Wesley, how did this happen to you?" I asked. He had taken a much harder tumble than I had, and I had gone down the length of a winding staircase.

He groaned again as an additional wave of pain passed over him. "Um, it was an accident."

"How was it an accident?" I asked patiently. "Where did it happen?"

"The—the rear entrance," he said. He bravely sniffed and blinked away tears.

"You fell?" I said, holding my breath for his answer.

"Um. Uh, yes, maum." He rocked back and forth over his clutched knee.

His answer was too hesitant. "John Wesley, I know how much it hurts, but you must look at me. Look me in the eye."

He lifted his gaze to mine. I hated to ask the next question. "Are you telling me you fell at the door . . . or on the steps?"

The rear exterior stairs were old, unevenly set slate ledges, and so it was reasonable to think he might have tripped on them, particularly if he was moving about in the dark.

His gaze slid away. "On the steps, maum. Please don't send me away."

Send him away? To where? I didn't even know where the boy was half the time. "You needn't worry about that, John Wesley, I promise you."

He gave me a tremulous smile. "Thank you, Miss. I-I . . . this hurts terrible bad."

We needed a surgeon, not Dr. Killigrew, who would merely prescribe from afar for John Wesley. The boy needed someone who could mend bones. Did I dare work outside Killigrew's authority?

I instructed Nurse Harris to clean and then put a salve on

the skin around the open wound. It would be utterly useless until the bone was repaired, but it would at least make John Wesley feel he was being cared for. I comforted him as best I could as Harris worked.

As the nurse rubbed the ointment, whose pungent odor was not disguised by the addition of attar of roses, around the edges of the lacerated knee, I turned back to see what Mary was writing down. I saw her eyes grow large in horror at Harris's ministrations. I suppose I no longer blocked her view of what was going on with John Wesley's knee and she could now see for herself how mangled it was.

To my own horror, though, Mary brought a hand to her mouth as she began to involuntarily heave. Her pen and notebook clattered to the floor as she jumped up and practically dove behind the screen that shielded the chamber pot from the rest of the room.

She must have been disgorging everything she'd eaten over the past week based on the sound of the sickening spew erupting out of her. I could hear it spattering the pot and, I feared, everything else.

John Wesley, though, seemed greatly cheered by it. "Is my knee making her do that, Miss Nightingale?" he asked almost gleefully.

"I'm afraid so," I said.

"She's very loud." I saw a hint of a smile, even though shortly thereafter he winced as Harris pressed her cloth too close to the gash through which pulp and bone protruded.

I wasn't sure whether to see to Mary or to continue questioning John Wesley. I decided on a third route, which was to talk to Nurse Harris. I moved so that I would once more be blocking Mary's view when she emerged from behind the curtain.

"Let's wrap it as best we can until the doctor gets here," I said. Harris wordlessly capped the salve and left for the linen room. I soothed John Wesley as best I could as Mary exhausted herself behind the curtain and we waited for Harris to return.

Perhaps bandages were an item that needed to be stored in every room. I made a mental note that the Establishment needed bigger wall cabinets to hold what should be a list of common supplies to be within reach for each inmate.

Mary was in no condition to make a note about it. She groaned from behind the curtain and John Wesley responded with a grin that turned into a pained grimace.

Nurse Harris reentered the room with a rolled length of muslin. She set to work tenderly wrapping John Wesley's leg while I dislodged his hands from his knee, much to his great disapproval. I wasn't sure how effective this gentle immobilization would be, but, like the salve, it was a small ministration we could offer our loyal servant in the moment.

"Nurse," I said, as I stroked the hair away from John Wesley's sweat-beaded forehead. "I have had a disturbing report about you."

Harris didn't pause in what she was doing. "Yes?"

"You were overheard conniving with Mrs. Roper in a moneymaking scheme."

Now she stopped and looked me directly in the eye. "I believe I can guess with total accuracy that it was Mims Jarrett who spoke against me." She said this flatly, as if she already knew I wouldn't deny it.

I didn't.

"What is this scheme, Nurse? I will not tolerate antics, but if you tell me what you have done and cease doing it immediately, I will have compassion on you and Polly Roper." My tone was stern, but I held no advantage, for I still needed to keep everyone in place until I found Bellamy's murderer.

Harris sighed heavily. "Mims has never cared for me. She told the previous superintendent in Cavendish Square that I was stealing food from the kitchens and selling it to workhouses. I pay no attention to her, and your predecessor did not either."

"Why does she dislike you?" I asked, thinking that Margery Frye had an equal dislike.

She shrugged. "Because I do not permit her to know me well. Mims has an overwhelming curiosity that will one day result in a bad end for her."

I had many questions. "What is it she seeks to know that you keep a secret? Is there something unsavory about you of which I should be aware?"

Harris gazed steadily at me, as if considering whether to share something, but ultimately simply responded, "I am like most women, Miss Nightingale. Not a saint nor a demon. I do not allow little chits like Nurse Frye and Mims Jarrett to affect my life or work or relationships."

A supremely unsatisfying answer. "Do you therefore deny that you are involved in an illicit scheme here at the Establishment?"

Harris finished wrapping John Wesley's knee and expertly wound the end of the muslin back through the bandaging to secure it before answering. "There is no answer that would assuage your concerns, madam, as I intend to leave my past in the past and will dredge it up for no one. I am prepared for immediate dismissal if you deem it necessary."

Now I was really curious about a background so mysterious that Harris refused to discuss it at all. But I did understand the fierce desire to keep emotions and hurts buried. Provided there weren't evil deeds mixed into the burial dirt.

"You are a good nurse," I admitted. "I'll not pry into your affairs as long as they don't interfere with this hospital's operation."

She nodded solemnly, and our bargain was struck. How had she maneuvered me in such a way? Wasn't I supposed to be interviewing her intensely, if not outright castigating her?

My attention turned back to the long-suffering John Wesley.

I had finally made my decision. The doctor might be insulted if I summoned a surgeon without his recommendation, but I could deal with his potential dander later. The area surrounding Upper Harley Street was attracting many medical men. It did so not only because of its beautiful, spacious Georgian-era buildings that enabled doctors to double up private residences and surgeries, but also because of Upper Harley Street's accessibility to major train depots like Euston Station. Unfortunately, I had met few of these men thus far, and only a Mr. Fox came to mind. I opened my mouth to ask Harris to go out with another nurse to summon Mr. Fox, even if I knew nothing of his reputation, good or bad.

To my great relief, which I expressed in an unceremonious whoosh of breath, Dr. Killigrew arrived in that moment, accompanied by both his leather bag and a man he introduced as Mr. Brewster, a surgeon.

"When Charlie described John Wesley's condition, I assumed something was fractured," the doctor said.

Charlie stood in the doorway, twisting his cap in his hands. "You'll be all right then, J-J-John Wesley," he said. "The surgeon will f-f-fix you right up."

I didn't like the fear and mistrust that flickered in John Wesley's eyes at Charlie's words.

With Nurse Harris, Mary Clarke, me, the doctor, the surgeon, and of course poor John Wesley in the room, things were a bit crowded. I could at least shoo off Charlie Lewis, which I did.

Mr. Brewster immediately undid Harris's painstaking work, then prodded and manipulated John Wesley's leg, to which the boy responded with howling pain. Men were so rough and tumble with one another, even in such delicate situations. How in heaven's name did soldiers injured on battlefields manage to survive medical ministrations? No doubt most of them would prefer being left alone with their infections, wounds, and pain over being treated by one of these medical men.

"There, there," the surgeon rebuked him. "Be a brave lad, and don't cry like a little girl."

"No, sir," John Wesley said, trying to sound stout. "I won't cry."

Tears streamed silently down the boy's face, and I admit I felt great anxiety for him. Children are not only innocent but completely uncomprehending of why illness or accident has befallen them. Yet, they are far sweeter recipients of care than many adults who understand perfectly well that they are not immune to cholera, carriage accidents, or death in childbirth, no matter what their station in life. Perhaps it is that children must be unquestioning of their elders. Or perhaps it is because they do not yet have those fully blossomed traits of selfishness, pride, and anger.

Regardless, John Wesley's pain could cause me to weep in a way that Ivy Stoke, Hester Moore, or Alice Drayton never could.

As Mr. Brewster completed his examination, Mary finally emerged from behind the curtain, flecks of vomit drying on her dress. She sat in her chair once more and gamely bent down and recovered her pen and notebook.

I returned my attention to the surgeon as he made his pronouncement. "The boy has an open fracture of the patella, very dangerous. The area is swollen and bruised and will soon be infected. There is some hemarthrosis, so I will have to drain some blood collected in the joint space."

I swallowed. It would provide John Wesley with relief, but the procedure would be inordinately painful.

"You'll be a brave man about it, won't you?" the surgeon said to John Wesley, who only nodded mutely in return.

I nearly dropped to my knees in gratitude when Dr. Killigrew suggested, "Brewster, I have a new syringe I would like to experiment with. Why don't I give the boy some morphine before you begin ham-handing him?"

The surgeon took no offense and stepped away to give Killigrew room. The physician went into his bag and withdrew a metal syringe.

"This is Alexander Wood's new version of a syringe," the doctor announced, holding it in the air as if those of us watching were medical students. I suppose in some ways most of us were learning all the time.

"The Scotsman has been experimenting with using syringes to inject opiates directly to pain areas and has had great successes in trials performed on his wife. So today let us see what we can do for Master John Wesley."

Killigrew handed the syringe to me, so I knew he expected me to do the actual work for him. While I screwed the needle into the base of the device, he dug around in his bag for a vial of morphine. I inserted the syringe and pulled up on the wood plunger to draw the contents into the chamber until it was full. I noticed that the needle was finer than any I had seen before and also made of metal instead of the usual ivory.

Dr. Killigrew forced the boy downward onto his back so he would not be witness to his own injection. "Insert the needle at a place near the fracture and press the handle to release some of the morphine. Then move to another nearby location and inject more, and so on. He will get immediate relief at the injury site and should only feel the first prick or two."

I asked Dr. Killigrew how much of the opiate he intended to have injected into John Wesley's kneecap. He shrugged. "Syringefuls until he is more or less unconscious. A precise dosage isn't important."

I went to work on poor John Welsey while Dr. Killigrew stood back at a physician's distance and observed. The boy grunted out a long "uhhhh" when the needle first penetrated his skin. I endeavored to hold it as still as possible while I depressed the wood plunger to inject the opiate.

As Killigrew had predicted, the boy rapidly lost sensation in his knee. "Stop now?" I suggested as I finished off the contents of the syringe.

"No, let's do some more in his arm until he appears to be asleep. Since the morphine is injected rather than passing through the digestive system, it is not addictive."

We refilled the syringe together, and soon John Wesley was unresponsive and breathing deeply.

Mr. Brewster then set to work with his own bag of scalpels, probes, tubes, and glass jars, all of which he put to good use as he spread John Wesley's wound open further. Into it he inserted one end of a tube. The surgeon then knelt on the ground and placed the other end of the tube into his mouth and began sucking on it.

His face grew red from the effort, even as John Wesley lay there, oblivious. Eventually the surgeon removed the tube from his mouth and inserted it into the mouth of a jar, shoving it deep inside. The sound of blood splattering against the glass was loud, but not as loud as Mr. Brewster, who repeatedly spat against the floor.

"Forgot my pump," he said by way of explanation.

The room was becoming noxious, between the odors of blood, spirits, and Mary's vomit.

Poor Mary. Maybe she, too, needed some morphine injected into her. She was a putrid shade of green again from observing the surgeon's work.

Mr. Brewster now crouched over John Wesley so that we could not see what he was doing. We heard the clinking and scraping of tools; then he requested my assistance. "Find thread and needle," he said, nodding at his bag. I searched through the chaotic jumble, so unlike Dr. Killigrew's well-ordered carrying case, until I found the items lying at the bottom of the bag.

Mr. Brewster set to work securing John Wesley's skin together over his attempt to repair the fracture. Fortunately, the boy continued to sleep peacefully.

Was he sleeping *too* peacefully? As the surgeon knitted John Wesley's knee together, I moved so that I was near the boy's head. "Dr. Killigrew," I said, directing his attention to the boy. "Look at his lips. They have a blue tinge."

I ran my hand down the boy's arm and held up his hand. "His fingertips, too."

The doctor pursed his lips as he looked at the grimy little hand in my own. "Perhaps a little too much morphine, eh? It should dissipate."

His tone was unconcerned, and I wondered whether he was disguising his own unease. However, by the time Mr. Brewster had completed his stitching, John Wesley's skin had regained its normal color again. Within a few minutes, his eyelashes began to flutter and his fingers jerked involuntarily.

Dr. Killigrew nodded in satisfaction. "The boy should recover well. Keep his diet sparse until I return again next week. Everyone here seems to be a bit accident-prone, eh, Miss Nightingale? Perhaps this is the last of it."

I had no response for him.

"Miss Nightingale," Mr. Brewster said, holding out his closed palm to me. I offered him my open one and he dumped the contents of his hand into it. Bits of shattered bone sprinkled my palm. He used his other hand to brush what was stuck on his hand into mine. Nurse Harris immediately opened a desk drawer to retrieve a piece of linen and wiped my hand clean, pulling all of the pieces into the cloth and tying it up for disposal.

As Dr. Killigrew and the surgeon packed their respective bags and departed, I determined that I would keep a close eye on John Wesley. I felt as though his "accident" was somehow my fault, if it was related to Nurse Bellamy's death. And how could I think otherwise?

I sent Nurse Harris to the kitchens to have some beef tea and toast made. "Not a speck of grease in the tea, mind. Tell Mrs. Roper that. Have her cool the tea completely so that the beef fat can be removed, then reheat it to a good, hot temperature. And do not allow her to blacken the bread. It should be a nice brown."

She nodded and started to leave. "And a bowl of groat gruel," I added. "Oh, and a small cup of sherry." I had no idea what might appeal to the boy.

She acknowledged this request, too. "Nurse," I said, causing her to turn back to me a second time. "Make it all as tempting as possible. A fresh clean cloth covering the tray, spotless dishes, and so on."

This time I allowed her to escape to obey my directives. I was now alone with Mary and a partially conscious John Wesley. Mary was only in slightly better condition than the boy, but she looked up from her notebook and asked, "Do you want me to write down the diet you have ordered for John Wesley?"

"Yes, but I want to ask you first . . . why were you at the Establishment when John Wesley was hurt? Why were you not at your lodgings?"

Mary reddened, which was actually an improvement over her previous complexion. "Oh, Miss Florence, I didn't want you to know I was here, but, well . . . Miss Jarrett let me rest in one of the library chairs. I was worried about you and wanted to be nearby in case you needed me. I know I am of little significance in your care, especially with all of the nurses here, but if you had required any little thing that I might have been able to provide, I couldn't have lived with myself if I hadn't been here. I remember once while my darling Milo was ill. I had left him sleeping and went for a walk for some fresh air. When I returned, the poor angel had fallen from the bed and hurt his hand. I never forgave myself for not being—"

"Mary." I stopped her train of thought, for I knew the next station would be Melancholy. "You really are a silly goose, but you're my goose and I appreciate your concern."

She blushed again. "I just want to be useful."

John Wesley was becoming restless, enough so that he began thrashing to and fro on the bed as he awoke more.

I sat on the edge of the bed next to him. "There, there, poor lamb," I murmured, stroking his head. "The doctor says you'll be fine as a fiddle soon."

"Yes, Miss," he croaked without opening his eyes. Whereas his lips had been blue, now they looked parched.

"Nurse Harris has gone to get you some good beef tea. That will help."

He opened his eyes briefly and nodded before settling back into sleep again.

I decided it might be best if I loosened up his clothes and put him under the bedcoverings, which really needed to be changed after all of the surgeon's messy work. As I pulled his sweat-stained collar away from his neck. I saw a gold chain encircling it and disappearing down against his thin chest.

How on earth did a waif like John Wesley have possession of a fine piece of jewelry?

I pulled the chain out of his shirt, only to discover there was a locket at the bottom of it.

I used a fingernail to pry open the oval locket, which had a floral etching on the front of it. Inside was a lock of hair on one side and a miniscule scrap of folded paper on the other. I gingerly unfolded it.

It is a strange sensation to be both thoroughly shocked and completely unsurprised at the same time.

★ ★ ★

The paper contained a poem written in tiny script.

> *I worshiped Caro from a safe place.*
> *I dared not draw near,*
> *For fear of being rebuffed.*
> *But she invited me with her face,*
> *The shadows became clear,*
> *And now I am loved.*

What terrible verse. It read like something a schoolboy would write. An educated schoolboy, for certain, but it was not the work of a sophisticated Lothario.

How had John Wesley come to be in possession of the locket Miss Jarrett had said Nurse Bellamy wore all the time?

I considered removing it from his neck but decided against

it. It would be better to ask the boy about the necklace without dangling it in front of him.

I had just finished tucking it back into his shirt when Nurse Harris returned with a food tray, exactly as I had asked for it. Did the woman have no outward faults?

She set the tray on the desk, and soon the aroma of the plain food caused John Wesley to more fully awaken. But the tea, toast, and gruel couldn't combat the odor of the vomit and blood. I gingerly helped him into a seated position and pulled a chair next to the bed so that I could feed him myself. "Nurse Harris—" I began.

As if reading my mind, she went to work at throwing the window open wide and removing the bedcoverings.

"Goose," I said to Mary. "I'm afraid you will need to empty your chamber pot. I cannot allow it to remain in here."

"Me?" Mary squeaked.

With great efficiency, Harris handed the bundled-up knot of soiled bed linens to Mary and said, "We will go downstairs, and I will show you where it can be emptied, in case you need to do so again." Harris picked up the stinking ceramic bowl and escorted Mary out of the room.

The room already smelled immensely better. I offered John Wesley some beef tea, which he gulped out of the cup while I held it up for him. The gruel he rejected, but he was willing to nibble on the toast.

Once he had a bit of nourishment in him, I said gently, "John Wesley, I couldn't help but notice that you have a locket around your neck. It is quite handsome."

He touched the locket through his shirt. "Yes, maum."

"Who gave it to you?" I asked, not expecting the truth from him in my first probe.

"No one. I found it." He reached for the second piece of toast I held in my hand, and I let him take it.

"You found it," I repeated. "Where, exactly, did you 'find' a valuable gold locket, John Wesley?"

"It were just lying on the floor, as if it wanted me to find it. I didn't sell it or anything." Now he was starting to sound defensive.

I nodded. "You did right by not selling it. Because that locket is very important."

His eyes opened wide. "Important?"

"Yes. It could be the very thing that helps me figure out what happened to Nurse Bellamy. You know who she is."

He bit his lip. "That nurse what died."

He swallowed the last of the toast, and I tried offering the gruel again. "She did die, and I'm worried that someone brought her to harm."

He wrinkled his nose at the dish, and I put it down again. I would not offer it again. It was my philosophy that a patient should never be required to eat anything unappetizing, no matter how nourishing. "And . . . you think this charm"—he again touched his chest where the locket lay beneath—"made her die?"

"No, no," I assured him. "But this looks to be Nurse Bellamy's necklace, so I need to know how you came to find it. Perhaps then we can know who took it from her."

Understanding dawned in John Wesley's ten-year-old eyes. "So you mean whoever took it might of kilt her?"

"It's possible, yes." Now I offered him the sherry. He took

a couple of sips and refused the rest, choosing instead to lay back against his pillow. He reminded me of a miniature adult, his forehead pulled together in a frown, obviously deep in thought.

"Do you want to tell me where you found it?" I suggested.

"Well, Miss Nightingale, I don't want no one in trouble . . ." I wondered what he knew, for his gazed traveled nervously around the room.

"The only person who could possibly be in trouble is whoever stole her necklace. You do want to catch a thief, if not an outright murderer, don't you?"

This seemed to confuse and agitate the boy even more. "I wouldn't want anyone to know I told you. I mean, what if the thief were to come after me for being a tittle-tattle? Maybe you should keep it, Miss." He presented his neck to me so that I could remove the chain.

Did John Wesley have more information than simply where he'd found the locket? "I promise I won't tell anyone where you found it, and I will keep it safe for you," I said, lifting it over his head. "How is that?"

He seemed satisfied with my assurance. "I found it in the secret room," he told me.

"The secret room? What is that? *Where* is that?" I had no idea what he was talking about.

"Downstairs, ma'am. Behind the linen room. Jasmine showed it to me."

I looked at him quizzically. "The cat showed you to a room?"

He grinned. "I was helping her chase a rat through the kitchen. It were a big one, it were. The rat went through a little hole in the bottom of the wall, and Jasmine tried to follow. She could only get her paw in at first. Then she took her paw out and put her face in to look for him. She got stuck that way. I helped pull her away from the wall, and as I pulled, well, half the wall moved a bit, didn't it? I got poor Jasmine out, and she saw that the wall had moved, too. She went behind it and I followed her again. Next thing I know, I'm in a little room 'tween the kitchen and the linen room."

"And the locket was in this room?" I asked.

"Yes, maum. It was on the floor, right in front of me."

So somehow Nurse Bellamy had known about this secret room. Was this where she was meeting her inamorato? I wished to see this room, although John Wesley would be in no condition to show it to me anytime soon. I also didn't want the little scamp blabbing to anyone about having shown it to me as part of a murder investigation. Moreover, I didn't want any of the staff to witness me searching for it. I needed to have a look at Persimmon Jarrett's sketch again. That way I could determine if she had discovered the room without directly asking her about it and invoking her considerable curiosity.

"How clever of you to have found it. Is there anything about the room you can tell me?"

He bit his lip and looked down. "You can hear a lot when you're inside it."

"A lot? Of noises?" An old home like this was bound to creak and scrape with regularity. "Or do you mean voices?"

"People talking." John Wesley winced, and I wasn't sure if it was pain in his knee or from what he was revealing.

"John Wesley," I said. "You must tell me the truth. Did

you overhear something that I should know about?" I stroked his hair once more to comfort him. Or perhaps it was to comfort me, as I had the feeling he was going to reveal something particularly unpleasant.

"Maybe, Miss. I'm not sure. I saw a leather strap that would pull the wall closed from the inside. I knew that if I closed it, it would help Jasmine trap her rat. It were easy to pull, even for me. When I closed it, I saw that the ceiling was way up above me. Very far. There was a little window way up there, so I had a little bit of light."

An old laundry chute or dumbwaiter converted into a hiding place, I was betting. Surely it had been done prior to the home being turned into a hospital. The basement hadn't seen much renovation, so the secret room was probably easily missed. Now I wished I had paid attention to the history of the property, which hadn't mattered a whit to me in becoming superintendent. I strained to remember what Lady Canning had told me—something about an aristocratic family owning most of the area. It came back to me slowly. Harley Street had been named for Edward Harley, the Earl of Oxford, who had acquired the area in the early eighteenth century. The estate had passed on to his daughter, who married the Duke of Portland, hence the nearby Portland Street and Portland Place. It was still in the Portland family, wasn't it? Yes, yes, the area was in the possession of the fifth duke, and hadn't Lady Canning once told me he was a veritable lunatic? Building underground tunnels and odd, unused buildings on his property and such things that only someone inordinately wealthy could afford to do?

It made me wonder if he hadn't personally owned No. 1

Upper Harley Street and had the room built for some bizarre purpose. But no, my memory dimly recalled that some other lord had built the house much earlier in the century.

"What did you do in the room by yourself?" I said.

"I wasn't scared at all!" John Wesley exclaimed to a question I hadn't asked. "I watched Jasmine eat the rat. She tore its head off, she did. She—"

"But then you heard something." I didn't want John Wesley wandering off into details about the cat's dining habits.

"Yes, maum. I heard Charlie first, and then that nurse come into the kitchen."

"That nurse? Which one?"

"The one what were taking care of me today."

Why would Nurse Harris privately meet with our manservant?

"You are absolutely sure of this, John Wesley?"

He nodded and winced again. "They talked in low tones, but I could hear some of it. I heard Charlie tell her that he would protect her from harm. Then I heard a disgusting noise. Miss Nightingale, I think he might have kissed her." His expression was one of utter revulsion.

I would have laughed if I hadn't been so appalled by what he was telling me. I simply couldn't believe that Harris would engage in an affair with Charlie Lewis. She was so reserved and standoffish, and Charlie was so, so—*Charlie.*

"Is that all you've witnessed from the secret room, John Wesley?" I asked, putting a finger under his chin and chucking him gently. I hoped the labored smile on my face was putting him at ease.

His breathing relaxed, but his expression was wary. "What do you mean?"

What I meant was that if he hadn't been seen by Charlie and Nurse Harris, then surely he had been caught as a witness to some other event, a deed odious enough that someone might have wanted to see the boy dead. Or badly injured.

But I simply shrugged. "Oh, I don't know. Like maybe you saw some of the other nurses having a talk."

He considered my question, and I didn't like how long it took him to answer me. He responded with a shrug of his own. "Not that I 'member," John Wesley said.

I sighed inwardly. Perhaps he hadn't witnessed something but had *done* something that he thought might make me angry. Something as silly as taking some food without permission. But the firm set of his lips told me I'd get nothing further from him on it.

I had one final question for John Wesley. "I want to ask you one more thing. And I want you to be as truthful in your answer as you have been about the secret room." I raised an eyebrow in a silent request for his honesty.

"Yes, maum," he replied solemnly.

"Did you really fall down the steps on your own? Or were you . . . helped?"

John Wesley shook his head firmly. "I didn't see no one behind me, Miss, I swear."

I hoped his response hadn't been *too* confident. I hadn't seen anyone behind me, either.

In that moment, Harris returned with Mary right behind her. Harris carried fresh bedcoverings, and set right away to remaking John Wesley's bed. She was as gentle as possible in working around the boy, but it was no use.

"Ahhhhhh," John Wesley cried, leaning over and gripping his leg below the knee. "Oh, Miss, ohhhhhhh, it hurts."

The morphine had worn off. "Nurse Harris," I said. "Go to the medicine case and retrieve—"

Harris stopped me, once more reading my thoughts. "I checked there while I was away, knowing that the boy would need more pain relief eventually. There is none in the case."

How could that be? Laudanum was a staple. Of course, all the nurses had keys. That would change immediately. My thoughts flew to Margery Frye, but there was no time for it now. "Go to the chemist and purchase more."

She flew from the room without question. I now addressed Mary. "Goose, please take this tray down to Mrs. Roper." I wanted no congealed or limp food to remain in front of a patient. So many doctors thought that food should remain a constant at the bedside. I thought that to wake up hours from now to gelatinous gruel would make John Wesley even sicker. He could have a fresh tray later.

Mary, too, obeyed without question, but in her case she was probably relieved to flee from the boy's suffering and moaning.

Now I just had to keep John Wesley calm until Harris returned. Between his injury and my own, as well as the onslaught of distinct and unrelated revelations I was receiving, I was suddenly very fatigued.

★　★　★

I spent some more time with John Wesley, ensuring he got a dose of laudanum and giving Nurse Harris care instructions for the boy. He didn't seem afraid of her, and I was too exhausted to confront her yet again. Mary helped me to my bedchamber once more, and this time I insisted that she return to her lodgings for the evening.

My sleep was mercifully uninterrupted until I was awakened by bullfinches chirping outside my window and sunlight flooding my room. A quick check of my watch told me it was nearly ten o'clock in the morning. I felt inordinately better, with only a few bruises as reminders of what had happened to me.

After relieving myself and getting dressed, I was eager to get to work in many ways. Although Nurse Bellamy was always at the forefront of my mind, I wanted to spend time developing some of my nursing plans as well as to visit the inmates.

As far as my investigation was concerned, though, Persimmon Jarrett was at the top of my list.

She sat at her desk in the library, her nose buried in Charlotte Brontë's latest novel, *Villette*. Pastry crumbs littered the desk next to an empty plate, and she held a cup of tea in her hand as she read.

I was doubting the wisdom of paying Jarrett to do as little as she did.

She greeted me politely, and I responded, "You showed me a diagram of the building layout yesterday. I would like to see it again."

"Yes, Miss Nightingale, right away." Jarrett closed the book and stood up, reaching into her pocket and pulling out a ring with several keys dangling from it. She selected one, nodded to me, and bent over the same desk drawer where

I had seen her place the sketch yesterday. The lock moved with a soft thud and Jarrett pulled the drawer open.

It was empty.

She jerked her head up at me. "I don't understand. Where is my drawing? I locked it up here after showing it to you, Miss Nightingale."

"I remember. Who else has access to your keys?"

She held up the ring and looked at it disbelief, as if it had intentionally betrayed her. "No one, Miss. I mean, I do not wear my keys at all times. I suppose, well, I leave them in my top drawer here if I leave to visit the toilet or run an errand."

By errand she undoubtedly meant a trip to the kitchens.

"Who was in the library yesterday?"

Jarrett considered this. "Let me see . . . Nurse Harris brought Mrs. Moore in and read to her for a while. Oh, and Charlie Lewis came by to repair a broken windowpane. I don't recall much of anyone else. There was so much to-do about John Wesley, of course."

"Did you leave to visit him?" I asked. I had a sneaking suspicion that her keys had been available for the taking for much of the day.

"I, well . . ." She shoved the key ring down into her dress pocket. "John Wesley is such a dear boy, so I had Mrs. Roper give me a couple of tarts to take to him. We ate them together. It was after you had gone off to bed, and he was all alone. I felt sorry for him, what with such a terrible fall he took. But—but—I see you are unhappy with me, and I am ever so sorry, Miss Nightingale." Repentant tears welled up in her eyes.

"That's enough, Miss Jarrett. I'll not have you blubbering

about. We have enough troubles. So you know for certain that Nurse Harris and Charlie Lewis were here. For how long were you away in John Wesley's room?"

"Probably about an hour. No, wait." She pursed her lips in concentration. "After seeing Mrs. Roper, I arrived in his room around seven thirty, and he said his dinner tray had just been cleared away. We had our tarts, and then I remember the clock striking nine, and then Nurse Harris came in and told me I had to let John Wesley sleep. So I was there around ninety minutes."

Enough time for half of Marylebone to have wandered in, lifted the key, and stolen the floor layout.

The real question was, why had it been stolen, unless for nefarious purposes? Did someone want to know of a good escape route . . . or did they want to cover up any seeming evidence of their escape route?

"Who knew that you had made that drawing, Miss Jarrett?"

"No one," she replied, too defensively.

I arched an eyebrow at her.

"Well, I may have had to ask Mrs. Roper where some of the basement doors lead. It can be quite dark and scary down there. Oh, and that kind doctor saw me working on it one day and offered to help me step out rooms. He said his foot was exactly twelve inches long, so he could accurately measure rooms and corridors for me. He told me the most humorous joke, Miss Nightingale. Why is a hen on the fence like a penny? The answer is, head on one side, tail on the other."

Jarrett tittered, but I remained stone-faced. I didn't think

Dr. Killigrew had any earthly reason to steal the diagram, but it was obvious that anyone could have done so. Once more I regretted not keeping it when I had held it in my hands.

I left Jarrett to check in on some of the patients. My next-to-last stop was Hester Moore's room. She was not as shy and was less agitated than normal, which I attributed to the absence of her overbearing brother.

However, even though we weren't full at the moment and Dunstan Moore could afford the weekly fee, she could not remain here as though we were a hotel.

"You seem improved, Mrs. Moore," I said.

She was sitting up in bed, a lace cap neatly arranged on her head. The bedcoverings were folded down to her lap in a precise manner, and a tray of paper, envelopes, pen, and ink jar were spread across her lap.

It wasn't the picture of an invalid.

"I admit I am feeling a little more content in my mind, Miss Nightingale. I was just writing a letter to Dunstan. He's with Mr. Brunel, you know. Such important work he's doing. The Leviathan will be the life's work for both of them, I think. And yet Dunstan takes time from his busy schedule to write to me. Isn't he truly the most loving of brothers?" She waved an envelope at me that had a thickly stroked and slanted handwriting across it.

"Very loving," I replied. "Perhaps you would like to write in the gardens and take in some fresh air?"

Hester frowned. "Oh, I don't know if Dunstan would want that. It is so much safer inside, don't you think?"

Was this a reference to Nurse Bellamy? If so, wouldn't she consider the *exterior* of the premises to be safer?

"The courtyard is walled, Mrs. Moore. Other than being victimized by a low-flying pigeon's droppings, I cannot see what harm could come to you."

She still hesitated, and no amount of my cajoling would convince her to leave her room.

In fact, Hester changed the subject entirely. "Dunstan asks about you, you know."

It was a disturbing thought. "How so?"

"He asks . . ." She lifted his letter from the tray. It was in the same heavy scrawl as the envelope. "Oh dear, my sight isn't what it used to be, and sometimes it takes me a moment to focus on writing. Let me see . . . yes, he asks how you are faring in your investigation into that nurse's death."

It's none of your affair, Dunstan Moore, I thought with a vitriol that surprised me. Why did the man bother me so much?

I replied pleasantly to Hester, "I am happy to report that there have been no more deaths and I expect this was just a singularly unfortunate incident. The police do not even believe there is anything to worry over."

Hester Moore jotted a few notes, then looked up and tilted her head at me. "Miss Nightingale, is that a bruise on your cheek?"

I self-consciously put a hand to my face. Did I think I could block her view of it that way and make her forget it? I lowered my hand and said brightly, "Yes, I was on my way to the kitchens to get some refreshments for an inmate and tripped on my skirts."

An expression of concern spread across her face. "To think that I might have just been lying here, peacefully sleeping, while you were injured somewhere. How terrible. I am glad to know you were not seriously harmed."

I suspected she was also glad for an additional juicy tidbit of gossip for her brother.

I left Hester Moore to her letter writing and went to John Wesley's room for my final visit before setting out on my grandiose plan of accomplishments for the day.

He was sleeping, no doubt thanks to another dose of opiates, but even in his sleep he was doubled over, clasping his bandaged knee. I still wasn't convinced he had merely had an accident.

★ ★ ★

Even without the missing floor layout, I decided that if a young boy and a cat could find the secret room, then so could I. I crept downstairs for the first time since my own attack, gripping the handrail fiercely to ensure nothing else would befall me. In my dress pockets were Harris's knife, the note Mrs. Alban had given me, and Bellamy's locket. After the theft of the first note, I felt a need to keep all of these clues on my person. Nevertheless, I felt like a superstitious old woman carrying talismans.

The basement was humming with activity. In the kitchen, pots and kettles burbled and whistled on the stove's top, and the makings of pie crusts lay all over Mrs. Roper's worktable. I could hear her arguing with someone at the rear entry door. The weekly laundress and her young assistant were dropping off bundles of sheets in the linen room. The assistant was a miniature replica of the laundress, presumably the woman's daughter. Both were red-faced and huffing from their loads and merely nodded at me as I came into the kitchen.

I removed the most insistent, shrill kettle from the heat, just as the cook walked back in, holding a bag.

"Pardon, Miss Nightingale, I had to give the grocer's boy a piece of my mind. He delivered the limpest runner beans I've ever seen. And them ripe right now! I've half a mind to start visiting that costermonger I've seen lately a few blocks from here. Her vegetables look better than these awful things." She tipped the bag into a pot of boiling water and the green pods disappeared in a violent rumble and hiss.

It gave me an idea. "I believe that is a splendid idea, Mrs. Roper. You'll want to visit her before she sells her choicest items, won't you?"

"Well, yes," she hesitated. "But I have all of my dishes going . . ."

I felt deceitful but proceeded anyway. "You say she's only a few blocks away; you couldn't possibly be gone a half hour."

Mrs. Roper frowned. "True. I'll be back quick as a wink, then."

She whisked off her apron and tossed it onto a hook screwed into the passageway between the kitchen and linen room and left through the back. Within a few moments, the laundress and her daughter had brought everything in, and it lay heaped upon the linen room table. I signed for the laundry delivery and told them that one of the nurses would take care of sorting it all. With everyone gone, I locked the rear door, although there was little I could do about anyone coming downstairs.

I stood in the middle of the linen room. Where was the secret place John Wesley had found? The entire room was lined with shelving and cabinets. There was practically no wall whatsoever exposed. Had the boy been mistaken? Had the false wall been in another room?

I walked back into the kitchen itself, blessedly quiet now that I had turned down the burners. I walked along what exposed walls there were but could find no evidence of a shifting wall. Perhaps the larder . . .

I went in and out of each and every closet-sized space attached to the kitchen, each with its own function: storage of dry goods, storage of dishes, a place to wash pans, and so forth. Charlie Lewis's tiny room was down here, too, furnished sparsely with a bed, a small chest of drawers, and a lamp. Tools covered the chest and much of the floor, and the room smelled of spilled lamp oil.

Finding nothing obvious anywhere, I even got on my hands and knees in the kitchen rooms, thinking that perhaps Jasmine had unlatched the wall by hitting something along the floorboards. Then I did the same in the linen room, the laundry room, the scullery, and, of course, Charlie's room.

Nothing.

I stood once more, wiping my hands against my skirt, thankful that I was in my usual gray garb. Surely the boy hadn't made it up. John Wesley was a scamp, but he wasn't a liar.

I returned to the kitchen to begin my search again, feeling anxious because I knew Mrs. Roper would return soon.

Where in the world could this secret room be?

I walked to the end of the basement nearest the servants'

staircase and turned around to face the downstairs. If I stood just so, I could effectively see a straight line through the various doorways of the basement all the way to the rear door. Each section was separated from another by a small, coved passageway. The kitchen and linen room, though, had a much deeper passageway between—

I practically ran to the place that separated the kitchen and linen room. Standing in the middle of the passageway, I pressed along the wall to one side, then dropped to my knees. I could find no way to spring open the wall. I rose once more and removed Mrs. Roper's apron from its hook, tossing it onto the back of a chair. It was instantly obvious that this was the place. I had been looking for a long piece of flat wall inside a room, but the secret room was actually accessed from in between the rooms.

I found an indentation along one of the outer corners of that side of the passageway that enabled me to get a firm hold and pull this section of wall away. It was on a very clever interior hinge, not visible from within the passageway itself. Inside the space, which was only about four feet wide but nearly twenty feet deep, were a couple of wood chairs, a narrow mattress on the floor made up with fresh linens, and a bench along the wall with some of life's daily accoutrements: a comb, a washbasin, a teacup, a few chamber sticks with half-burned candles in them, a few open jars containing powders and creams, and a cracked handheld mirror.

Far above me were small skylights that let in a little filtered light this far down, enough so that I did not require a lamp to be able to see.

I took a deep breath. The air was mostly stale and dry,

although there was just the faintest hint of floral perfume in the room, probably from the cosmetics jars.

If they hadn't gone out of fashion centuries before this home had been built, I would have thought this was a priest's hole. What had the owner been thinking when he'd had this installed in his basement?

The walls were actually papered in here. Because it had had little exposure to the elements over time, the old Georgian flocked pattern, imitating a damask fabric of robin's-egg blue and cream, was perfectly intact. I stood there several more moments, deciding that it could be a lovers' nest, for certain. Was it Nurse Bellamy's? If so, with whom had she been sharing it?

CHAPTER 13

I quickly closed up the secret room, replaced Mrs. Roper's apron, unlocked the rear door, and returned upstairs with a tray of tea and biscuits that I had quickly assembled. I hadn't had anything to eat yet for the day, and I was famished. By this time, Mary had arrived at the Establishment and was waiting for me in the library. I sent her to the kitchens to get her own cup so that she could partake of the repast with me and instructed her to meet me back in my study for privacy, despite the fact that Miss Jarrett had not yet reported for work. Jarrett was one of few who did not live on the premises, and she clearly had difficulty meeting a scheduled arrival time.

I shook my head. So many problems to work through, and I could accomplish so little until Nurse Bellamy's death was solved.

Over tea, gingersnap cookies, and almond macaroons, I confided to Mary the vision I had for a proper hospital, unlike any that England had ever seen.

"You may not know, Goose, that I traveled to Egypt and throughout Europe before I came here. I toured hospitals to investigate their practices."

Mary's cheeks pinked a little, my nickname for her apparently still pleasing her.

"Of course, my parents believed me to be on a version of the Grand Tour with our family friends, Charles and Selina Bracebridge."

Mary nodded. "I remember Milo speaking of them. He told me that if you saw their carriage in the drive, not even chains could prevent you from leaping out of the schoolroom to go and greet them."

Ah, I remembered that well, also. The Bracebridges had always treated me as an adult, even when I was a young child, and had taken my desires and dreams seriously when my parents would not. So seriously had they taken me that they had been willing to engage me in a year-long "grand tour" of Egypt and Greece. The trip had enabled me to put thousands of miles between Richard and me.

Licking one's open and salted wounds is much more easily accomplished without others observing the messy process.

The brilliant landscapes of the Nile and the Aegean had meant little to me, although I spent considerable time documenting everything I saw. My brightest moment had been when I stumbled upon a baby owl being taunted by some boys at the Parthenon. I rescued the owlet, named her Athena, and carried her about in my pocket, which she adored. I adored her right back, loving the trilling and *hoo-hooing* sounds she made when I dropped her into my pocket. I added a pair of tortoises, whom I named Mr. and Mrs. Hill, to my retinue, as well as a cicada I called Plato.

Athena eventually ate Plato, which ended my animal collecting.

However, none of it was enough to completely eradicate Richard from my mind.

The Bracebridges had surprised me, though, by routing us back through Berlin so that I could visit a place called *Kaiserswerther Diakonie*, located along the Rhine.

I had read of Pastor Theodor Fliedner and was very interested in visiting his facility. It wasn't exactly a medical school. He had instead designed a training center and hospital based on the early Christian diaconates, so that he focused on training young women to care for the needy sick. This training included both theology and nursing skills. I wholeheartedly agreed with his unique approach, since it was based in the Christian notion of charity.

Early Christian women, who became known as deaconesses, had been encouraged to wander into the streets and find people who were sick, injured, or otherwise stricken. They would care for the needy and return to their own homes at night. Not only did this help a suffering society, but it gave many women purpose and meaning in a time when they had few opportunities.

I empathized with those early church women, as my mother had been determined to see my mind—which men like my father and Milo Clarke had filled with knowledge and curiosity—emptied of all ambition. I needed purpose and meaning, and Pastor Fliedner had shown me how my passion could be molded into something valuable.

Moreover, the pastor's hospital had been clean and cheery, in direct contradiction to most British hospitals, which were full of filth, wretchedness, and squalor. There was even a phrase in the everyday British lexicon, "hospital smell," which referred to the overpowering stink of hospital wards that usually led to nausea.

My tour of Kaiserswerth had turned into a stay of two weeks. During that time, the Bracebridges and I sent letters back to my parents, extolling the wondrous beauty of Schloss Benrath's gardens, the Rhine, and the Prussian marketplaces, so that they wouldn't know what I was truly doing.

I had returned home, brimming with hope and full of ideas. Mother was appalled, of course, but even worse was Parthenope. She had noticeably declined in health because of her anxiety over my absence, and all of a sudden I found myself needing to be in attendance on her at all hours, else she would mope and weep. I read with her, allowed her to sketch me, sang with her, and was generally inseparable from her for the next six months. My familial slavery quickly took its toll on me, and I sank into my own depression. If it was possible, I became even sicker and more depressed than Parthe.

It had been my own serious decline that finally convinced Mother to let me return to Kaiserswerth and enter Pastor Fliedner's complete training program. Thus far, it had been the most wondrous and extraordinary period of my entire life, other than my idyll with Richard.

The diakonie had expanded into an orphan asylum, an infant school, and a school for training schoolmistresses. I had slept in the orphan asylum and worked both there and in the hospital for such rigorously long days that I had hardly taken out ten minutes for meals and to send my things to be washed. I had even been permitted to be present at operations, which I hadn't dared report to my mother, lest she faint dead away at the indecency of it all.

Upon my return to the family home, I had known I was close to freedom. I had blatantly made plans and sought out an opportunity to employ what I had learned from Fliedner. Parthe slid again, and this time was carted off to the queen's physician, Dr. James Clark, who delivered the knife that finally cut the cord between my sister and me. He told her that the only effective cure would be for her to learn to live without me.

I could have happily kissed Dr. Clark.

On a trip out to Wilton House to visit Elizabeth Herbert, she had told me of the open supervisor's position with the Establishment, a position that had reopened with the facility's move from Cavendish Square to Harley Street.

So here I was now, finally liberated to do the good works I had known I was meant for since my divine visit in 1837. Yet I was in thorough paralysis because of the murder that had occurred a week after I walked through the door.

Well, it was time to work on both.

"Yes," I said to Mary. "The Bracebridges were instrumental in helping me realize my dream. I just hope it hasn't turned into a permanent nightmare."

"Oh, no, Miss Florence, it won't be. You will succeed in ways you can't imagine, I'm sure of it. And one day your family will recognize your achievements." She made a move as if to hug me, as if I were still a child, but hastily checked herself and sat back down.

However, the encouragement warmed me. So few people were ever on my side. "Goose, you are a treasure."

She blushed again.

"Now, let me tell you what I wish to implement," I said. Mary opened her notebook and dipped her pen in the ink bottle that sat on a side table at her elbow. She looked up at me expectantly.

"I want to create an instruction manual for nursing. There is simply nothing adequate in existence. We will start with the qualifications of a nurse. As it stands now, a nurse is qualified if she merely breathes, and even then that breath might be rank with spirits or poor hygiene. Not so here at the Establishment."

"But Nurse Frye . . ." Mary ventured.

"Yes, and Nurse Wilmot, too," I agreed. "Once I have developed my list of requirements, perhaps I can convince them to leave of their own accord, once they realize for themselves they are not fit for service. Let me see, I believe a nurse should generally be between thirty and fifty years of age."

Mary looked up in surprise. "You don't prefer that it be a young, energetic woman?"

I shook my head. "I want her to be old enough to have had a little experience, yet not too old or infirm so that she would be prevented from performing duties requiring strength. So she should be somewhere between my age and yours, Goose."

Mary bent her head down and wrote.

"That is the age requirement. Now, as for temperament, the qualified nurse must have a kind and gentle disposition, for she will frequently have to endure the whims and caprices of the invalid." I thought of Alice Drayton. Then I thought of Hester Moore and thought that perhaps I should add "the whims and caprices of the patient's family" as well. However, I wouldn't want that memorialized on paper.

"The proper nurse must have the confidence to exert her authority when necessary, while reining in her temper so as not to create anxiety in those who are in her charge." Hmm, perhaps my requirements would cause me personally to be disqualified.

"Is that all?" Mary asked, dipping her pen into the ink.

"No, there is one more quality for a proper nurse." Here I thought of Nurse Harris, wondering if she were friend or foe. "She must be someone who strives to make herself indispensable to both patient and institution."

Mary obediently wrote it all down.

"The good nurse will understand that sanitary conditions are of paramount importance, both in patients' surroundings and for themselves personally. A clean uniform, clean skin and hair, and sweet breath will demonstrate for the patient that the nurse takes her role seriously. Diseases such as cholera are, I believe, spread through noxious air. Cleanliness helps prevent these miasmas from forming."

Mary looked up, confused. "M-y-e-a—"

"M-i-a-s-m-a," I said.

She nodded and bent her head down once more.

"Then there is the patient's diet." This was a topic upon which I could lecture for hours. For my notes, I would keep it simple and sermonize more on it when I had the nurses together and could address them directly. "The first rule in invalid cookery is that the food itself should do half the work of the patient's weak digestion. The nurse should seek recipes for simply dressed fish, light soups, plain roasted meats and poultry, simple puddings, and so forth."

The scratching of Mary's pen was soothing, and I leaned back to stare up at the ceiling as I thought more about everything I had learned.

"Furthermore, a nurse should never put before a patient milk that is sour, meat that has turned, an egg that is bad, or vegetables that are undone. Any spoiled articles should not be handed off to the patient with the notion that he won't notice, but the nurse should quickly whip up something else in a few minutes."

Mary looked up again. "But you have a cook here."

"Indeed, and a luxury it is, since Mrs. Roper cooks exclusively for invalids and knows what to do. But many nurses work in private homes where the cook rules the kitchen with an iron skillet and will brook no suggested modifications to his cooking. In such case, the nurse must be resourceful— exerting authority while controlling her temper—and find a way to prepare appropriate foods for the patient."

Mary developed that dreamy expression again. "I, of course, had total control over dear Milo's diet, although I suppose I might have had benefit of training. He didn't always care for my soups and tended to wrinkle his sweet nose at them. I suppose it's almost as if I was a nurse while Milo was so sick. He never complained, though. Such a darling man. I never had to exert authority over him. How I miss him."

I was on the verge of confessing how much I missed someone, too, but caught myself. There was no point in both of us mourning aloud. In any case, I wished to finish my dictation.

"I'm sure Mr. Clarke appreciated all you did for him, especially since you took care of him until the very end, Goose." I gave her an encouraging look. "But if we finish up the list of nurse requirements, which will be a small part of the nursing instruction manual, then one day *any* woman will know how to take care of her sick husband, child, or parent, right?"

"Yes, you are right, Miss Florence. What else would you like to say about the requirements of a nurse?" Her pen was freshly dipped again and poised over the paper. A drop of ink splashed out of the nib and made an irregular blotch on the page. She frowned at it but moved down below the mark to continue writing.

I finished up with my thoughts on a nurse's duty to ensure that meal times are neat and tidy and that she not dribble tea into a saucer or soup down a shirt front. The utmost care was to be taken not to soil sheets, bedgowns, pillows, or any other piece of cloth the patient touched.

"All of this," I concluded, "will ensure that the patient will not only be comfortable but will wish to partake of the food offered. Next to cleanliness, nourishing food is the most critical component of good health."

As I dictated my final thoughts on the matter—to which I was sure I would add later—I heard wailing erupt from the ward of inmate rooms. It wasn't so much a wailing, really, as a terrible keening.

It was John Wesley.

CHAPTER 14

Poor John Wesley was suffering terrible pain with his knee. Although I knew he had been through a gruesome operation, I was also concerned that he was receiving too much laudanum.

But laudanum was the least of his problems, for if an infection set in due to the surgeon's work, the boy would not likely survive. Thus far, he had not presented a fever, nor confusion, nor nausea, so thus I did not believe he had an infection. My greatest hope was that he would continue to somehow ward off such symptoms.

Regardless of my concerns about laudanum, I gave him a half dose of the medicinal tonic, waited for him to settle back against his pillow, inspected and changed his bandages, then went to gather up the nurses, instructing them to meet me in the kitchens.

They all sat around the worktable—now cleared of its pastry-making supplies—and I sat at the head. Polly Roper attempted to excuse herself, but I told her that she was to be part of the conversation.

First, I discussed my opinion of John Wesley and that we

should reduce how much laudanum he received, at least until Dr. Killigrew returned and ordered otherwise. I also stated that in the afternoon I wanted him out of his sickbed to learn how to use a crutch, and that I expected the other nurses to work with him each day as well. I didn't want a ten-year-old boy to become a coddled, permanent invalid like Hester Moore.

Their expressions were much what I would have expected. Nan Wilmot was smug, Margery Frye was openly hostile, Marian Hughes was blank, and Clementina Harris's features were carefully schooled into calm repose, although she had made sure to select a chair as far from Frye as possible.

Mrs. Roper was agitated, rocking back and forth and picking at herself as though she had fleas, which I attributed to her discomfort at the group of us invading her domain. She didn't tend to mix much with the others, unless what Jarrett had said was true and Polly Roper was actively engaged in a plot with Wilmot and Harris.

It was difficult to believe that one of these women might be a murderess.

I put it away in my mind. If I was to sweep out the evil debris from the Establishment, I couldn't allow myself to be afraid of some dirt.

"I have brought you together to tell you of my thoughts regarding invalid cooking."

Frye made an impatient noise. "Isn't that for Polly to know?"

I truly hoped that Margery Frye was guilty of some wrongdoing that I could eventually prove. The thought of her being hauled off the premises in chains actually gave me a warm feeling.

"It is for all of you to know," I replied with firm conviction. "As nurses, you must not be reliant on *anyone* except yourselves for the care of inmates. This means everything from knowing how to clean"—I gave Nan Wilmot a sharp stare, under which she had the good grace to shrink—"to performing everyday household tasks, and especially how to cook."

Grumbling passed around the table, but I rapped on the scratched and scarred wood. "A good nurse does whatever is required of her to ensure her patient's comfort. Although we do rely on Mrs. Roper's considerable talents, it is imperative that everyone know how to prepare dishes like egg wine and rice milk."

I turned back to Mary, who sat in a corner, and asked her to record the recipes. Then I had Mrs. Roper assemble ingredients for me, and together we prepared egg wine, mixing together a beaten egg, a half cup of cold water, sugar, and nutmeg. I asked her to pour it all into a saucepan, and then I added a cup of sherry to it. "An egg is very nutritious, and it is beneficial to add it where you can," I said as Mrs. Roper stirred the warming concoction.

After the cook poured the saucepan contents into a large cup, I passed the cup around the table so that each nurse could taste the result. All of them seemed openly surprised that the mixture tasted pleasant, and naturally Nurse Frye took a couple of extra swallows. Seeing that everyone noticed, she defended herself. "My taste buds are dull today. I need more of it to get the flavor."

We then stepped through the makings for rice milk, a more solid provision for a patient than simple egg wine. Once more using a saucepan, I had Polly simmer some rinsed rice in milk. Once it was tender, I added sugar and nutmeg.

"Nutmeg not only flavors well but aids in digestion," I instructed them as Polly put spoonfuls in egg cups for the nurses to try. "You will want to find ways to use it for patients, who so often develop intestinal problems just from lying around with other ailments."

The rice milk was clearly not a favorite with Frye, but she gamely ate what was put before her.

"As good nurses, you should all be able to develop quick-thinking recipes for your inmates that Mrs. Roper can easily prepare or you can prepare on your own if she is busy. Keep basic principles in mind: patients love sugar, and it will cause them to ingest something otherwise revolting. Nutmeg is good for digestion, as is arrowroot, although I think flour can be substituted for arrowroot's thickening properties while providing more nutrition. Broths of all types are restorative but must have good flavor—whether it be from beef, chicken, veal, or mutton."

To my surprise, Frye had become interested in what I was saying, sitting up straighter and frowning in concentration. "Miss Nightingale, what of coffee?" she asked. "Is it as helpful as tea? Sometimes I am asked for a pot, but I always deny it because I assume tea is much more nutritious."

"Fetch me your supply of coffee beans," I said to Polly Roper, then addressed the nurses. "I believe a great deal too much credit is given to tea by some, and too much criticism is made by others. We English crave it beyond all reason, and I count myself among those who must have several daily cups.

A little bit of tea or coffee can be quite restorative, but too much—particularly of coffee—will impair what little powers of digestion the patient has. However, when we see that one or two cups of tea makes the patient feel better, we think, 'How much better might four or five cups be?' and yet this is not the case. Coffee is generally a better restorative than tea, but is also quicker than tea to disrupt digestion. Thus, you must use good judgment in determining how much of either to give the patient and not simply give in to her demands.

"I shall demonstrate for you how to make nutritious coffee. Ah, thank you, Mrs. Roper." The cook had returned and handed a tin to me. I rattled it and heard the telltale sound of beans. However, upon removing the lid, I was immediately dismayed. There was an awful fuzz growing on the beans. "I presume you haven't been using these? They are covered in mold spores."

Mrs. Roper shrugged. "They came over from Cavendish Square and I put them on a shelf. No one ever asks me to make it."

"Dispose of these and obtain more from the grocer. Buy no more than a pound of beans until we see how much we might use now that we understand its benefits. Do not keep any coffee for more than a couple of months, and only ever grind what you are about to use."

The cook nodded and took the beans away.

"Then I shall simply explain the proper making of coffee for an invalid, which is a fairly simple matter," I said, wondering what other stored foods might need review. "To make a large cupful of coffee, first bring a pint of milk to nearly boiling in a saucepan, then stir in a half ounce of ground coffee.

Boil them together for three minutes, then let it settle off the heat for five minutes. Now, how might the coffee be made even more nutritious?"

Nurse Hughes raised her hand tentatively. "An egg?"

I smiled. She had been listening. "Yes. A beaten egg in the empty coffee cup, then mixed with the hot coffee that is poured over it."

The nurses were all paying rapt attention to me now. Was it my imagination, or was there the tiniest glimmer of respect in Margery Frye's expression?

"Tomorrow we will gather again to discuss cleanliness and how it prevents the miasmas that contribute to the spread of diseases. I am of the firm opinion that—"

There was a thud against the rear servants' door so loud that we all started in unison.

Polly Roper smoothed her apron. "That must be Gideon, the butcher's boy, with the beef joints I ordered. He's a clumsy little oaf. I'll just pop out and take the delivery."

She scurried out of sight, and in a moment I heard the door locks unlatching, and then it opened with the squeal of rusted hinges that had not been replaced in decades. So much more could have been done in the building's renovation.

However, the creaky hinge was inaudible over Mrs. Roper's shriek, which could not possibly have resulted from being offered a tainted cut of meat.

I jumped up and ran through the kitchen, linen room, and laundry to the rear door, stepping short at what I saw.

Persimmon Jarrett lay face down on the floor, sobbing, blood pouring from one wrist onto the old, tiled floor.

Chapter 15

Jarrett's hair was tousled, if not downright ratty, above her shaking shoulders. She was clad in a drab brown dress that was immodestly bunched above her knees, and there were a variety of scratches and bruises on her exposed skin.

I permitted myself two seconds to absorb the scene in front of me before snapping to action. "You will boil some water," I instructed Mrs. Roper, "for the nurses will need clean water to address her wounds."

She immediately obeyed me, most likely so she could flee the dreadful scene. I knelt down next to Miss Jarrett. "You little simpleton," I said quietly but not unkindly. "What happened to you?"

With Polly Roper gone, Mary and the nurses clamored into the room, but all were thankfully silent.

"Miss Nightingale, I am so sorry," Jarrett said, struggling to rise to her knees. Harris got down on her own knees on the other side of the librarian, and together we gently lifted her into a seated position.

I ordered the other nurses to prepare a room, to go to the linen room for bandages, and to summon Dr. Killigrew. Again.

Dr. Killigrew was spending more time at the Establishment lately than at his wealthy clients' homes.

For once, Nurse Wilmot moved as though she was not drugged. A tiny bit of progress.

Marian Hughes returned first with bandages, which I instructed her to press against Jarrett's wrist to arrest the bleeding. The librarian whispered her thanks.

Harris loosened Jarrett's clothing as best she could so that the woman could breathe better.

"So sorry," Jarrett repeated, snuffling now as Harris and Hughes worked on her. With Hughes pressing the now blood-soaked cloths against Jarrett's wrist while holding the cut arm up in the air, Harris began inspecting her for other injuries. I was pleased with my nurses' zealous and efficient tending of the injured woman.

"She has a very large contusion on the side of her head, Miss Nightingale," Harris announced as she ran her fingers carefully over Jarrett's scalp.

The librarian winced as Harris probed the area more. "No blood, but she took a nasty blow."

"Tell me what happened," I said, pulling a handkerchief from my pocket and offering it to Jarrett. She made quite a sight. Her one arm was raised in the air like a child desperate to answer a schoolmaster's question, and the other was wiping a piece of linen across her nose while a nurse picked at her head like a chimpanzee removing fleas off a fellow monkey.

"It happened about—I don't know, what time is it?"

I consulted the watch pinned to my dress. "It is half past two."

She frowned, confused. "Oh. Then I was out longer than I thought."

"Out?" I said. "Outside? Or do you mean unconscious?"

"I suppose both. I just wanted to help you." Her voice cracked and the tears began streaming again.

"For heaven's sake, girl, tell me how this happened." Persimmon Jarrett was achingly frustrating, and it was causing my temper to flare again.

"I thought I might be able to assist you by keeping an eye on the Establishment, to see if a stranger came around and tried to sneak in. I failed." The word "failed" was drawn out in a cry of anguish.

"Miss Jarrett, you still haven't told me what happened to you." What was keeping Dr. Killigrew? Was I too impatient in expecting everyone to appear in an instant?

"Right." She snuffled one last time. "I hid among the boxwoods. I thought that in this dress I would blend into the gardens. I was in what I thought to be a good spying position, and the next thing I knew, I felt a cold, hard . . . object . . . strike me. I fell sideways and woke to find my . . . my . . . wrist bleeding. I tried to get up and fell again, and I woke up again with my wrist against . . . against . . . a sharp stone, and bleeding anew. It hurt so much. Who would do this to me, Miss Nightingale?"

She wiggled her coagulating wrist for emphasis and Nurse Hughes shook her head at the librarian.

First me, then John Wesley, now Persimmon Jarrett. All of us attacked, but all in a somewhat clumsy manner, as if the attacks were warnings being issued and not truly attempted murders.

In fact, they were exceedingly amateurish attempts, particularly compared to the thorough job done on Caroline Bellamy.

The one thing that struck me as unusual was that whereas John Wesley and I had been pushed down the stairs, Jarrett's wrist had been cut. An echo of Bellamy's death.

I still had no idea who might be behind it all, nor the purpose of all of the bloodshed and batterings.

More important, I didn't know how to stop it from happening again.

★   ★   ★

Dr. Killigrew checked Jarrett over and determined that the cut was neither deep enough nor the blow to her head strong enough to put her in any mortal danger.

I had him accompany me to the rear gardens, and together we found the spot where Jarrett had been attacked. She had been hiding between the brick wall that separated the Establishment from its neighboring property and a short line of old boxwoods that rose in front of a section of the wall. Several branches were snapped and lay bloodied on the ground, and there was a pool of dried blood that seemed to mark where her wrist had been draining out until she managed to wake and stumble her way down to the kitchens.

Poor, stupid girl. Although I had to admit that she really had chosen an ideally concealed location from which to view anyone coming and going from the rear of the building. It just wasn't concealed enough for her to avoid detection. Of course, knowing Jarrett, she had probably sneezed or coughed at the wrong moment while crouching back there.

"Here you are," Dr. Killigrew said, holding up a brick from the wall. We searched the wall and found a location on the opposite side of the gardens where the brick had fallen out. Or been chiseled out.

"Do you have any suspects now?" he asked, replacing the brick into its proper place but with the bloodied side in the wall.

I shook my head. "I can find fault with everyone inside the Establishment, and yet I cannot find *enough* fault with anyone."

"Hmm," he speculated. "Perhaps you should be looking elsewhere."

I frowned. "Where else is there to look?"

"If the murderer is not obviously here, he might be more obviously found elsewhere, and find him you must. Who is associated with the Establishment who does not reside here?"

I considered this. "Well, there is Lady Canning, of course, but that's a preposterous notion."

He nodded in agreement.

"Then there would be all of the committee members. And their wives." I remembered the conversation I'd had with Lillian Alban, happy to not have had any subsequent visits from her. "Beyond that, there would just be the inmates' relatives and the routine people who come by in the course of a day. Delivery boys, the postman, and the like."

"And me, of course, Miss Nightingale. You should also consider the fact that I am a regular visitor." Killigrew smiled broadly at me, and I returned the smile.

"Yes, doctor, I shall put you at the top of my suspect list.

Pray, what is your reasoning for the mayhem you have caused in my life?"

He spread his hands. "It could be any number of things. What are the seven deadly sins? Let me see . . . sloth, envy, gluttony, avarice . . . what are the others?"

"Lust, pride, and wrath," I finished up for him.

"Of course, of course. Well, you may be sure that the murderer's reasoning is one or more of these sins." Dr. Killigrew then expressed to me his grave concern regarding what was occurring at the Establishment, especially since it might result in my dismissal, a fact I was acutely and miserably aware of. I didn't need constant reminders about it.

"Think on my suggestions. You are shrewd and resourceful, Miss Nightingale. You will find the answer."

★ ★ ★

With Dr. Killigrew gone and Jarrett situated in a room resting comfortably, I sent Mary on an errand to purchase sundry supplies that would have her wandering from shop to shop throughout Marylebone. I needed a chance to clear my mind away from the Establishment and decided upon another visit to Elizabeth Herbert. She would be both a comfort and a wise counselor. I rather regretted now refusing her offer to ask for her husband's help in my situation.

Liz welcomed me as warmly as usual, but this time her face was etched with worry as we sat down.

"I've been a bit frantic about you, dear one. What I'm hearing—is it true that you nearly died from a fall?"

I assured my friend that reports of my injuries were

exaggerated. She looked at me dubiously. "In any case, I am glad to see you feeling robust, and relieved that you thought to come see me as soon as you were well. I wanted to send you a note, but Sidney wouldn't hear of it."

I was puzzled. "Why on earth not?"

"Sidney greatly admires your courage but is concerned about the outcome of your venture. And as you know, Sidney is worried he may soon be prosecuting a war in—"

We were interrupted by the arrival of the man himself, Sidney Herbert, leaving me puzzled as to why Sidney's work as secretary of war had anything to do with my work as superintendent of the Establishment. We stood as he entered, and he smiled upon beholding his wife, as though he hadn't seen her in years instead of having parted ways with her after breakfast toast and sausages. It was hard to believe that he had once been besotted with society beauty Caroline Norton, who, unable to obtain a divorce from her foul and despicable husband, had ended their torrid affair. He had married Elizabeth Ashe à Court-Repington the same year, and had seemed to easily transfer his affections from Norton to Elizabeth.

Now, Liz returned the adoration in kind, and once more I swallowed bitter-tasting bile.

If I hadn't been so insistent on nursing as my destiny, I might now be living in a fine home with laughing children and a handsome man delighting daily in my very presence.

Instead, I was on the verge of disaster on all fronts.

Enough, I told myself. My situation at the Establishment had been divinely granted, and I would face any hardships with fortitude and concealed pain.

Herbert greeted me with his hands on my shoulders and a kiss to both cheeks. His cologne was vaguely flowery.

"Ah, Florence, how good to have you here to entertain my lovely Elizabeth. But I am quite certain you two were gossiping about me as I came in, and you must tell me why." He sat in the middle of a settee, leaning back with his legs crossed and one arm laid casually across the back of the sofa. It was a relaxed position, but I sensed that he was tense.

Liz must have noticed it too, for she said cheerfully, "I don't know about you, my love, but I am famished. Florence, won't you stay for luncheon? I insist that we save talk of anything save the weather and the new infant Prince Leopold for the dining table."

"To the contrary, dearest, I believe the only topic of conversation that can be had pre-luncheon regards our own little Mary, George, Maud, and Sidney."

Thus did we spend the next hour discussing the Herbert children, particularly George. He was three years old now, and his father already had grandiose plans for the boy to rise higher than his father. Little Sidney, just seven months old, was making extraordinary gains at crawling and eating whatever would fit in his mouth. Several odd glances passed between Sidney and Liz as they gushed over their children, and finally I could stand it no more.

"Is there some secret lurking in this room?" I asked, just as a subtle bell tinkled from somewhere nearby and we rose to go to the dining room. "I'll not be able to digest any food whatsoever unless you share it with me."

Sidney nodded at Liz, and she said, beaming with

happiness, "Very few people know yet, but we are expecting another child in the spring."

So soon! "Why, that's wonderful news," I said, going to her and embracing her tightly. "I am already imagining the engraved rattle I will purchase for him or her." How was it possible to be at once so filled with both joy and envy?

Sidney's grin threatened to split his face in half. "I'm thinking it will be another girl this time, as beautiful as her mother."

Liz rolled her eyes, but she was obviously pleased by the compliment. "I have the feeling that I will produce nothing but boys for you from this point forward."

We sat down to a glorious mayonnaise of salmon as well as braised carrots, buttered peas, and potato croquettes, luxurious fare compared to what I consumed at the Establishment despite Mrs. Roper's considerable talents, and no doubt my own digestion would suffer later. At least now Mrs. Roper could prepare some rice milk for me if I needed it.

Our dining conversation turned serious across the damask tablecloth, with Sidney discussing meetings being held at the War Office. "Lord Aberdeen has ordered the British fleet to the Black Sea to demonstrate to Tsar Nicholas that Great Britain will not tolerate Russian aggression. The Russians simply cannot be permitted to gain territory and power at Ottoman expense."

Sidney took to his subject with zeal. Soon enough he was arranging salt spoons, glasses, knives, and a variety of nuts, fruit, and sweetmeats from the silver epergne centerpiece to demonstrate exactly how the Russians were wrongfully taking territory. "I find the tsar's claim that he is attempting to protect the rights of Orthodox Christians in the Holy Land from the Turks to be more than a little outlandish," he said, waving an almond in the air.

Liz watched avidly as her husband piled up filbert nuts, cut dried plums, and laid out the curved-edge fish server as part of his explanation. As for me, I saw something else entirely. It was obvious from listening to the man in charge of the War Office that negotiations with the Russians were at an end, no matter what the newspapers might say. That meant that Her Majesty's soldiers were at the beginning of their ordeal.

"How many doctors will go with the troops?" I asked. "I've heard much about troop numbers, tents, and bullets, but nothing about food, clothing, and care." I was far more focused on the casualties of men's political dealings than on the strategies and tactics of winning bureaucratic conflicts.

Sidney's mouth formed an O at my question. I had clearly rattled him. "I, well . . . I suppose that the War Office is more concerned with ensuring that this is a quick effort. If it comes to pass, that is. We don't intend for this to last more than a couple of months, as our spies tell us that the Russian commanders are old and incompetent, much like their muskets. Besides"—now Sidney seemed to have regained his mental footing—"Englishmen are made of stern and hardy stuff. A few passing bullets won't stop them from doing their duty, and most are experienced enough to wrap a few bandages themselves."

I was appalled by my friend's cavalier dismissal. I was already considering the amount of morphine, laundering facilities, eggs, tea, and fresh water that would be needed to care for injured men. "Don't be foolish," I snapped, suddenly agitated. "There will be more than 'passing bullets' and you know it. The men will need not only rescue from the battle-field but decent restoration to health. Particularly after the surgeons get to them."

But Sidney Herbert shrugged, ready to change the subject by reviving Liz's and my earlier discussion prior to his arrival home. "Speaking of surgeons, it has reached my ears that you are having an inordinate number of visits from surgeons and doctors, but for your staff, not your inmates."

"Lady Canning told you," I said flatly.

Sidney shook his head. "Actually, no. Cyril Matthews has kept me abreast of the goings-on at the Establishment. He seems concerned for your well-being. Lady Canning is, too, but mostly from the perspective of keeping her treasured venture afloat. Matthews has expressed great interest in you personally."

Now it was my turn to be discomfited. "How do you know him? And why would he do that?" I had met him only the one time in Roderick Alban's offices at the Royal Exchange. He was surely a busy man. Why would he be concerned with the superintendent of a small hospital?

"Cyril is a liaison between the government and the Royal Exchange so that we can monitor trade dealings, especially those with hostile countries. I've asked him about you myself, actually. He says his interest is impersonal, that he would like to see Parliament be more concerned about the health and welfare of its citizens, and he believes that forward-thinkers such as you, Florence, will bring about monumental change in the country."

I may have believed my life's work to be God-breathed,

but I certainly did not view myself in such lofty terms. "He is very kind, but for the moment, I would be grateful to simply discover who has killed one of my nurses."

"Yes, that," Sidney said, now rearranging his culinary troops back into their original places as food and dining ware. "I know you did not wish it, but Liz has been asking me to intercede on your behalf, Flo, to bring influence to bear upon the police to take your nurse's death more seriously. I hate to disappoint my wife, but I don't think it will be possible."

With the table back in order, he continued. "Liz recommended you to Lady Canning for the position you now hold, so essentially that recommendation comes from me as well. I didn't mind, of course. We both have great faith in your competence, and Liz made a very impassioned speech to her about your great intellect and passion for nursing. However, the queen herself knows that Liz—we—recommended you for the position, so your success or failure reflects upon me. If I were to ask for a special favor to assist in solving a murder that occurred under your auspices—particularly after only a week in your position—it would seem as though our trust in you was misplaced. Neither your reputation nor mine would be helped for it, and I suspect the queen would happily see you removed." Sidney shook his head dolefully. "I'm sorry, but you will have to do this on your own, Flo."

I had been doing so up until this point, anyway, and I certainly did not want my friend placed in an uncomfortable position. I was about to say so and emphasize that I had not requested his help and so felt no loss in not receiving it, but Liz was not yet ready to give up.

"But Sidney," she said, protesting with the great charm

she possessed. "Don't you think that it would further your own career to put Florence's case before the queen? Flo has so many ideas for nursing that could be of great benefit to hospitals across the country. You would be the éminence grise who secretly initiated a modern reformation, only not of faith, but of healing. We just need to see this delicate situation resolved."

He laughed gently. "My dear, I am no power broker remaining hidden behind the draperies. Besides, you know the queen's position on women in elevated positions. Herself excepted, of course. Remember her apoplexy over that Elizabeth Blackwell woman going to America, then Paris, for medical training, then coming back and attempting to enter St. Bart's? It was probably for the best that Blackwell returned to New York City."

Thus I preferred not to have royal notice. At least not while I was in such a precarious position. I could only imagine the queen's reaction to my situation.

But Liz was not to be deterred. "What about the prince? He is very interested in helping society improve. He also has great influence over Her Majesty. Might he not be able to help?"

"Perhaps," Sidney said doubtfully. "But Albert is far more interested in scientific invention as a way to advance society. Besides, he is adamantly against British involvement in the Crimea, so I wouldn't exactly consider him an ally at the moment."

With that, he rose from the table, an indication that luncheon was over. He was soon on his way back to his offices.

"Don't worry, dear," Liz whispered to me as I embraced her once more before leaving. "I will talk to my husband, and you will receive the help you need. I promise."

She was so firm in her opinion that I needed his help that I didn't argue. Besides, Sidney Herbert struck me as being quite firm in his decision, and I didn't believe that even his wife's impending delivery and all of his indulgence in her that that entailed would result in his changing his mind.

Perhaps, though, Cyril Matthews could be an objective source of assistance. He had mentioned wanting to meet with me in a few weeks. Maybe I should visit him sooner.

★　★　★

I returned to a hodgepodge of bustling activity at the Establishment, my penance for leaving the building for just a couple of hours.

First, there was the wretched Alice Drayton, who was carrying on like a banshee so that anyone in the building could hear her. Nurse Wilmot was with Alice, wild-eyed herself from dealing with the inmate's hysteria. "I don't know what to do, Miss. Do we need restraints? She says Nurse Bellamy has stolen a cameo pin from her."

"No, no, no!" Miss Drayton shouted from her bed, lunging out as if to slap Wilmot, who deftly stepped out of reach. "Not Bellamy, you insipid little tramp. It was that boy!"

I did not know if the woman had come into the hospital with any sort of fine jewelry. With Mary at my elbow once more, I asked her to make a notation that inmate belongings required cataloging. I then calmed Miss Drayton down as best I could, although she was quite irrational. I clasped my hands in front of me and said softly, forcing her to be quiet herself in order to hear me, "I am sorry your brooch is missing. Did you witness it being stolen?"

If I had hoped my slow actions would help the situation, I was mistaken. Alice Drayton proceeded to rail on about the perfidy of Nurse Bellamy, John Wesley, Nurse Wilmot, and Polly Roper, then threw in Dr. Killigrew and me for good measure. Everyone appeared to have either stolen from her or tried to murder her. I no longer put any credence in her tale of Nurse Bellamy having once tried to murder her.

The woman was dotty.

I decided in that moment to try something else. "Miss Drayton, it has been a couple of days since I checked on your progress. Open your mouth now, will you?"

My request startled her into obedience. I was even more startled, for her ulcers were completely gone. Dr. Killigrew's urine cure had really, truly worked. It didn't make sense to me, given that disease spreads and multiplies through miasmas. Perhaps it was that the amount of urine she quickly drank, mixed as it was with sugar and water, did not produce enough noxious air to harm in conjunction with whatever restorative properties her urine might have.

I could not understand how urine could cure one of *anything*, but I couldn't argue with the result.

"Miss Drayton, I do believe you are ready to go home now," I pronounced.

"What?" she said, confused. "No, I need a cup of tea. Tea. I told that girl *hours* ago that I need a pot, but she just ignores me."

Wilmot held up her hands—the nails of which appeared to have finally come in contact with a scrub brush—and shook her head. I guessed this was the first she was hearing about Alice Drayton's need for tea.

"Nurse Wilmot will get you a lovely pot of tea, Miss Drayton, while we send word to your sister that you are quite well now."

But Alice Drayton was off in her own world of complaint and grievance. "How many times must I ask? Even a *dying* person would be offered tea . . ."

At least she had stopped her infernal howling.

"What of Dr. Killigrew?" Wilmot asked hesitantly. "Don't he have to give the say-so for her to leave?"

"In this instance, we might have to take matters into our own hands." Yes, I was going against my own rules for showing doctors their proper respect, but I preferred to endure Killigrew's chastisement over another moment of Alice Drayton.

From Alice Drayton's room, I dragged Mary with me to see John Wesley. Harris had the boy on a crutch, and together they were attempting to exit the room for an amble down the hall. Mary and I stepped back to give them room.

The boy gave me a wave with his free hand, but even that effort seemed difficult for him. His injured leg was straight under the firmly wrapped bandages, but he was clearly in excruciating pain. His lips trembled as he attempted not to cry out. He relied heavily on Nurse Harris to help him limp along on his good foot.

I wanted to ask him about Alice Drayton's accusation, as bizarre and unreasonable as it had been, simply because I had so few trails to follow. I wasn't even sure what her stolen brooch—if it even existed—had to do with Nurse Bellamy, other than Alice's ranting about both her and John Wesley having stolen it.

As I observed the boy struggling gamely to take a few

steps down the hall, I realized this was not my moment. "Nurse Harris, I don't think the boy is ready for this yet. Let's let him rest a couple more days."

As Harris returned John Wesley to his room, I took off again with Mary in my wake, intending to take care of several tasks before going to see Mr. Matthews. I reached the bottom of the staircase and put my hand to the carved lion newel, a fancy of the lord who had once lived here, and it was there that Polly Roper stopped me.

"Miss Nightingale," she said. Polly was perspiring as though she had run a great distance. "I've been working on some recipes ever since you left, and I thought you might like to taste . . . ?"

I was impressed that she had taken it upon herself to heed my advice. My other work could wait. I followed her down into the kitchens, where she presented me with an array of burbling pans over the cooktop fire and ceramic dishes laid out on the worktable. There was also a pitcher full of golden-yellow liquid on the table.

"What is this?" I asked, pointing to the pitcher.

Her eyes just about disappeared into their sockets as she grinned with pride. "I invented a nourishing lemonade, Miss. Would you like to try it?"

She got cups for both Mary and me and poured samples into them. I was pleasantly surprised. The drink was sweet, syrupy, and quite tasty. "Delicious," I pronounced. "What's in it?"

Mrs. Roper became more animated than I had ever seen her before. "I took your recipe for egg wine and modified it for lemonade. I boiled water and poured it over lemon rind and sugar in the pitcher. While it cooled, I worked on some of these other dishes here, such as these stewed rabbits in milk, and mutton jelly, and—"

"Mrs. Roper," I said. "First tell me about the lemonade."

"Oh, yes. So when the mixture cooled, I strained it, added sherry, some finely beaten eggs, and quite a bit of loaf sugar. For more flavor, I rubbed a few lumps of sugar over the strained rinds until they turned yellow and added the lumps to the drink. I briskly stirred it all, and you are drinking the result."

"Well done," I said warmly. "A fine offering for the inmates."

"And this is my stewed rabbit." She indicated a large pan resting on the burners, which had been turned down to a low flame. "I made a nice little sauce of flour—not arrowroot—mixed with milk, a blade of mace, a little salt, and a pinch of cayenne. I cut up two rabbits and put them in the stewpan, poured the sauce over the meat, and simmered it about half an hour until the rabbit was quite tender. Using young rabbits is the secret, Miss Nightingale, to having it come out soft and flavorful. I think that is what you would want." She dished a bit of it out for me.

It, too, was heavenly. Perhaps I would no longer consider Herbert House a place to seek out fine dishes. "Mrs. Roper, your cooking will make this hospital famous."

Her cheeks were pouched like a chipmunk's from smiling so hard. "I am still working on a mutton jelly. Tomorrow I plan to work on some flavorful broths. Perhaps something that would be a good tea substitute for those who want too much of it."

"Well done," I repeated.

Yes, Polly Roper would make us famous. Unless she'd had anything to do with Nurse Bellamy's death.

Between luncheon at the Herbert home and sampling Mrs. Roper's wares, I was quite sated. Mary and I went back upstairs, and now I was determined to reach my study to accomplish some work. But Marian Hughes found me.

"Miss Nightingale, you should know that Miss Jarrett is in very restless sleep. She's having terrible nightmares over her attack."

That wasn't surprising. "Mrs. Roper has made a new lemonade. Get a cup of it and wake Miss Jarrett to drink it. It will settle her nerves, I believe."

Hughes nodded, then added shyly, "And Miss Nightingale, I have a sample uniform to show you. When you have a few moments . . ."

I realized I wasn't going to accomplish anything I had planned for that day because the interruptions wouldn't cease. Cyril Matthews might have to wait until tomorrow. However, I was most interested in seeing what Hughes had produced. "Bring it to me in twenty minutes."

Twenty minutes later, Hughes, Mary, and I were in my study. I opened windows while Mary turned the gas lamps up as far as they would go to ensure as much light as possible. Meanwhile, Nurse Hughes unfolded her cloth bundle, revealing to me a uniform that was . . . interesting, to say the least.

Actually, it was dreadful.

It wasn't the design that caused me to wince; it was the awful color of the uniform. I had asked for gray. This was an odd shade that, when the fabric was shifted in different directions, had a green cast to it. It wasn't simply plain as I had wished; it was spectacularly . . . ugly.

However, she had followed all of my specifications precisely, and it was well constructed. I inspected the stitching on the inside of the dress, and it caused me to stop, blinking, not sure if what I felt was disbelief or terror.

Hughes's stitching was a zigzag pattern identical to that I had seen in Nurse Bellamy's clothing. Clearly Hughes had known Bellamy to a greater extent than she had admitted. It didn't mean she was guilty of anything, but the subterfuge was troubling.

CHAPTER 16

"What is this?" I demanded, thrusting the fabric out to the nurse.

"Miss?" she said, her colorless gaze switching between Mary and me in confusion. "It is the uniform you wanted."

"So I see. This stitching, though; where did you learn it?" It wasn't my real question, but I would get to that.

"I-I-I've always sewn that way, Miss. I came up with it myself. I find it holds a seam well, although you can't use it in every situation, certainly not in tight corners or small arm-holes or—"

"Yes, yes, I see," I interrupted, not interested at all in a sewing lesson. "How well did you know Nurse Bellamy? Tell me the truth this time."

"Miss Florence," came Mary's voice floating quietly to my ear. "Perhaps we might wish to let Nurse Hughes sit down for a moment."

I was instantly embarrassed. My temper was frayed into tatters, it would seem. "Yes, of course. Sit down, Nurse."

Hughes took a chair gingerly, as if she'd been beaten and was covered in bruises. Why was I ill-treating someone with so much promise? Was Caroline Bellamy's death completely destroying my focus?

"My apologies," I began, still holding the dress in my hands. "You have made a well-constructed uniform, although I do wonder at your choice of fabric color."

"You do not like it," Hughes said, glancing down, crestfallen.

I would not be dishonest to spare her feelings, but I did check my caustic tongue. "It is an unusual color to be sure, just not what I had in mind when I asked for gray. Where did you purchase it?"

"I asked Miss Jarrett to place the order for me some weeks ago. She has much better grammar and handwriting than me. I had it stored in the linen room and had planned to use it for some nice curtains I thought to make for my room. I thought the color might be close enough to what you wanted." Hughes bit her lip. "So you do not want me to make the uniforms, then?"

"I didn't say that. I want you to make another one, but next time show me the fabric first." I gently laid the uniform across her lap. "Now, let's discuss you and Miss Bellamy. You must have been more friendly with her than you told me before, at least enough to have made a dress for her."

She shook her head. "Actually, I adjusted a couple of her own skirts for her. I have made things here and there for the staff, when I'm asked. She had recently come into some very nice dresses—very fine silk poplin. They were used, but hardly. Caroline never told me—"

"Nurse Bellamy," I corrected, holding back a sigh.

"Yes, Miss. Nurse Bellamy never told me how she got

them, but she showed them to me while we were still at Cavendish Square."

Was that significant? I had no idea. The dresses were no longer among her things.

"Beyond clothing, did the two of you have anything in common? Did you socialize?"

"A little. She wasn't much of a socializing sort. I don't think she cared much for working at the hospital. We walked to Regent's Park Zoo together once and had cups of chocolate at a café on the way back." Hughes began folding the dress I had so rudely shaken at her a few minutes before.

"And did you learn anything about her?" I was frustrated to have to draw each piece of information out of her. Surely she understood that I was asking her to tell me what she knew about the enigmatic Caroline Bellamy.

"Well, she did tell me that she didn't have much money, but none of us do. I don't know if she had any schooling." Hughes frowned, trying to remember.

Thus far, I wasn't learning anything.

"Oh, yes, Nurse Bellamy did once tell me that she had a scheme for lifting herself out of the Establishment and into a better life. She wouldn't tell me what it was, and I figured it was just boasting. Plenty of women do it, Miss Nightingale. Our lots are sometimes harsh, and we think if we can imagine a way into society and then think on it hard enough, it might come to pass. Of course," she added, "employment at the Establishment is already a step up, which is why I thought she was just being silly and trying to impress me."

I didn't care that Nurse Bellamy found employment at the Establishment not to be high enough for her. I was still focused on Hughes telling me that Bellamy had found a scheme for riches.

I needed to talk to Nurse Wilmot, whom I still had not confronted after Persimmon Jarrett had revealed she had overheard a plot between her and Polly Roper.

I hated the thought that my newly invigorated cook might have to be fired.

★   ★   ★

Again I was prevented from doing what I wanted to do, this time by the late afternoon mail delivery. Inside the stack of bills to be paid and letters for inmates was a letter to me from my mother.

I considered just tossing it up in my bedchamber to read later but then decided it was always best to drink a necessary poison without first dwelling on how terrible it would taste.

It was nothing unexpected, just a reiteration of how disappointed she was that I wasn't writing to her daily and how beneficial Mary would be in my life.

Poor Mother. If she only knew.

Ah, but then my mother reached the real point of her letter.

> *—and it has come to our attention that someone has died at the Establishment, and not a patient. Neither you, daughter, nor Mary has written to me of it. Me, your own flesh and blood, Florence. Without an assurance that I am mistaken in the gossip I have heard, I must assume that I was COR-RECT in saying that this position is too DANGEROUS for you, and surely you will AGREE to this.*

Mother ranted a bit more, but I was already folding the letter back up. Presumably it was Lady Canning keeping my mother informed. I couldn't say that I blamed her. If anything happened to me, my parents would throw her into the Thames themselves. She absolved herself of any guilt by telling mother everything. I had no time to haggle and bicker with Mother over this.

The already-indispensable Mary was still at my elbow, quietly waiting for whatever I needed.

"Goose, will you take care of this?" I handed her the letter.

She pushed her glasses up the bridge of her nose and quickly scanned Mother's missive. "What do you wish me to do?"

"Write to her. Tell her I've said to you that ten people could be murdered in my bedchamber while I sleep, and still I will not give this up and return to Embley Park."

At the expression of shock on her face, I added, "This is a critical moment for you. For if you report this to Mother, she will dismiss you as completely unable to manage me. Do not protest; I know that was the reason for your hire. I would, of course, hire you from my own purse immediately." That purse, ironically, was a generous allowance from my father, but I wouldn't quibble about such details now.

Mary gasped. "Miss Florence, you are testing my loyalty."

I nodded. She was truly the only one at the Establishment I *did* trust at the moment, but I had to know that she was truly, unequivocally, on my side.

She folded the letter and thrust it deep into her dress pocket. "I am your dedicated friend, Miss Florence, and even if your mother tries to attach my head to a pike, I'll not abandon you. I will write to her of your intent to remain at the Establishment."

I smiled and embraced her for the first time. It was good to have a friend at hand. She could never replace Liz Herbert, but my time at the hospital would be much easier if I could empty my mind of its troubles on someone who did not either report to me or have power over me.

★ ★ ★

As if the Establishment had turned into an orphanage ward full of unhappy infants, now I was summoned to Ivy Stoke's room. I left Mary behind so I could visit the inmate privately.

"Miss Nightingale, I believe I am getting worse. The air is so thick in here, don't you thiiiiink?" She was wheezing again. The window was only cracked open, so I threw up the sash to let in more fresh air. She was not comforted by that, so I retrieved one of Killigrew's specially prescribed cigarettes and offered it to her. She made all manner of exaggerated expressions as she smoked it.

I waited impatiently for her to finish. I had so much to do.

"Oh, Miss Nightingale!" she exclaimed. "Have I shown you the new trick Jasmine can perform? If I hold up a little piece of meat from my tray, she will put her paws together as if in prayer, saying grace. It is the most amusing thing . . ."

I escaped Mrs. Stoke, but before I could finally seek out Nurse Wilmot, I was stopped short by a scene I was surely not supposed to see.

I backed up on my toes to maintain silence and peered into the library again.

They must have believed themselves to be hidden in between two rows of bookcases, but it was a plain and terrible vision for me.

For there were Charlie Lewis and Clementina Harris, leaning in close together and whispering. I couldn't make out their words, nor could I read Harris's expression, since her back was to me. But there was no mistaking that hair. Charlie was apparently taken with it, for he gently reached for one of her long, auburn loops.

I would not watch any further. I tiptoed away, disappointed. I was very unhappy with this, and not because of any awakened longing for Richard. I could not have this sort of congress between my staff members. The mission of this hospital was to care for sick women, not to be a sanctuary for secret trysts.

Moreover, I wanted my nurses fully focused on their work, not daydreaming and wondering when they might catch a glimpse of their lovers in the corridors.

Perhaps another requirement for nurses should be that they be reserved in nature and free of romantic entanglements.

I did hate the idea of losing a worker like Harris, though. Even as comely as she was, she had the many innate qualities that made her a good nurse.

At the rate that I was making these judgments, I would end up with no one except Mary by the time it was all over.

★ ★ ★

I searched around for Nurse Wilmot but was unable to find her. I returned to my study, where Mary was tidying up around my desk.

I expressed my frustration at being waylaid so many times before having time to find Wilmot, then being unable to find her. A tiny part of me worried that she had permanently fled.

"Oh," Mary said. "I know where she is. She took Miss Drayton for a walk. Said they would return in an hour or so."

"An hour!" I burst out angrily. "You are saying that my nurse took an inmate—who is wandering in her mind—out into the congested streets of London for a *walk*? Heaven knows what could happen to Miss Drayton if Wilmot loses sight of her for even a moment. And I've sent word for Miss Drayton's sister to pick her up . . ." I could only imagine the scene when Alice Drayton's sister arrived, only to find there was no one to take home.

I felt like a firework that had just had a lit match put to its wick. I took a calming deep breath. It would do no good for me to behave like a madwoman, as good as venting my anger and frustration would feel.

"Miss Florence, may I show you some more work I did on your investigative charts? I filled in more blanks and—"

I held up a hand. "Not now, Goose. I need to clear my mind."

I abruptly left her standing there. I went to my room and changed into a better day dress, selecting one of deep burgundy edged in black piping. I also grabbed my black cloak from its hook. The September weather was becoming very chilly.

I was under no illusion that I would be able to find Nurse Wilmot and Alice Drayton. There was no point in even attempting to search the streets, alleys, and shops that lay scattered across the neighborhood. I stood on the stoop of the

Establishment, watching as an omnibus turned the corner from Harley Street into Weymouth Street, its ten or so passengers sullen and quiet in the nippy air.

As usual, coal smuts drifted through the air, landing invisibly on my ebony cloak.

Across the street, a boy stood next to an iron barrel that contained a brightly burning fire. He warmed his chapped hands over it, for a moment not caring about hawking the newspapers stacked on the ground around him.

A carriage being pulled by two horses hurried by, the driver sitting with his coat collar pulled up so far it was as though he had no neck.

I smelled the roasting of meat in the distance. Lamb, in fact.

Now I knew I was hungry, for my stomach responded longingly to the meat's aroma.

Perhaps I would find the street vendor offering the lamb and buy a pasty or two for myself.

But then I realized that the fragrant aroma was actually coming from inside the Establishment.

Mrs. Roper, you are outdoing yourself, I thought.

And, with that, I no longer felt a desire to leave. I would eat here much as I slept, worked, studied, and supervised here. I went inside, shaking my cloak off on the stoop first before passing back through the door.

How had everything changed in just a few minutes?

There stood Alice Drayton, dressed and wearing a hat, leaning on Nurse Wilmot with one arm and holding a walking stick with the other. Charlie Lewis was just bringing her trunk into the entry hall.

"Where—where did you come from?" I gasped.

Wilmot looked at me quizzically. "From Miss Drayton's room, Miss."

I exhaled impatiently. "Did you not take Miss Drayton off the premises?"

"Yes, but not very far. And we had a nice read with the spiritualist, didn't we?" she hinted, turning to the inmate.

Alice tittered. "That Madame LaMotte was quite interesting. And that gentleman with the long mustache whom we talked to was so very kind, wasn't he? Even when he—"

Nurse Wilmot stopped her with a conspiratorial, "Now, we won't want to be telling the secrets of your fortune, will we, Miss Drayton?"

"What?" Alice Drayton was already confused again, and I had little interest in more details of their visit with a fortune-teller now that the inmate was safe at the Establishment again. Obviously I couldn't speak to Wilmot about what she was doing with Polly Roper as long as my nurse was with Charlie and Miss Drayton. I left them to rejoin Mary in my study.

I learned later that Alice's sister had never arrived, and eventually Miss Drayton was moved back to her room. Alice seemed quite content that her sister had neglected to come for her, and she chattered quite happily when I visited her after she was reinstalled in her room. As for me, I realized that I had been entirely too hasty about ejecting the inmate. Physically recovered as she might be, perhaps it made sense for me to keep not only my nurses, but the inmates as well, close at hand until I determined who had killed Caroline Bellamy.

CHAPTER 17

I was unsure if Cyril Matthews would appreciate my appearing unannounced at the Royal Exchange but plowed ahead anyway.

The Exchange was just as busy and clamorous as it had been on my first visit. I quickly made my way up to Roderick Alban's offices, hoping that I would miraculously manage to find Mr. Matthews, and only Mr. Matthews, there.

The door to Alban's rooms was ajar, and I knocked lightly on it. Receiving no response, I removed my gloves and shoved them into my reticule so that I could rap more loudly. Still no answer. I was disappointed that no one was in, but it had been foolish to think I could expect a busy man to be sitting behind a desk all the time, as though he had nothing to do but wait upon me.

I knocked once more and called out, "Sir? Mr. Matthews? Mr. Alban?"

Still no answer.

Now I was downright curious. Why would the door be open if no one was there?

Perhaps I could leave him a note, stating that I would return again tomorrow. I pushed the door open further and walked in. I had only taken a few steps before I stopped, chilled in place as though I had just been dropped into a subarctic forest. The garish green walls were like a grove of pines, still and sentinel over what they had witnessed. My mind simply could not understand what my eyes were seeing.

Slumped over a desk on the opposite end of the room from the inquisition table and chairs was Cyril Matthews. His face was cheek down in the midst of scattered papers. I knew immediately from his ashen skin and slackened jaw that he was dead and had been dead for some time. Perhaps a day or more.

I slowly approached the man's body. His right arm was on the desk, circling around his head like a halo. The other dangled limply at his side. And what was this?

On the floor beneath his suspended hand was a piece of paper. I picked it up and turned it over. It contained a single line.

Dead as prommised

I let it flutter back to the ground, so many thoughts whirling through my mind that they threatened to overwhelm me. The note, written in the same hand as the one I had found among Nurse Bellamy's papers and the note Lillian Alban had given me, seemed to be informing Mr. Matthews that he was dead. As he most certainly was. Was this a murderer taunting people he was about to kill? The idea was both breathtaking and ghastly.

Or was its purpose to inform Mr. Matthews that someone else was dead? If so, Mr. Matthews would have known exactly who was now dead, given that it was not signed.

Was this relevant to my own investigation or just a very unhappy coincidence? I had no idea, but I folded the note into a small square and shoved it deep into my dress pocket.

I needed a doctor. No, this man was beyond a doctor's help. I needed the police. Surely they would not think *this* to be a suicide.

CHAPTER 18

I found an errand boy to go and summon the police. Who should arrive shortly but Douglas Lyon, the constable who had come after Caroline Bellamy's death and who reminded me so much of Richard.

He frowned upon seeing me, and I knew he recognized me but could not quite place me. I reminded him of our previous meeting and he nodded, remembering. "You seem to have had great misfortune of late." He said it kindly, without irony.

"I'm afraid so," I replied. "And the misfortune is greater than you know."

His brown eyes softened and his expression became one of concern, and all of a sudden I wished I had swallowed my rash words, for the man was going to melt me. "However," I said briskly, drawing my hands together primly, "What is important is your investigation, and I shan't interfere with it."

Lyon gave me a curious look but didn't pursue whatever I might have meant by my great misfortunes. I told him of my connection to Cyril Matthews and how I had met him on only the one occasion. As I told the constable what little I knew about the dead man, he examined Matthews's body, running his hands over it and loosening clothing here and there. Finally, he nodded. "He hasn't been stabbed or shot. There was no blood anywhere to indicate he had been, but I had to be sure. He may have had a crisis of his heart or perhaps he suffered an apoplexy. However, if I were a wagering man, I'd say he was poisoned."

That surprised me. "Poisoned? By what? How?"

He didn't answer my questions but instead presented one of his own. "How well did you know the man? Can you tell me anything about him?"

I thought back to the brief meeting I'd had with him. "He was congenial enough. A very pleasant manner." I suddenly remembered Matthews rubbing his temples. "Oh, he did seem to be suffering from a headache when I met him."

"Ah," Lyon said, nodding knowingly. "I've seen this before. I venture to say he has died of arsenic poisoning."

"Arsenic!" I exclaimed in horror, remembering dotty Alice Drayton's claims. "How?"

"It's mixed with copper to make the deep green colors that everyone has become so fond of using to dye their walls, furniture, and clothing. I would stake my life that that is what happened to the man."

"But how can that be?" I asked, walking over to the wall. I rubbed two fingers against the paper and then showed him my unstained skin. "I cannot rub the arsenic off, so how is it possible that he could have ingested it?"

He lifted both hands. "I do not know. But it is more common than you might think, with the new fashion of dark walls, to find people suffering from headaches, throat constrictions, and nausea inside homes papered this way. The moment they go elsewhere, their symptoms clear up. I will say also that the wallpaper manufacturers make the same argument you just made."

Was it possible that the arsenic in the wallpaper created a miasma that settled into the lungs? I had so many questions at that moment, but only one created a burning sensation inside my stomach. Was it coincidental that Mr. Matthews had begun using Roderick Alban's offices at the same time that it had been redone in arsenic-laced papers and upholstery? Was it even more coincidental that Alban had practically stopped using this space now that it had been redecorated in this vivid color palette?

★ ★ ★

It was of no surprise to me that Lady Canning swept into the Establishment the next day while I was giving my nurses a lesson on bleaching muslin.

They needed to know how to do so and not always rely on a laundress to do it for them. It would also save money if I could eventually dispense with the laundress's services altogether, given that we had laundry facilities in the basement.

May was really the optimum month for bleaching muslin, but I didn't intend to wait until next spring to continue lessons for my nurses. I had shown them how to dissolve a pound of white, powdery chloride of lime in two quarts of water, and now we had thoroughly soaked the long length of cloth for about twenty minutes, periodically lifting and airing it. I sent Frye and Harris outside together with the fabric to rinse in a bucket of rainwater and then lay it out across the bush line to dry. My hope was that working together in this way might cause the two of them to mend what I suspected were many quarrels.

Lady Canning arrived while Harris and Frye were outside and I was lecturing the others on how to whiten yellowed linens by soaking them in buttermilk. Charlie came downstairs to retrieve me, saying that my employer awaited me in the library.

I didn't waste time going to my room to change into more refined clothing and instead met her as I was in my plain working dress. I was sure I stank of the bleaching powder's sharp odor, but that simply couldn't be helped.

I held out a reddened hand to her and she shook it, although I caught her quickly shuttered expression of distaste. No doubt Lady Canning thought laundry was beneath me.

Two years ago, I would have agreed with her.

"Roderick Alban told me about Cyril Matthews, the poor soul," she said. "Cyril's wife is quite beside herself but is taking his funeral arrangements in hand with the help of his brother."

I was happy to know that Mr. Matthews had someone to care for him in death, but surely this wasn't the only reason my employer had come here today.

Lady Canning frowned as if deciding upon the right words to use. I invited her to be seated, but she refused, so I knew she had merely come to make some sort of pronouncement and would be gone.

"You should know," she began, "that both the men's and women's committees have been fully apprised of everything that has happened here. Nurse Bellamy, your fall, the attack on your librarian, and so forth. Now we have poor Cyril's death."

It was remarkable how quickly news traveled even when one didn't wish for it to do so. "I didn't think I should burden you regarding my—"

Lady Canning held up a hand. "Please allow me to finish, as I'm not sure that your withholding of more tragic events is really the worst of our problems at the moment. The committees have become gravely concerned about the future of the Establishment."

"No doubt Mr. Alban is urging their concern," I said sarcastically, instantly regretting it.

Lady Canning gave me a sympathetic look. "Roderick can be difficult, but he really is a wonder at fund-raising. Hence I must take his anxieties seriously. I do not wish to lose you, my dear, but I *cannot* lose him. Do you understand?"

Unfortunately, I did.

"I've spoken privately to several key committee members, asking them to reserve judgment until you straighten up the Establishment. They are willing, but for how long? And I'm not sure how long I can restrain Roderick. What I'm saying is, if you don't clear the Establishment's name quickly, my hand may be forced. Especially since . . ." She let her words trail off, but I knew what she was thinking.

Especially since I no longer had my defender in the form of Cyril Matthews.

★　★　★

I wanted my mind as bleached clean as the muslin, so despite the dire nature of Lady Canning's warning, I spent the rest of the day in instruction with my nurses and tending to patients. I slept in surprisingly blessed peace that night and awoke the most refreshed I had been since arriving at the Establishment.

I bathed, dressed, and had breakfast, ready to begin my investigation again. Mary then arrived as if she knew the exact moment to do so.

"Goose, today we shall examine our charts and attempt to make sense of them."

She seemed pleased by my cheerfulness, which I realized had not been present of late, and we secreted ourselves away in my study for several hours, writing and discussing. We ended up with a list that attempted to establish a relationship between Caroline Bellamy and everyone associated with the hospital.

Lady Canning—hired her
Roderick Alban—affair?

My nerves prickled about this. Would someone as arrogant as Roderick Alban have had an affair with Nurse Bellamy? Wouldn't his aim be higher? Lillian Alban's claims rose up in the back of my mind. Perhaps the better question was whether someone as disturbed as Lillian Alban would kill her husband's mistress.

Cyril Matthews—sympathetic to her plight
Charlie Lewis—affair?
Polly Roper—part of a riches scheme with her?
John Wesley—found her locket in the secret room (tryst location?)

*Persimmon "Mims" Jarrett—body found in library she
    manages; overheard talk about money scheme to include
    Bellamy*
*Margery Frye—believes Harris to be a murderess . . . is it
    relevant to Bellamy?*
*Nan Wilmot—witnessed Bellamy sneaking out; claims
    Bellamy was unsociable*
Clementina Harris—a prior murderess?
*Marian Hughes—socialized with her; altered her clothes;
    knew of the money scheme*

So who was the liar, Wilmot or Hughes? Had Nurse Bellamy been aloof and cold or merely particular about the company she kept?

Ivy Stoke—cat knows secret room
Alice Drayton—believed Bellamy to be poisoning her
Hester Moore—??
*Dunstan Moore—claims Bellamy told him she would be
    rich soon*

Moreover, if Persimmon Jarrett, Marian Hughes, and Dunstan Moore were all independently aware of some sort of money scheme involving the nurse, did that scheme make up a critical part of the answer?

As I examined our list, it seemed to me that only one person within the Establishment had been on any sort of admitted good terms with my dead nurse.

It was time to talk to Nurse Hughes again.

★ ★ ★

Mary accompanied me on a search for Marian Hughes. She wasn't with any patients, although Mrs. Stoke said she had been in earlier and was headed to the kitchen for some lunch. We went to the basement, and Polly Roper said Hughes had eaten but gone into the rear gardens for a walk. Outside, Charlie was digging up bulbs and told us she had only been out briefly before going back inside via the front door. Back inside Mary and I went, finally finding her in her room. Nurse Hughes sat in her chair next to her bed, picking through a box of buttons that she had dumped onto the coverlet.

"Miss Nightingale," she said, gathering up the button cards. "Did you require me to do something? I'm still waiting on some fabric to start the new uniforms."

I sat down on the edge of the bed across from her while Mary remained in the doorway. "You needn't put these away, and I'm not worried about the uniforms for the moment. I just want to ask you some questions."

She blinked those bland, colorless eyes at me. "Me? What sort of questions can I possibly answer?"

I picked up one of the button cards. The button secured on it was brass and appeared to be a souvenir of the queen's 1840 wedding. It held a relief of Victoria and Albert facing away from each other. I put it back down.

"Nurse, I would like you to tell me more about your background." Hughes shrank back against her chair. "Is there something about your life I should know?"

"I don't think so, Miss. I am very ordinary." She was sounding skittish.

"I understand. But you seem to be the one person within the Establishment with whom Nurse Bellamy had any sort of relationship, and I'd like to know why. It would be helpful to me to know what you had in common, beyond her desiring you to alter her clothing. For example, did she share your love of buttons?"

Hughes frowned. "Not especially. No one thinks they are anything but silly." She picked up the Victoria and Albert button card and stroked it, almost as if it were a pet.

They were odd, I had to say, but there was no harm in them. "Did Nurse Bellamy have a collection of any sort?" I knew the answer to this, for I had been through the woman's room.

She shook her head. "No, Miss. No collections that I know of."

She wasn't going to make this easy for me. "You said your parents are gone. Was Nurse Bellamy also an orphan?"

She slowly nodded her head. I had landed upon something. Both women were orphans and both had ended up as nurses. "I remember you told me you had been a nurse elsewhere, in Southwark, wasn't it? How did you come to that position?"

I thought my question innocent, but to my surprise, tears welled up in Hughes's pale-blue eyes. "To be truthful, Miss, I didn't want to do it," she whispered.

Most women did not; hence it was a profession mostly occupied by the worst of women. But Hughes appeared to have been scared by the position. I kept my voice low and calm. "Did you not have a choice in the matter?"

She sniffed and shook her head. "No. I had to take care of myself somehow and it was all I could think of to do. You see, it all started after my papa died. We lived on a nice estate up north, in Lancashire. But it was entailed, and when Papa died, my cousin who inherited turned us out. Poor Mama. We had very little besides the clothes on our backs. We made our way to London, because Mama heard that there was opportunity here for a woman willing to work." She sniffed again, and I asked Mary to fetch a handkerchief from somewhere.

"Mama was willing to work, but no one told her that she needed a skill—sewing, cooking, and the like. She found a bit of work as a maid here and there, but no one wanted to have to house a child along with her, and no one much believed that she was a widow and not a woman who hadn't gotten herself into trouble. You understand my meaning, Miss."

I did, and I shivered. How likely was it that this would have happened to my own mother had my father died when Parthenope and I were younger?

"So Mama's opportunities got fewer and fewer until finally she, she—"

Mary returned in that moment with a handkerchief, which I gave to Hughes. She held it up to her face, patting her eyes and nose.

"Until finally she . . . ?" I prompted her.

Hughes sighed. "Until she was finally reduced to that profession that no woman wants. She did it for me, I know. So we didn't starve."

"Of course she did," I murmured sympathetically.

"Well, eventually Mama did fall into trouble. She went to a woman to, you know . . ." Hughes looked at me, pleadingly. She didn't want to have to say it.

"To take care of it," I said to help her, even though I felt sickened over the whole sad tale she was telling.

"Yes." Now Hughes's voice was barely a whisper and I had to strain to hear her. "Mama took sick with a fever afterward, and she died. She only had a single dress, the one she was wearing. It was repaired a lot of times, and the buttons on it were all mismatched as they had been acquired in random ways. I took the buttons as memories, and I suppose I keep adding buttons to keep Mama's memories alive now that I earn a little money."

I nodded. "And then you managed to find work as a nurse?"

An expression of pain passed over her face. "Not how you might think. Mr. Maxwell, the man I was nurse to, well, he was the one who . . . who . . . got my mother in trouble. He was a regular customer. I think he felt guilty about what happened, so he took me on as his nurse. He was an old man, you see, and it seemed like work I could do, fetching him pillows and tea and the like. But it turned out he was hoping I might eventually take my mother's place when I was old enough. I avoided him as long as I could, and then I just ran away."

I was silent for several moments, acutely aware of how often the laws of entailment sent women and children into poverty. Perhaps Mother hadn't been quite so unreasonable in expecting me to rescue the family fortunes.

"About Nurse Bellamy," I finally said. "Did she have to endure what your mother did?"

Hughes shook her head. "I don't think so. But only because she *enjoyed* men's attentions. I don't mean she was paid or anything, only that she enjoyed spending time with men who made her happy."

But perhaps Bellamy *had* been paid. In dresses and other finery. And in assurances of a golden future. But who had made promises like that?

And hadn't she been a married woman escaping an abusive husband, according to Lady Canning? How did all of this fall together?

★ ★ ★

Just as it was no surprise to have had an unexpected visit from Lady Canning, it was also no shock to receive a note from the Herberts requesting that I call on them.

They were with their eldest son when I was admitted into their drawing room. Sidney was on the floor with George, setting up random objects on the Turkish carpet to demonstrate Russia's perfidy to his three-year-old son. Liz sat in a chair by the window, picking idly at a piece of embroidery as she watched her husband and son.

For his part, George stared blankly at his father, then picked up an antique Chinese blue-and-white snuffbox that apparently represented part of the tsar's armies and proclaimed, "Mine!"

George then shoved the piece into the furred sporran he wore over his kilt. It was all the rage these days to dress young children as Scottish Highlanders.

Sidney burst into laughter. "Now, that's the way to take care of the Russians, my boy!"

Liz shook her head and smiled. "Florence will think we are raising zoo animals."

Sidney rose, lifting the boy with him and holding him up high so that the boy looked down upon him. It resulted in great giggles from George. Sidney was as affectionate with his children as my own father had been with Parthenope and me. I shuddered to think that Liz could ever turn into my mother, but the woman before me seemed to be cut from gentler material.

A young woman in a starched white apron and collar over a modest, dark-blue dress entered. "Shall I take him now, sir?"

"Thank you, Molly. Have someone bring tea, will you?" Sidney lowered his son to the ground, and George obediently scampered after his nanny.

"Now then," Sidney said to me, as Liz rose to join him. "I believe it important that we talk, before ugly rumors begin. It never ceases to amaze me that, for a city of three million, a false bit of gossip can travel from Paddington to Bromley in the time it takes to pour a cup of souchong."

We all sat down. While Sidney and Liz sat together on the settee, I occupied a delicately carved chair with an overstuffed seat.

"I know from the police that you were the unfortunate one who found Cyril Matthews's body," Sidney said. "It must have given you quite a fright."

I didn't wish to be jaded and tell my friend that very little surprised me anymore, so I simply nodded and Sidney continued, "I understand the police believe it was an accidental death from poisoning . . . by the room's wallpaper?" He raised an incredulous eyebrow at me.

I nodded again. "The constable says it is becoming common

in rooms with dark-green decoration, what with arsenic being used to make the deep color."

Liz's gaze took in the drawing room, which was done in gold and varying shades of blue. Her expression was one of relief that their home was in no danger.

"The police say that they believe it to be an accident," Sidney said. He was obviously well informed, but presumably the death of someone serving as liaison between the government and the Exchange would be of great interest to someone like Sidney Herbert. "However, I am wondering what you think."

I may have thought myself impervious to surprise, but I had been wrong. "Pardon me? You want my opinion on Mr. Matthews's death?"

We were interrupted by the arrival of tea. With a warm cup flavored with three sugar cubes at my side, I was ready to address Matthews's death. "There was a letter at the scene—"

"Yes, we know," Sidney said.

I was confused again. How could he possibly know about the note I had concealed on my person before Constable Lyon came? "You do?"

He set aside his teacup and went to an antique table that sat along one wall. He lifted the top, which was extravagantly inlaid with other woods to create a picture of a tree with wide-spreading branches. He pulled a piece of paper out and brought it to me. "Roderick Alban cleaned out the office and found this."

I took it from him, already dreading whatever it was. I scanned the long missive but didn't comprehend it, although I mentally registered that it was not in the same handwriting as the other notes that had come into my possession. It appeared to be a formal list of accusations against Matthews, and I saw my name mentioned.

"What is this?" I asked in confusion, handing it back to Sidney.

"It would seem that Cyril was contriving to involve himself in the Crimea to his own profit. He was urging certain members of Parliament to vote on going to war in the Crimea. Meanwhile, he was setting up several business relationships at the Exchange that would enable him to serve as a conduit for materials and supplies that would eventually be sold to the army. He would have made a hefty profit for himself, but some honest soul at the Exchange wanted to stop Matthews before it went too far. He sent Matthews this letter to let him know that he would reveal him to us if he did not cease his scheming."

Liz also put her teacup aside. "Sidney hasn't found the man yet, since it wasn't signed, but he has confirmed that Mr. Matthews was indeed conspiring with men both in Parliament and at the Exchange. I'm sure he will eventually find him, won't you?" She offered her husband a look of utter devotion.

I was still confused. "But what does it all have to do with me?"

"You were part of his plan, Florence." Sidney glanced down at the letter as if to pick up details. "He intended to be the sole purveyor of medical supplies to the army and thought that he might also round you up in that. Knowing that you were friends with us, he planned to express a great deal of interest in your work so that he could inspire your confidence in him. Then he would use you to influence me into making him into the powerful mogul that he so desired to be."

I could hardly believe that the pleasant man I had met was in reality so abominable. I would have more easily suspected it of Roderick Alban.

"It would seem that the arsenic poisoning, which must have been happening gradually over the course of the time that he was using Alban's offices, finally did him in." Sidney picked up his cup of tea once more. "Anyway, I wanted you to know about it from me personally, lest you hear anything different from members of the Establishment's board."

I had much to contemplate. First, though, I need to show Sidney what I had. I silently pulled the one-line note from my skirt pocket, where I had kept it for safety. I unfolded it carefully and showed it to him. Liz read it over his shoulder.

Sidney drained his cup and returned it to the tea tray. "What is this?" he said. Now it was his turn to show surprise.

I explained to him how I had come into possession of it, fearful that he might bark at me for concealing it. However, he merely grunted and gave it back to me. "So perhaps it wasn't arsenic poisoning and someone did us a favor. After all, he would have eventually ended up in a noose for what he was doing."

Sidney seemed to consider the matter closed, but my mind was bedeviled by questions. Presumably the man who had sent the list of complaints to Matthews was not the same man who had sent the death note, for if murder was the intended result, why bother with the litany of complaints? No, I did not think the writer of the one paper was the writer of the other. The handwriting was similar, but I didn't think it the same. So had Cyril Matthews been coincidentally suffering from slow arsenic poisoning when he was confronted by a murderer who killed him in an undetectable fashion? It was simply impossible to know.

Undetectable fashion.

Fashion.

I felt a mental nudging, as though someone were trying to offer me the correct physic to cure my own ailment of feverish ignorance.

An image of Dr. Killigrew flashed through my mind. He had said to me that the motive for the murder had to be among the seven deadly sins and had ticked them off for me. "Lust, pride, and wrath," I had said, helping him with the incomplete list he had formed.

Perhaps the motive included all three of those sins.

More images flashed through my mind. The attacks on me, John Wesley, and Miss Jarrett. Nurse Hughes's ghastly uniforms. Not to mention Alice Drayton's belief that she was being poisoned by Bellamy. And the stolen floor plans. Oh, dear heavens. What a complicated web, but it had a pattern I should have understood the moment I first walked into Roderick Alban's rooms at the Exchange.

CHAPTER 19

I did not yet understand everything, but I knew I had to return to the Establishment. There was a murderer in the hospital's corridors who might still strike again, for there was one person who surely remained a threat.

I stood abruptly. "I must leave," I announced. "I believe Nurse Bellamy's killer might attempt another murder in my absence."

"What?" Liz cried. "Whom do you believe to be the murderer?"

"I cannot be sure," I said, hesitant to make an accusation until I had confirmed my fears. "But I am certain that someone else is in danger."

"I'll come with you," Sidney said, also jumping up.

"No," I said. "Your presence will only confuse my staff." I was already heading for the front of the house without waiting for a servant escort.

I rushed through the streets like a Bedlamite to get back to the Establishment, attempting to puzzle out what I truly knew against what I suspected. I sincerely hoped that I was wrong, but when I considered Nurse Hughes's fabrics, Roderick Alban's activities, and Cyril Matthews's death—well, I could not be blamed for alternately shaking and sweating during my mad scramble back to the hospital.

I burst through the front door like a violent storm. The building was unusually quiet, although that may have just been my mind playing tricks on me.

Persimmon Jarrett emerged from the corridor where the inmate rooms were located. She moved tentatively, as though unsure of herself. "Oh, Miss Nightingale, there you are. Dr. Killigrew stopped by and told me I should try to walk—"

I did not care a whit about what Dr. Killigrew had to say. "Where is the rest of the staff?" I demanded.

Jarrett looked at me in complete bewilderment. "Pardon, Miss? I don't know—"

"Never mind!" I snapped. For the moment, the only important thing was John Wesley.

But I was stopped again by the emergence of Lady Canning and Roderick Alban from the library. "Miss Nightingale," Lady Canning began. "We've been waiting for you. We wish to discuss termination of your employ—"

I didn't give a whit about that, either.

"Later," I said, cutting them off rudely. I lifted my skirts again and tore down the corridor of the ward, almost barreling past John Wesley's room. As I feared, his bed was empty.

I ran back into the hall, shouting to whoever could hear me, "Where is John Wesley? Who has seen him?"

The boy was not recovered enough to be hobbling about on his own. In fact, I doubted whether he would ever walk again without a limp. Right now, though, I had to ensure his very survival.

Unfortunately, my disturbance caused not only the staff to come running but the inmates to begin wailing. How stupid of me. Soon they all joined the staff, Lady Canning, and Mr. Alban in the entry, which was becoming very crowded. How ironic that the same scene would be replaying as when John Wesley had first been injured.

"John Wesley is not in his room," I said as calmly as I could—another irony, given that I had probably discomfited everyone in fear. "I want everyone to look for him. Yes, even you," I said in response to the questioning look in Mrs. Moore's eyes.

I had my own idea as to where he might be, and the thought twisted my innards into paralyzing knots. Nevertheless, I clasped my shaking hands together and headed to the library, praying I would not find him in the same manner that I had found Nurse Bellamy.

The alcove was empty.

I laughed, a little too hysterically, for I was both relieved not to see him there and terrified because I was unsure where else to look. And, for some reason, everyone had simply followed me in here rather than obeying my instructions.

Charlie Lewis ventured to speak. "Miss Nightingale, m-m-maybe he went for a walk, like Alice Drayton."

Miss Drayton bobbed her head up and down. "I've been waiting to go for a walk, Miss Nightingale. Even a dying—"

I had no time for this. "The boy's knee is damaged. He could barely take a few steps, and only with help." I looked around. Nan Wilmot was in the room with all of us, so she hadn't taken him out. I did not see Polly Roper.

That's when I knew where to find John Wesley. I pushed through the confused sea of faces and made my way to the servants' staircase. I grabbed the rail with one hand and my skirts with the other and ran down as fast as I could, the gaggle of employees and patients quacking and making their way down behind me.

I felt like a duck leading my ducklings to a watering place.

I did not immediately see the cook downstairs. "Mrs. Roper?" I called out, as everyone backed up behind me at the base of the stairs.

She emerged from the scullery, wiping her hands on her apron. "Yes, Miss Nightingale?" She paused in confusion at the sea of faces before her.

"Have you seen John Wesley?" I said, trying to keep the urgency from my voice.

"Why would he be down here?" she asked. "He's injured."

"Exactly." I moved determinedly to where I knew the secret room to be. I didn't need to remove the apron since it was on Mrs. Roper's person. I found the depression along the joint of the wall again, and pulled the wall open. There was a collective gasp behind me.

Inside, John Wesley lay face up on the mattress, unconscious. At least I hoped he was only unconscious. I rushed to him and dropped to my knees, placing my hand on his chest. He was still breathing, but barely.

On the floor next to him was an open bottle of laudanum.

I suppose I should have been grateful that he hadn't been done in by an overdose of arsenic, which would have been swift but painful. But at the moment I was so filled with rage for the person who would do such a thing that I wasn't thinking quite rationally.

"John Wesley, dear boy," I said softly, rubbing my hand against his face. Was it too late for him? He moved his cheek just slightly against my hand, although he didn't open his eyes. *You will be well*, I thought with relief. I had to get the laudanum out of his system, but I needed him awake enough to vomit.

"Someone find me a bucket, and I need a nurse to bring syrup of ipecac. I also need a cup of fresh water and some wet cloths," I commanded, while I worked to bring John Wesley to some sort of consciousness. In a matter of moments, everything was next to me, placed by unknown hands.

For the next few minutes I massaged John Wesley's chest, tapped his face, and did what I could to awaken him. He was groggy and barely able to open his eyes, but it was enough to pour some ipecac down his throat and have him swallow it. It wasn't long before I got the desired result. I grabbed the bucket, which smelled as if it had been storing spoiled fish. I probably could have used this alone rather than the ipecac. Soon, though, he was vomiting his poor little stomach into it.

When he was done, he collapsed back against the mattress and I wiped his sweating face and mouth with a damp cloth. "Sleep now," I whispered to him gently, as if he were the son of my own womb.

Nurse Harris came forward to take over care of John

Wesley, but I blew all of my ire at her, stopping her with a sharp, "Stay away! I don't want anyone near this boy for the moment."

She backed away, rejoining everyone who was trying to peer into the narrow room, which was certainly no longer a secret to anyone.

Now that John Wesley was breathing normally, I rose and turned to face the assembly. I had a murderer to put into the hands of the authorities.

"There is someone here who has made several murder attempts," I said, as I walked out of the concealed room as everyone spread away from me and into the kitchen. "Two were successful, although one of those was an accident, missing the intended target. No doubt the murderer believes that the intended target is still within grasp, but I tell you today that the killing is over."

Most of the faces in the room were staring at me openmouthed in shock and disbelief. Ivy Stoke collapsed into a chair at the worktable, beginning to wheeze uncontrollably.

I stared back at them all, wondering if the guilty party would step forward. A foolish and naive thought on my part, for they stood frozen in their places. Very well, then.

"I've only been here a very short time, but it has been a time fraught with lies and deception. I have many ideas regarding patient care that I wish to implement, but someone here has thus far prevented it by forcing me to spend all of my waking hours ferreting out the truth about the death of a young nurse, Caroline Bellamy. The first question I had to answer for myself was not who would kill her but why she would be killed. To answer that, I needed to know who she was, but there was little information about her.

"Lady Canning believed her to have fled an abusive husband. But she was mistaken. Bellamy had never been married, and no one had followed her here. Lady Canning hadn't purposely lied to me, but it added to my own confusion."

I pointed to Persimmon Jarrett. "You told me that Nurse Bellamy was a loner and didn't associate with anyone. But then you"—I turned to Nurse Hughes—"told me that you had gone to the zoo and to a café for cups of chocolate with the nurse, stating that she was shy but not a complete recluse. It made me even more perplexed as to who Nurse Bellamy really was. Then Mr. Moore"—I turned to Hester—"said that Nurse Bellamy had some sort of quick-riches scheme, another nettlesome piece in this intricate puzzle. But was it possible that Mrs. Moore and her brother were part of that scheme?"

"I never!" Hester protested. "My brother is an upstanding citizen, a close confidant of Mr. Brunel, and would never—"

Yes, I knew all about the inestimable Brunel.

I continued. "But I could see nothing obvious linking the Moores to my nurse. Yet Bellamy did seem to have a secret life. Secret enough that although she had no family to speak of, an anonymous donor gave money for her funeral. How odd. What activities was Bellamy conducting outside the Establishment that this would be so?"

There were still no sounds in the room apart for my voice.

"Then there was the repeated tale that she was having strange gentleman callers late at night. That opened up so many possibilities. Had a jilted lover murdered her? That was the theory the coroner put forth. Or had her lover tired of her and she refused to let him go? Had they quarreled? Charlie Lewis lives here. Was it him? Was it the relative of a patient? Someone else?"

Finally there was a reaction from the staff. "Miss N-n-n-ightingale," Charlie said, his hat off and being ceaselessly worried in his hands. "I t-t-told you I would never be d-d-disrespectful of ladies."

I stared at him. "Yes, you did, Charlie. But I have heard tales regarding you and Nurse Harris, too. Many people have told me a variety of stories, and I have had to work my way through to the truth." I walked over to the secret room to check on John Wesley from the wall opening. He was still sleeping tranquilly, so I stepped back out into the kitchen.

Charlie Lewis's eyes were as big as one of Polly Roper's tea saucers by now. I noticed that Harris wasn't standing anywhere near him and was in fact standing apart from the rest of the group.

I returned mentally to the scene of the murder. "The killer choked Nurse Bellamy with a rope, but then, I believe, realized that it looked too obviously like a murder. The hanging and the slashed wrists were clumsy attempts to make it look like suicide. Nurse Bellamy wore only one boot, which suggested to me that perhaps she had been dragged into the library. That meant she was either dead or unconscious at the time. Given that her wrists were cut after death, my guess is that she was already dead. However, it is no simple thing to haul dead weight into the air to make it appear to be a suicide.

"But none of this provided clues as to who had killed her, and I had to know more. In my search of the dead nurse's room, I found two very interesting items. Three, really. The first was a new jar of Crème Céleste, a product entirely too expensive for someone like Bellamy to have purchased. It was most likely a gift from her lover. Next were a stack of bills for finely made gowns, none of which were in her armoire. Why not? I'm fairly certain I know who is hiding them. The final item was a letter, written in a poor hand, accusing her of committing a sin. That sin was, of course, adultery. That letter was stolen from me—how our killer enjoys a good theft—likely thinking I wouldn't remember what that handwriting looked like.

"I interviewed my staff and ended up far more confused than before. However, a common thread I was able to document, thanks to the assistance of Mary Clarke, was that two or more nurses were involved in some sort of monetary scheme here. There were plenty of cross-accusations about it, but I finally realized that the simplest answer was the correct one. Nurse Frye was the organizer of the plan, I suspect, given her experience at Allen and Hanbury and the extraordinary amount of pharmaceuticals she had stashed here. I think the plot went something like this . . ."

I looked upward, imagining it all as if it were imprinted on the smoke-stained ceiling above me. "Nurse Frye concocted an idea whereby she could convince inmates not only to hand over whatever valuables they might have in their rooms but also to rewrite their wills to leave her all their worldly goods, such as they were. Such schemes are hard to accomplish alone, I imagine, and you enlisted Nurse Wilmot, whom you recognized as being as unscrupulous as you are."

"Unscrupulous!" Frye exclaimed, hotly defensive. "I've been a good nurse here. Never hurt anyone."

"That is debatable. By introducing substances into food and drink, you could decide whether a patient was sleepy enough to make a theft possible, or perhaps the inmate would be pliable enough to convince her to visit her lawyer for a little will change. Is that not correct, Nurse Wilmot? Is that not what you were doing a couple of days ago when you took Alice Drayton out for a supposed walk? No doubt your Madame LaMotte and the other attendees at the fortune-teller's were most helpful in convincing Miss Drayton to do as you wished."

Wilmot said nothing, but her face was flushed—whether from anger or mortification, I could not say.

"In fact, Alice Drayton believed that Nurse Bellamy had been poisoning her. I suspect her mind was too foggy to really know what was going on, and you convinced her that it was Bellamy—not you—putting substances in her tea. I can't imagine that you were collecting much from the inmates here, but perhaps you hoped that one day we might have a well-off merchant's wife. Or maybe you figured that, as long as you were collecting from everyone, it all added up. Somehow Mrs. Roper caught wind of what you were doing. Maybe she threatened to reveal the scheme—I like to hope that's what it was—or perhaps she saw a way to earn more than she did burning herself on hot pans in a dark kitchen all day. But Miss Jarrett overheard you chattering about your scheme. Surely it was impossible for you to believe you could keep it secret. It's a shame because, Mrs. Roper, you really are an excellent cook. Greed does spoil the stew, though, does it not?"

Roper glowered murderously at Miss Jarrett, her mouth

turned downward as she spat invective. "I should wring your little bird neck. You eat all day, have me make you special dishes, and then you do this."

"Shut up, you idiot," Frye shot back at Roper as Jarrett stood there stoically. "She doesn't know anything; she's just guessing."

That wasn't entirely true; I just hadn't been sure until that moment whether all three of them were involved together.

"No doubt you have sold inmates' items on the street so they will never be recovered. I can only imagine that you took the money and spent it foolishly. Particularly on gin, correct, Nurse Frye?" I realized I should stop calling her and Wilmot "Nurse," for they were going to be in jail before nightfall.

"What I found curious, though, is that Bellamy seemed to also be part of your little scheme. Several people attested to her talking about a method of becoming wealthy. Yet, was there a reason why she had to die for it? Had she betrayed you? Had she—"

Now Frye couldn't help herself. "Bellamy had nothing to do with us! She wasn't part of our plan at all! We aren't murderesses."

I smiled grimly. "No, Bellamy had another plan for improving her lot in life, but thank you for admitting your wrongdoing."

To my surprise, Lady Canning marched over to Frye, drew her hand back as far as she could, and slapped Frye. She used enough strength that the sound of her hand against the woman's face echoed off the walls and created an angry red blotch on Frye's cheek.

"Charlotte!" Alban exclaimed. "Striking a servant is so crass."

Lady Canning glared at him but did not attempt to give Wilmot and Roper the same punishment. She returned to her place next to him.

I was not yet finished with Roderick Alban, though. "The money scheme aside, there was still the problem of who murdered Caroline Bellamy. Clearly the killer was nervous about being found out, because first I was pushed down the servants' staircase into this room, then John Wesley fell down the rear outside staircase, and then Miss Jarrett was attacked, all in the space of a few days. Most shockingly of all, Cyril Matthews, a member of the men's committee for the Establishment, died of arsenic poisoning as a result of spending too much time in Roderick Alban's newly redecorated offices. What did the four of us have in common? Had I discovered something without realizing it was crucial to ferreting out the murderer?

"I have to suppose that once a person gets the taste for killing, it is a drug far more powerful than morphine. It is inconceivable to me that someone associated with a hospital should have this taste, but mankind is nothing if not full of rage and hate. The attack on Miss Jarrett resembled that of the original one on Nurse Bellamy, except that only one of her wrists was cut, and of course it wasn't postmortem. However, John Wesley and I were pushed down stairs, and Cyril Matthews died of arsenic poisoning. Why so many methods? Was I dealing with more than one murderer?

"Although he claimed otherwise, I wondered if perhaps

Mr. Alban had had the rooms redone in the poison-laced wallpaper and fabrics himself, knowing that he was receiving a new tenant he greatly disliked—"

"How dare you," Alban sputtered, inflamed with sudden anger. "I'll see you ousted from decent society. I'll—"

I held up a hand to quiet his righteous indignation. Roderick Alban was in no position to lecture me. "But I discarded the idea, because I couldn't see that your crimes extended to murder."

"My crimes!" Alban was outraged again. "What crime can you possibly accuse me of, Miss Nightingale? Charlotte, we were correct to come here today to dismiss her. We should—"

I cut him off once more. "I suppose your crimes are of a nature that would not see you imprisoned or hanged, sir. But you are the reason for everything. Let me ask, how did you know that Nurse Bellamy had been murdered prior to coming to the Establishment and dressing me down?"

"I—" He looked around and had the good grace to redden. "Someone came to visit me and let me know."

I nodded. "Yes, indeed. That same someone also tried to kill you, but because you turned your offices over to Mr. Matthews, well, we know the result. He died in your stead, as he was probably more sensitive to the arsenic than you were. I found a note next to the man's body that read, in poorly spelled wording, 'Dead as promised.' It took me time to realize that he had opened a note intended for *you*. It was a bold message to let you know that *you* were going to die as well. Our killer didn't know that you had largely stopped using your rooms at the Exchange."

Alban looked at me in shock. "But . . . if that is true, how am I guilty of a crime?"

"An excellent question," I replied. "Only today did I realize that John Wesley was in danger for having found the secret room. He's a boy, and it wouldn't have occurred to him not to talk about it. The floor layout—which no doubt contained the whereabouts of the room—had been stolen, so there was no physical evidence, and the murderer had no idea that I knew about the room. But John Wesley would surely lead someone to it, and then the lovers' nest would be discovered. Correct, Mr. Alban?"

"What lovers' nest?" Alban said, aghast. "I have never killed anyone in my life, although you have sorely tried me, Miss Nightingale, and you might be the first were I so inclined."

I nodded again. "No doubt that is true. But you were fully aware of the room, weren't you? Since it is where you and Nurse Bellamy used to meet. Nurse Wilmot told me she had witnessed Bellamy slipping out through the kitchens, but in reality Bellamy was merely entering the secret room. To wait for you. You were her mysterious visitor."

The room was as silent as a graveyard for several moments. Then Lady Canning cleared her throat. "Excuse me, are you saying that Roderick Alban, a member of the men's committee and an esteemed member of the community, was having a tawdry affair with one of the nurses here?" She sniffed in disgust. "What you suggest is preposterous."

I smiled sadly at her. "Nevertheless, it is true. Mr. Alban is not as discreet as he believes himself to be, though. I can assure you, sir, that your wife is fully aware of your activities, given how careless you are with your clothing. You left a note in your jacket about an assignation, and it took quite a bit of talking for me to convince Mrs. Alban that *I* was not your inamorata."

Now Lady Canning's face was ablaze with fury. "Sir, we are supposed to be above reproach. How can we build a reputable hospital if the very people who are supposed to—"

"Leave it, Charlotte," Alban demanded, cutting her off. "Not in front of servants."

Lady Canning snapped her mouth shut, but I was sure he would hear about it later. His wife would also be dressing him down once she knew the entire truth.

"But the assignation was not with Caroline Bellamy, was it? It was with someone else. The same someone who informed you of Bellamy's death."

Alban refused to respond.

"Does this sound familiar, Mr. Alban?" I withdrew Bellamy's locket from within my dress, pulled out the tiny piece of paper, and read the poem aloud. Finished, I looked up at Alban and saw him standing nearly immobile except for the opening and clenching fists by his side.

"You gave this locket to Nurse Bellamy as a present, and our killer yanked it from her neck in anger. Do you know where I found it? Around John Wesley's neck. Do you know where he found it? Why, right inside the secret room."

"But why—oh," he said, understanding finally dawning in his eyes. "Surely not . . ."

"Yes. Our killer was quite unhappy about your affair with Bellamy. The note in your jacket was from the killer, not your ladylove, and it was a warning: 'Tonight at the usual place.' You probably considered it an invitation, and you ignored it.

But it wasn't an invitation to you, it was an announcement that Bellamy would be killed in the place where you used to meet her, which was the secret room that John Wesley now occupies. I suspect the murderer hoped you would accept the invitation and then Bellamy would be killed right before your very eyes.

"How do I know that was the location of the murder? Because I found a dead rat under Nurse Frye's bed, and later realized that it had probably made its way into the secret room and eaten arsenic from one of the jars in there, then crept around and coincidentally died in Frye's room. After all, Jasmine had proved that both she and rodents could find their way into the room. A little arsenic to make Bellamy sick and therefore pliable, then an elaborate and painful strangulation with a rope. That way Bellamy would understand how angry the killer was. It is a testament to our killer's deep and malicious evil that a relatively quick poisoning was simply not enough."

There was eerie silence in the room as everyone seemed to be collectively holding their breath over my accusation while waiting to see what Roderick Alban would do. Men like Alban were not usually called out for their peccadilloes at all, and certainly not ever in front of an audience of lowly hospital staff.

Finally, he confessed. "Yes, I did love the girl; does that surprise you, Miss Nightingale?" It didn't, but what did surprise me was Roderick Alban passing a hand over his face as he drew in one great sob. Remembering himself, though, he quickly drew upright. "It was not an acceptable relationship, of course, and I knew it could not last forever, although I did for her what I could. I even paid for her funeral. I couldn't attend and I couldn't grieve, yet it didn't seem right that she would have a pauper's burial."

I could never approve of Alban's adultery, but I could at least bring him the comfort of unmasking Bellamy's killer.

CHAPTER 20

"Sir, I am sorry that Caroline Bellamy can never be brought back, but today you may at least stand before the one who put her in her grave."

Alban's expression was bleak. I don't think he quite believed me.

"Miss Jarrett," I began, turning away from Alban and toward the librarian. "You have long been in love with Roderick Alban, have you not? And you had some idea that he was in love with you."

The woman had been so calm and unruffled since we had all tumbled down into the kitchens that I assumed she would continue as such and placidly deny her infatuation. But apparently she was tired of hiding herself.

"He *was* in love with me! He found excuses to come to the Establishment regularly and didn't stop even when we moved to this location. He was ever so nice to me, even bringing me pastries at times. He loved me," she insisted, "until Caroline came along and stole him from me."

Alban's jaw dropped. "Are you suggesting that because I was pleasant to you, and brought leftovers to the Establishment from the baker and personally offered you one, that I was in love with you?"

Jarrett seemed confused, but only for a moment. "No, you showed you loved me by your constant attentions. An important man like you has no need to come to the hospital, but you did, and you always sought me out for a greeting. That's why you took me up on my offer to redecorate your offices, because you loved me. I knew that one day you would set me up as your mistress and I would have nice lodgings and dresses and food."

"What?" Alban exclaimed, his countenance full of disgust. "You pestered me with magazines and drawings about the current fashion for deep colors in interior design, and I invited you to try your hand at my offices because you seemed so enthusiastic on the topic. You said the previous superintendent wouldn't hear of the old building being redone when there was a move in the offing, and I completely agreed with her. It would have been a waste of raised funds to do such a thing. All the while your intent was to kill me?" Alban's disbelief was something to behold.

Jarrett's chilling nonchalance was even more frightening to behold. "You had wandered away from me."

Alban put a hand to his chest, and I thought perhaps his heart was ailing him. He said slowly, "Are you saying . . . you little ninny . . . that you killed Caro . . . because you believed that once you did . . . I would take up with *you*?"

"No, of course not. I knew she was simply a distraction in the way of our being together. But you became too enamored of her and seemed to forget me. I don't know what witch's brew she must have given you, for she wasn't as pretty as me and certainly not as smart." Jarrett crossed her arms, her expression petulant.

"She also wasn't an icy-hearted murderess," I said, but neither of them was listening to me.

"When I saw you had lost all interest in me, I was angry. I couldn't allow her to have you. I also couldn't allow you to leave me."

His breathing was ragged. "I should kill you . . . myself."

We didn't need another murder in the building. "Lady Canning," I said. "Perhaps you should escort Mr. Alban home and . . ."

But Lady Canning was shaking her head, almost in wonder. "You've made quite a remarkable accusation, Miss Nightingale. How did you know it was your librarian?"

I considered this briefly before replying. "Sidney Herbert made a comment to me about Mr. Matthews being killed in an undetectable fashion via arsenic. It made me think of who might have been doing things in an undetectable way here at the Establishment. It occurred to me that Persimmon Jarrett was the only one who had had the opportunity to deceive me continuously in unprovable ways. She presented a floor layout of the building to me intentionally so that I would think she was helping me; then that layout was 'stolen' from her desk. She offered me information about a money scheme being conducted. That was indeed true, again lulling me into her confidence. She even placed her victim in the library, her own space. Who would suspect her of putting the body in the place most associated with her? Her greatest trick, though, was making me think she had been attacked in the rear gardens by the killer. She even slashed her own wrist—but not too deeply—to echo Bellamy's postmortem slashing and bashed herself in the head with a brick. Very clever, that."

Jarrett smiled even as she stood with her arms crossed, hugging her waist, proud to have been called such. Certainly I had never used that word in connection with her before.

"It was all quite inventive. You made the terrible decision that they both had to die. First you redid Roderick Alban's rooms; then you waited a short time and killed Caroline Bellamy. I imagine you fed her a little arsenic somehow. The ill effects of the arsenic would have made her more pliable for the violent death you intended for her. I don't know how you got her body to hang in the library alcove, though."

Jarrett shrugged. "She was no match for me," she boasted. No doubt she had been waiting for her moment to brag about how canny she had been.

"One afternoon with both you and Mrs. Roper out, I invited her to sit with me in the kitchen for late tea. The inmates were all abed, and everything was quiet so I knew she could spare the time. Somehow as she drank, she caught on to me and began to run. I tore off her locket in the struggle and later tossed it into the secret room for safekeeping so I could sell it later, but that stupid boy found it.

"I saw it around his neck later and tried to take it from him the night he came back late, but he put up such a fuss after I . . . er . . . helped him down the stairs that I wasn't able to get it back. The little guttersnipe nearly woke the entire neighborhood." She shook her head in disgust at the inconvenience John Wesley had created for her.

Poor John Wesley had probably known that someone had pushed him down the stairs—even if he wasn't quite sure who—and had been too terrified to tell me. How remarkable it was that fear could make skilled liars of both adults and children.

Jarrett was quite animated now that she was reaching the climax of her story and was even pantomiming what came next. "While Caroline was still awake enough not to be dead weight, I yanked her by the arm and took her and my length of rope up to the library. She was getting quite sleepy by then, and it wasn't much work to choke her once I got her in the alcove. Once I had strangled her, I fashioned a noose from one end, something I learned from a *Punch* cartoon. With that tightened around her neck, I threw the other end over the chandelier, tied it to the leg of the table in the alcove, and pulled it until she was dangling properly. I held the rope, pushed the table back, climbed on and tied the rope up around the chandelier, then arranged the table to look as though it had been kicked away. Thus did Bellamy hang herself."

I was surprised she didn't curtsy to the audience as if having completed the final act of a great dramatic play.

I continued my telling of her sordid tale. "I suppose I must give you credit. You wrote notes that made me believe that they were done by someone wholly uneducated, but that is not true about you, is it, Miss Jarrett? You became a librarian because of your excellent writing and grammar skills, and even Nurse Hughes said she had you help her order cloth because of your talents."

"Yes, I even gave her some leftover green fabric that I had, a good way to get rid of it, but I told her I had ordered it special just for her. Didn't matter to me that she would use it to make uniforms because I would never have to wear one."

"Speaking of fabric, if someone were to search your lodgings, no doubt we would find the dresses Mr. Alban purchased for Nurse Bellamy."

Jarrett stared back at me incredulously. "You are a half-wit if you believe I would have kept them. I cast them, one a day, across the street into the paper boy's fire."

Her disregard for others was astounding and sad, but I plowed on, determined to have every bit of confession from her. "Showing me the floor layout was a game for you, wasn't it? A pretense that you were helping me. You knew I'd eventually ask for it again and you would innocently tell me it was missing from your locked desk. I imagine you had originally drawn it as a way to inform Mr. Alban of the various places you could meet, and in combing through the Establishment, you came across the secret room down here. In doing so, you realized that he and Bellamy had found it first and were using it."

Alban looked so miserable I thought he would retch, as Mary would in witnessing something so distressing. Speaking of Mary . . .

"As I said earlier, our killer—you—enjoyed theft. You stole a page from Mary's notebook and then moved the notebook to another location. I suspect the page itself wasn't important; it was just a way of distracting Mary so that you could fill me full of your poisonous lies about the floor layout. Ah, poison," I repeated. "Why did you have to fill John Wesley full of laudanum? Wasn't shattering his knee enough for you? You had to attempt to kill him a second time as well?"

"Stupid boy. Who would miss that street urchin?" she spat out. "I couldn't trust his ten-year-old mouth. He knew of the room and he had found the locket. He sealed his own fate when I caught him watching me as I tore the page from the little coward's notebook." She sniffed in a belittling manner in Mary's direction. "Anyway, I didn't wish to be cruel to him, so I gave him the laudanum. If you hadn't interfered, he would have simply gone to permanent sleep, and I would have been just as surprised as you when we found his rotting body."

I joined Alban in his desire to kill her myself. I had to maintain composure, though. "Indeed," I said, clasping my hands together as I always did when asserting control of a situation. "I'm afraid the surprise will be all yours, Miss Jarrett. Charlie, please go and fetch the pol—"

But the astonishment was suddenly all mine. Persimmon Jarrett had somehow gotten possession of Clem Harris's knife and now had it pointed threateningly at me. I patted my dress pockets. They were both empty except for the locket and the notes. Good God, how stealthy she was. I wasn't even sure when it had been stolen, as I had been carrying it around for so long that I no longer paid attention to it.

I paid attention now, as Jarrett backed away, the knife still thrust forward as she edged her way to the stairs.

"Be silent, say nothing more, or I will, I will—" Jarrett looked frantically around the room. Clementina Harris was still standing off to the side by herself. A terrible, calculating smile spread across Jarrett's face, and before I could shout a warning to the nurse, Jarrett acted. She leapt over to Nurse Harris, grabbed one arm and twisted it behind Harris's back, and put the nurse's own knife to her throat.

I had to give Harris credit. Although she rolled her eyes back so that just the whites showed, demonstrating her very real fear, she remained calm and silent. She didn't struggle against Jarrett's rough handling of her.

"Maybe I should cut your pretty locks off instead of slicing your neck," Jarrett snarled, the sharp, rusted knife tip indenting Harris's flesh. "You've always been too haughty and proud of your hair."

Harris closed her eyes. The only sign of her fear now was her shallow breathing and her throat bobbing slightly as she swallowed nervously. I admired her bravery but was fearful that I could do nothing to save her.

Alban looked at Jarrett sadly but also with contempt. "How could you do this?" he demanded of her. He extended his hands out to his sides, palms up in dismal query.

Her response was one of rage as she shrieked, "How could I do it? How could *I*? *You* are the monster who abandoned me for that . . . that . . ." The librarian had no words.

"I loved her, and you took her from me," Alban declared flatly. "For that, *you* are the one who should die."

CHAPTER 21

But Jarrett had not come this far in her dark journey to allow the object of her affection to hinder her escape.

Jarrett drew the knife across Harris's neck, and a crimson line instantly formed along the blade's track. While everyone gasped, the librarian tossed Harris off to one side, where the nurse hit the floor with a loud thump. Jarrett then dashed madly up the stairs, skirt in one hand and the knife held over her shoulder as if she would stab anyone in her way. Who that would be, I didn't know, given that everyone was down in the kitchens except for Alice Drayton.

Oh, no.

I pointed at Hughes. "Take care of Nurse Harris," I commanded as I picked up my own skirts and pushed my way past the sea of faces to chase the crazed librarian up the stairs.

Jarrett moved quickly, for by the time I had arrived on the main floor, I could hear her already stomping into Alice Drayton's room. I had never moved so quickly in my entire life, my feet seeming to fly of their own volition. I hardly felt the flooring beneath me as I swiftly followed her. She would have to kill me before I would permit her to harm that poor woman whose only current crime was being unable to move herself out of bed.

Jarrett stood over Drayton's bed, her face wet with perspiration as she held the knife over Miss Drayton's chest. "If I can't do the boy, it may as well be you. There is blood to be paid for what I have suffered. I should have done this long ago anyway, you irritating old cow. Listening to you blathering on and on about nothing is enough to drive anyone insane. I should receive the keys to London for dispatching you."

Her voice woke Alice, whose eyes flew open at the hideous apparition over her. She made a strangled noise, and it seemed to please Jarrett, for she relaxed a moment and laughed. It was a maniacal sound that made my scalp tingle. "Perhaps it was better that I waited until now. The fear on your stupid brainless face is worth it. I—"

"Stop!" I commanded loudly from the doorway. "Put that knife down, Persimmon Jarrett, or I swear I will, will . . ."

She turned to me but still kept the knife poised over Drayton. "Or you will what, Miss?" Jarrett's voice was both derisive and sneering. "If you step into this room, I will plunge Nurse Harris's knife straight into the biddy's heart. She's a weak thing; it should take only a moment before it stops pumping blood. I won't even need to cut her wrists afterward, will I?" Her face glistened with sweat, but she was smiling in malicious pleasure. Her eyes were dilated, with a glimmer of absolute evil in them. It was a frightening visage.

I remained still, fearing that any movement on my part would cause her to carry through with her threat. She laughed again, this time in a higher pitch. "You are not the important woman you thought you were, now, are you, *Florence*?" She enunciated my first name very deliberately and mockingly.

"There is no need to harm Miss Drayton," I reasoned. "She has done nothing to you."

"No?" she replied, now looking back down at her intended victim. "She chattered on about Nurse Bellamy trying to poison her, didn't she? I thought she might expose me with her foolish talk, somehow make people think I was the one doing the poisoning."

Alice whimpered like a scared child but remained instinctively still herself.

How had Jarrett gone from a sheepish, ridiculous fool to this insane harridan in mere moments? Of course, she had probably been unhinged for much longer but been able to cleverly conceal her true self.

I was desperate for a weapon. I glanced furtively around. What was there?

In that moment, though, salvation arrived in the form of a bundle of gray fur. Jasmine came casually strolling through the corridor in her usual way, tail twitching as she looked this way and that, probably wondering who might drop a little food down to her. It gave me the only idea I had in my panicked mind. As she rubbed her face down against my booted foot, I slowly leaned down, keeping a wary eye on Jarrett the entire time. The librarian, however, was paying no mind to me and Jasmine. She was instead wholly focused on Alice Drayton, hissing final threats to the poor woman.

"Be yourself," I whispered, picking the cat up and tossing

her at Jarrett. Being a feline with a finely honed sense of well-being, the cat ensured she landed upright, all four sets of claws firmly entrenched in Jarrett's back.

A dead-center hit.

Jarrett howled in pain, letting the knife clatter to the floor. I confess it gave me great joy to watch as she performed a bizarre, wriggling dance to try to remove Jasmine from her back. The cat did not appreciate being frenetically tossed to and fro and dug in deeper, which only resulted in Jarrett screeching and cursing even more loudly. I was emboldened enough to enter the room and hastily grab the knife from the floor while the librarian lurched and swayed her way out of the room and down the corridor.

I looked down at Alice Drayton, tucking the knife securely into my dress pocket so she could no longer see it. "Are you all right?" I asked quietly. Her eyes were round globes of horror.

She nodded her head as she settled down, blinking several times as if to erase the past few minutes from her mind.

"Miss Nightingale?" she said.

"Yes, Miss Drayton?"

"That woman is barmy."

I laughed. "That she is, dear lady." She joined me in nervous laughter.

Jasmine must have remained lodged in Jarrett's skin, for her piercing cries of pain reached us from the entry hall. Except now I heard a plethora of other voices, which I assumed was the gaggle of everyone residing or working at the Establishment coming up to see what had happened. Then I heard the sound of the front doors flying open and what almost sounded like a melee of shouting.

"Don't worry," I assured Alice, squeezing her fleshy shoulder reassuringly. I then headed out to the entryway.

It took several moments to take in what was happening. Jarrett was curled up on the floor with a constable standing over her, his foot on her arm as if daring her to move. Douglas Lyon was also in attendance. Jasmine was back in Ivy Stoke's arms and the woman was cooing at the feline, who reached up and affectionately licked her owner's face.

As far as I was concerned, Ivy Stoke and Jasmine could remain lodged at the Establishment forever.

Nurse Harris had been brought up and was also on the floor where John Wesley had once lain. While she moaned, Marian Hughes was on her knees, bunching up linens to put at Harris's neck to staunch the bleeding. Who knew how much more damage had been done to the poor woman by dragging her up the stairs, but there was no point in thinking about it now.

Hughes looked up at me, again seeming to read my mind. "It's not a deep cut," she said succinctly before returning to her work.

Mary stood in a corner, turning ashen as she observed blood spattering on Hughes's hands, face, and clothing.

Charlie Lewis was at Lyon's side and had seemed to take on a newfound confidence. Charlie was busy pointing out Roper, Frye, and Wilmot, all of whom began wailing and casting blame on each other as they were rounded up for arrest.

This wasn't a hospital for the sick; it was absolute Bedlam.

Conspicuously absent now were Lady Canning and Roderick Alban. I presumed Lady Canning had scurried Alban out the rear servants' door to prevent him from doing anything he might later regret. And how he would keep this from his wife, I had no idea.

I cleared my throat to make my presence known. Lyon looked away from what he was doing and smiled. "Miss Nightingale, I wondered where you were."

"How did you know you were needed?" I asked in amazement.

"Mr. Herbert sent for the police. He said you might be in serious trouble. I volunteered to come. Seems like you've had considerable excitement here today. We had planned to come through the rear so as not to alarm your neighbors, but then we heard screaming in here and decided that saving someone was more important than propriety."

I thanked him and joined the rest of the patients and staff in gawking at Jarrett's sorry, caterwauling removal from the premises. Then I ensured that John Wesley was brought upstairs and that Harris was transferred to a room. Finally, I sent Charlie Lewis out for Dr. Killigrew. Charlie was more than eager to perform the task. I only hoped it was the last time I would need Killigrew in such a hurry.

The inmates returned to their rooms, and no doubt they would wish to gossip all about this as I went around to see them later in the evening. However, I felt as though I were finally in charge of what was happening inside the walls of the Establishment.

I walked back into the entry hall, where Mary remained. She had barely taken two frightened steps.

"Well, Goose," I said. "It's all over now. There's nothing more to fear."

Clearly I had no idea what I was talking about, for Mary promptly turned around and threw up in the corner.

CHAPTER 22

Once more I had a member of the Establishment in a hospital bed. How fortunate Nurse Harris—and I—had been that Jarrett was sometimes sloppy in her methods.

I stood at Nurse Harris's bedside, where she sat up against plumped pillows, her hands clasped on top of the neatly made coverlet. Despite the horrific attack on her and the bandages now adorning her neck, she was still and composed. How did she manage that?

I confirmed that she was comfortable, then decided it was time to have the truth from her. "I have never understood why you are so secretive, Nurse. Your husband is dead, you carry a sharp knife about you, you skulk about with Charlie Lewis while avoiding the other nurses . . . What is this all about?"

Nurse Harris sighed and turned her somber green-eyed gaze to me. "I do regret that Charlie believed me to be interested in him. He was quite persistent in his attentions, and I truly didn't wish to hurt his feelings."

I frowned. "Did you believe Charlie would become angry?"

"Not really, not him. Although I couldn't be sure. I certainly could never predict my husband's anger. Regardless, I could not allow myself to find anyone else. I'm not free to marry, and if Ralph were to find me . . ." She let the words trail off.

That information stopped me. "I thought you were grieving your dead husband. You implied that he was a great loss to you."

She gave me another of her serious looks. "A desperate woman is willing to do anything to protect herself. Besides, it was not truly a lie. The man I married was not the man he turned out to be, and I did mourn the husband I thought I had wed. And I had heard how dangerous London was. A knife would protect me from both the city and the brute, if he found me."

I tried to imagine Richard turning into anything other than what he was. I could not conceive of it.

"Why was the knife bloodied?"

She shrugged. "I took it out of Ralph's possession. I'm sure it had seen the scruff of many animals." She winced and put two fingers to the bandages wound around her own neck. "Although I believed I could get lost in London, I was also not naive enough to think that Ralph wouldn't attempt to find me."

"Is Clementina Harris really your name?" I asked.

She nodded. "It is common enough, and I didn't think I had enough deception in me to learn to respond to anything else. I gambled that Ralph would never look for me to be working in a hospital in Marylebone. Thus far, it has worked, since my only enemy has been another nurse."

"Why do you suppose Nurse Frye had such loathing for you?" Was there no low point to people's anger and hate?

"I think because I knew her secrets—the liquor, the medicines—and she knew none of mine. She wanted to know that she held something over me, but I never permitted it. I was never surprised when she spoke out against me, although I admit I was taken aback when she found my knife and gave it to you."

There was still another unanswered question. "John Wesley overheard you once while hiding in the secret room. Charlie was saying he could protect you, and then, according to John Wesley, you kissed Charlie."

Harris looked puzzled for a moment, then laughed lightly. "Hardly. I told Charlie that Nurse Frye enjoyed persecuting me, and he believed he could be my bulwark against her. Very chivalrous, I suppose, but unnecessary. As though a slattern like Margery Frye would frighten me. To distract Charlie, I suggested we have slices of Mrs. Roper's leftover mincemeat pie. No doubt what John Wesley heard were sounds of enjoyment. As you know, Charlie's room is downstairs, and sometimes he would wait for me, knowing I would be down to fulfill some patient's request for food or tea. It was always innocent, of course. He was ostensibly just looking for a tool or cleaning something from the garden or some such thing. But it was almost as if he knew the sound of my footsteps on the staircase."

"Why did you not report him to me?" I said.

"Report what, Miss Nightingale? That Charlie Lewis was lovesick?" She shrugged. "I didn't wish to embarrass him. As long as he committed no harm against my person, I had no quarrel with him."

Charlie Lewis must be admonished to leave the nursing staff alone, no matter to what extent he thought he treated them with respect. I would not have my nurses molested by unwanted attentions. Perhaps it was time to consider another manservant, although at this point practically my entire staff was turning over. Nurse Harris, though, I would keep and protect as best I could.

EPILOGUE

August 1854

I picked up the brown paper-wrapped package from the afternoon mail. The postman had beat on the door with his truncheon before shoving it all through the large slot and letting the pieces scatter to the floor. I had repeatedly asked him to just leave the mail and not announce his presence for fear of disturbing napping inmates, but he completely ignored me. Twice a day or more, then, I heard the *thump-thump-thump* of his arrival, then the creaking of the mail flap as he tossed in letters and packages.

A year had passed since Persimmon Jarrett had been dragged away from this entry hall. I still vividly remembered her protesting her arrest loudly and with vehemence, screeching at the officers that she had been most justified in her actions.

I had been summoned to testify at her trial, another sad spectacle that I worried would bring unwanted notoriety to myself and the Establishment. Instead, it served only to make us famous.

After Jarrett's short trial and inevitable hanging at Newgate—which was private rather than a public exhibition thanks to Dr. Killigrew's intercession—I had received a note of recognition from the queen herself. Moreover, Sidney Herbert now sought my advice regarding medical improvements for soldiers now being sent to the Crimea. Poor, brave lads. Herbert's plans had all come to fruition. How good for England that Mr. Matthews's plans, meanwhile, would *not* be realized.

John Wesley had largely recovered and talked incessantly about joining the army, when he was old enough, "to thrash them Russians." I didn't have the heart to tell him that he was many years away from a uniform and that his permanent limp probably wouldn't allow him to do much beyond sitting at a desk.

Nurse Harris, too, bore permanent marks. They were covered well beneath her collar, and she carried on as ever before, if perhaps with a bit more reserve.

Naturally, only Harris and Hughes remained of the original group of nurses. Wilmot and Frye, as well as Polly Roper, were still in Bridewell Prison, and I had replaced them all. I had sternly lectured Charlie Lewis, and his contrition was sincere enough that I was certain he would give Harris a permanent wide berth.

Roderick Alban had also decided upon a wide berth, but that was beneficial for me. I never saw him again after the day Jarrett was arrested. As a result, I was given a free hand in the running of the Establishment. I had instituted strict rules regarding nurses' behavior to avoid any of the chicanery I had experienced. We now had Hughes's revised uniforms, and I insisted that they be clean and starched at all times.

All of my nurses knew how to prepare meals, manage linens, give injections, clean wounds properly, and keep rooms aired and clean. The Establishment smelled fresher than I had even intended it would that first week I arrived.

The expansion to the attached rear building had taken place, so now there was a proper surgery and more inmate rooms. No longer would people be operated upon in their beds.

Mary was helping me create a nursing manual, which was still just pages upon pages of my thoughts on the care of invalids. Despite her weak constitution, she had quickly become a true friend to me.

I hefted the small package in my hand. It weighed less than a pound. I untied the package's string and the paper fell away. Inside was a red-leather volume only slightly longer than the length of my outstretched hand. In gilt lettering, I read:

The Hanging of Nurse Bellamy:
An Accurate Account of a Curious Murder in Marylebone
By
Dunstan Moore

That certainly explained the man's overwhelming curiosity.

I flipped through the first few pages. The book was dedicated to me.

For Miss F.N., who never surrendered,
neither to danger nor evil

I smiled. I supposed I could understand why Moore never let on what he was about, for without question I would have thrown him out on his ear.

I decided that I would begin reading his book that very evening in the library—*my* library, now a peaceful place with no dead bodies and no murderous librarians.

I did not think we needed to hire a replacement for Miss Jarrett.

Nor did I think we would henceforth have any further troubles at the Establishment. After all, once one has dealt with two murders, what surprise or turmoil could possibly throw one into any upheaval?

The other bits of mail that caught my eye were an official-looking envelope and an envelope in very familiar handwriting. Both stood out among the rest of the scattered pieces on the floor. I placed Moore's book on the entry table and gathered the remaining mail. I tossed it all onto the table with the book except for the two pieces that had piqued my curiosity.

I realized who had sent the letter in such familiar handwriting. It was from Richard. My hands developed uncontrolled tremors as I picked it up. I was torn between wanting to run to my bedchamber with it to read it in secret and not wanting to waste another moment before tearing it open. My mind ran wild with what it could contain. Had he received an important posting somewhere? Had someone died? *Please God, don't let it be an announcement that Annabella is with child.*

My impatience asserted itself over my desire for privacy and I opened the envelope right there in the entry hall, scanning the contents quickly. He had enclosed a poem, not *for* me per se, but for me to read and critique.

> *I had a dream of waters: I was borne*
> *Fast down the slimy tide*
> *Of eldest Nile, and endless flats forlorn*
> *Stretched out on either side,—*
> *Save where from time to time arose*
> *Red pyramids, like flames in forced repose,*
> *And Sphinxes gazed, vast countenances bland,*
> *Athwart that river-sea and sea of sand.*

Richard had always been disposed to the writing of poetry, ballads, and the like. I much preferred his treatises on church matters. But why was he suddenly desiring my opinion on a few lines of poetry? Was he simply extending an olive branch of friendship?

I reread the poem slowly. It referenced a dream of sailing along the Nile, a place I had been three years ago. Was he trying to evoke a particular emotion in me, or did he merely want the opinion of someone who had also been there? My emotions were always such a jumble where he was concerned.

I put the letter back in its envelope to decide upon later. I just wasn't sure my heart could endure a correspondence with Richard, no matter how innocent.

All thoughts of Richard were tossed aside in an instant, though, as I opened the second letter. It was from Sidney Herbert's office at the War Department.

Elizabeth had been attacked in her carriage by a madman. Could I come right away?

I trembled, not only for my friend but for myself. Was it possible that my new life meant that I would never be settled and at peace for very long?

Author's Note

Florence Nightingale (1820–1910), was a remarkable woman of the Victorian era. Her lifespan was longer than Queen Victoria's (1819–1901), and she arguably changed the world at least as much as the woman who wore the crown.

Born into a wealthy family, Florence was named for the Italian city in which she was born while her newlywed parents were still on the Grand Tour. She was destined for a life of ease and comfort. She referred to her childhood home, Lea Hurst, located in Derbyshire, as "charming," with its thirteen bedrooms, additional coach house, and acres of gardens and grounds. Lea Hurst later became the Nightingale family's summer home, and Florence returned there in 1856 after the Crimean War.

Because the Nightingale estates were entailed, her mother, **Frances "Fanny" Nightingale (1788–1880)**, intended that Florence and her sister, **Parthenope Nightingale (1819–1890)**, would deliver the family from eventual financial ruin through brilliant marriages and their resulting children. Parthenope, also named for the place where she was born, was willing but unable to attract an appropriate suitor. Florence attracted many suitors but was unwilling to make a match.

Fanny nearly lost her mind over her recalcitrant younger daughter, especially when she rejected the proposal of **Richard Monckton Milnes (1809–1885)**, for whom Florence had a genuine and abiding affection.

However, Florence claimed she had had a divine visit at the age of seventeen in which God told her he was setting her apart for a special task. She never veered from her confidence in this divine appointment, no matter how many tears her mother, and eventually her sister, expended on her. Her father, **William Edward Nightingale (1794–1874**), also known as W.E.N., actually supported his daughter's desire to pursue a different path, but Fanny was a force unto herself, and he tended not to cross her directly.

W.E.N. focused on giving Florence the best foundation he could, taking her education in hand personally and teaching her mathematics, science, and languages. All of this knowledge would serve her well in her lifetime.

Florence did travel to Egypt and Europe on an extended visit with the Bracebridges and did eventually manage to get a stay at Kaiserwerth to train with **Pastor Theodor Fliedner (1800–1864)**. Upon returning to her family, Florence later said, Fanny and Parthenope acted as though she "had come from committing a crime." When Florence was invited to become the superintendent of the Establishment for Gentlewomen During Temporary Illness, her mother and sister wept, wailed, and refused food. Her sister began having mood disturbances, and Florence herself became nervous and irritable.

It was Florence's friend, Elizabeth "Liz" Herbert, who

recommended her to Lady Canning for the post at the Establishment. **Sidney Herbert (1810–1861)** had married the twenty-four-year-old **Elizabeth Ashe à Court-Repington (1822–1911)** in 1846, and together they had seven children. They were a formidable and influential match: he was an ambitious politician who became the secretary of war and later the first Baron Herbert of Lea; she was a passionate advocate of Florence's work. Through Elizabeth, Sidney came to be an advocate for Florence's hospital reforms.

As an aside, Herbert ran Wilton House, the Pembroke family estates in Wiltshire, for most of his life. His elder half brother, the twelfth Earl of Pembroke, lived in self-imposed exile in Paris, so the estates fell upon Herbert's shoulders. I spent several happy hours here in 2013 and can attest to it being a wonderful place to visit. Despite the magnificence of it, the estate feels like a family home, especially since it is still occupied by the Pembrokes (currently the eighteenth Earl and Countess of Pembroke) 450 years after it was built.

Lady Charlotte Canning (1817–1861) was the driving force behind the Establishment, intending to serve women who were too wellborn to be in a workhouse hospital yet not of enough stature to warrant at-home visits from a doctor. Lady Canning was a lady of the bedchamber to Queen Victoria for over a decade, yet all of that exposure to wealth and nobility did not affect Lady Canning's passion for serving an overlooked segment of society. Her husband, Charles, would eventually be appointed governor-general of India. While there with him, she contracted malaria and died in her husband's arms in 1861. Thoroughly shocked by her death, Charles followed her to the grave less than a year later.

It cannot be overstated how lowly the nursing profession was when Florence Nightingale burst upon the scene in 1853. Long considered work for thieves and drunkards—with some justification—it suffered a reputation on par with prostitution. As such, it is understandable why Florence's mother and sister were nearly hysterical when she announced her desire to become a nurse herself. To this upper-class family, it was tantamount to Florence announcing that she was going to enter a brothel. She persevered, though, and in a great irony, Fanny and Parthenope would one day be her most enthusiastic supporters. What Florence had failed to do for her family's future with marriage, she succeeded in doing with her own personal fame.

The Establishment, as I call it, was founded in 1849 by Lady Canning and a group of philanthropic women. Originally located in Cavendish Square, it was moved to No. 1 Upper Harley Street (now 90 Harley Street) in 1853, just prior to Florence's arrival. The building now contains a clinic and is in an area that started its great influx of medical professionals in Florence's day. Although I show the hospital as having only single rooms, it did also have three four-bed wards, known as "cubicles," which were sectioned off by curtains.

Florence did not actually enter the hospital as its superintendent but was instead promoted to that position within a year of arriving. However, it worked better for my story that she be in this position of authority right away.

Yes, cigarettes were considered a cure for asthma. They *didn't* work. Yes, drinking urine was a cure for thrush, an oral yeast infection. It *did* seem to work.

Florence insisted on having a free hand in the hospital's

management, although she was viewed with suspicion by a great number of people associated with the hospital who were unable to comprehend why a wellborn woman like Florence would wish to engage in such an effort. Florence overcame it all with her willful personality. She was sometimes sharp, sometimes sweet, and always extremely intelligent and curious. She certainly never tolerated stupidity in others.

Florence was also a lifelong adherent of miasma theory, which held that many contagious diseases were spread through bad air, known as *miasmas* (ancient Greek for pollution). Even though she was incorrect, as a result of this theory she was an early proponent of throwing open windows and doors to let as much air and light into a sickroom as possible. This was in a time when sealing off a room like a tomb was considered the most effective way to treat illness.

Queen Victoria would have been among those looking askance at Florence. The queen was not an admirer of women who overstepped their bounds by moving into professions rightfully occupied by men. She, of course, made an exception for herself as the reigning monarch of Great Britain. Victoria particularly did not like women who attempted to enter fields like medicine, although she would later come to mightily praise Florence. That, however, is a tale for another book!

ACKNOWLEDGMENTS

I had been casting about for an idea for a new historical mystery series to complement my Lady of Ashes series about a Victorian undertaker when Florence Nightingale popped into my mind. This was not entirely a coincidence, as my mother—whom I lost in October 2015—had been a nurse in her earlier years. During her long-term illness, we spent an inordinate amount of time in hospitals in the MedStar system. Over the course of about ten years, I met numerous nurses who gave their all under sometimes very trying circumstances. I believe my mother lived longer than might seem possible because of the tireless work of so many caring nurses. To you all, I offer my sincere—if inadequate—thanks for tending to, and loving, my mother.

I tentatively proposed the idea of fictionalizing Florence Nightingale to my agent, Helen Breitwieser, who said, "Eureka!" With that same enthusiasm, she shared the project with Faith Black Ross at Crooked Lane Books, and I am deeply grateful to both of them for their passion in turning Florence Nightingale into an amateur sleuth.

This marks my tenth published book, and with each one,

I receive the help of numerous people. The Hair Company actually books my appointments for extra time so that I can sit in a chair and spend time writing while the chaos of a salon whirls around me. Jackie and Lauren, you are the best.

I know it is cliché to talk about writers sitting in coffee shops to write, but I do find that I can get a lot done in one, particularly at the BTB Coffee Shop. Penny, Heather, and the rest of the crew make sure I am well fed and well caffeinated during the hours I spend there.

The usual suspects—my husband, Jon; my brother, Tony; and a plethora friends—all pitched in in different ways to ensure I delivered my manuscript on time. I'm especially grateful to my sister-in-law, Marian, who combs through each of my manuscripts with a meticulous thoroughness that is astounding. Love you, sis.

I am also blessed with an amazing assistant, Ruth Martin of Maplewood Virtual Assistance, who manages me so quietly and efficiently in the background that I hardly know she's there. I would be lost without her.

Cruce, dum spiro, fido.